GOLD BULLETS

GOLD BULLETS

CHARLES G. BOOTH

COACHWHIP PUBLICATIONS
Greenville, Ohio

Gold Bullets, by Charles G. Booth
© 2025 Coachwhip Publications edition

Cover: *California Miner with a Pack Horse,* by Henry Raschen
(CC BY-SA 3.0 Oakland Museum of California, Museum
Donors Acquisition Fund; https://creativecommons.org/
licenses/by-sa/3.0/deed.en); Colt .45 cartridges (CC BY-
SA 3.0 Hmaag; https://creativecommons.org/licenses/by-
sa/3.0/deed.en)

First published 1929
Charles G. Booth, 1896-1949
CoachwhipBooks.com

ISBN 1-61646-614-6
ISBN-13 978-1-61646-614-5

1
The Gold-Mounted Pistol

There was nothing in Nathan Hyde's note that even re-
motely suggested a connection with what was to happen
that night. If there had been I should have quailed a little
for I am getting on for that sort of thing. Not that I am
old—at sixty-nine one has hardly begun one's declining
years—but I have reached that time of life when my carpet slippers, a newspaper, and a crackling fire in my den,
Polyandria purring in front of it, mean a good deal to me.
My garden, my books, and my collection of pistols fill my
active moments and Lucy, my niece, gives me such contact
with life as I desire. Certainly as much as is good for me!

The note, which was written in Hyde's cramped hand,
asked me to drop in and see him about an old pistol he
thought might interest me. I don't care a great deal for
Hyde—he is as smooth as a mahogany walking-stick—but
his shop, a sort of antique-secondhand establishment, is
the only one of its kind in San Felipe, and he has an uncanny faculty of getting his hands on the rarities collec-
tors barter their souls for. The shop has a telephone connection, but Hyde is something of an antique himself and
he never uses the instrument unless a note by mail or mes-
senger will not serve his purpose as well. I remind Lucy
of this when she accuses me of being old-fashioned. Lucy

calls his shop the "Pirate's Cave" and Hyde, she insists,
is a reincarnation of Captain Kidd. There is a good bit of
the polished old pirate about him and when I think of his
prices I incline to her opinion.

It was early afternoon. I had nothing to do and Lucy,
for a wonder, had left the car at home so there was no
reason why I should not see Hyde at once. San Felipe is
a town of thirty thousand or so, but like most California
cities it covers a good deal of ground; and as Hyde's shop
is in the center of the town while our modest bungalow is
on the outskirts I had some distance to go.

Magnolia Avenue is the loveliest thoroughfare in the
city and I drove along it with pride. Magnolia and pepper
trees, with here and there a hibiscus, grace both sides of
the avenue. None of the home sites is less than an acre,
many of them are planted to oranges and figs and all of
them are well kept, so the avenue always is a bower of
beauty. And yet, thirty years ago the San Felipe Valley
was a sun-burned waste of sage and cactus, lizard and rattler and the like its only animal life. But that was before
Andrew Ogden, our first citizen, brought water and accomplished another of those miracles which are the wonder of
the Southwest.

Andrew is my next-door neighbor and my friend. His
wealth has left him unspoiled and we have much in common. In fact, there is between us that fine quality of
affection which men achieve so rarely in their friendships.
And if, at times, during the nine years we have known each
other, I have felt a restraint upon his spirit, had a sense
of looking upon a mask instead of the man himself, and if
his antecedents are a matter of conjecture, what of it? My
feeling was probably nonsense. But if it were not, hasn't he
the right to seal what chambers of his memory he chooses?
It is known that we are cronies and I have to discourage a
good deal of casual inquiry about Andrew.

Jerry Ogden, Andrew's boy, and Lucy have cemented our friendship. Lucy, I see, is wearing a handsome sapphire. I shall be sorry to lose her for she has meant a good deal to me since Paul and his wife died, but Jerry is a fine lad and I am the last man in the world to stand in the way of youth. A lot of good it would do me if I weren't!

The building that houses Hyde's place, one of the first of a permanent nature to be erected in the town, is a dilapidated wooden structure with its second story hanging over the street like a frowsy head stuck out of a window. A lot of ordinary stuff, secondhand furniture and the like, crams the cavern of a shop, but there are a few good things, too, for Hyde has excellent taste and no scruples. From time to time I have come across some fine Indian ollas, excellent pieces of European pottery, a bronze or two, any number of arrowheads and metates, and a good bit of stuff from the old California missions. I love these things and leave them alone. Pistols are enough for a man of moderate means.

After the brilliant afternoon sunlight the weird gloom of the shop blinded me and I had to grope my way forward. There seemed to be no one about; and then I heard voices in the office at the rear. My eyes adapted themselves to the half light and as I approached the office I saw that Hyde was talking with Roy Hammond, a local lawyer. I am not keen about Hammond, but I know him well enough and I put my head inside the office.

"Good afternoon, gentlemen."

I wear rubber heels and I instantly realized that they had not heard me coming. Hyde was sitting at his desk. His hawk-like head went up with a jerk and he deftly slid a letter over some object on the desk. What it was I did not see, but I was to remember the incident later. Hammond was standing on the opposite side of the desk. He spun on his heel with a muttered exclamation.

"Excuse me, Hyde," I said, withdrawing. "I didn't know you were busy. I'll drop in later."

"Ah, Peebles! Nothing of the sort. Come right in," Hyde protested suavely.

He stood up, "long and lean and lank" as Mr. Coleridge's Ancient Mariner. Eighty if he is a day, and in startling contrast to the shabby atmosphere of his shop, Hyde affects the polished elegance of an old roue. But in spite of his morning coat, his striped gray trousers, and his pearl-gray spats he reminded me more than ever of Lucy's "reincarnated Captain Kidd." It wouldn't be hard to imagine him with a blood-stained sash around his waist and a cutlass in his hand directing the looting of a galleon.

"I was just going," Hammond muttered. "I wanted Hyde to bring some junk down from the house."

It was none of my business that Hammond had lied. He is a tall, heavily built man with a meaty face which I never saw cast in any expression but one of cultivated affability. In his younger days—ten or fifteen years ago—Hammond prospected through the desert mountains. A lucky strike gave him a small capital and he went in for law. Now he belongs to every luncheon club and fraternal order in town and I believe he has designs on the state legislature. He wouldn't be entrusted with any of my legal affairs.

"Don't go on my account," I begged, as he picked up his hat. "My business will wait." But he took his departure. "Well," I said to Hyde, "what have you got?"

"It may not interest you." Hyde's sly chuckle irritated me.

But when I saw him reach for his snuff-box, which he keeps in a pocket somewhere in the tail of his morning coat, I knew that he had something I wanted and that I should have to pay for it. The snuff-box, an elaborate affair of richly chased silver, had belonged to a French Louis and taking snuff from it is in the nature of a ceremony that Hyde always indulges in before and after pocketing a fat profit. But after much fumbling he withdrew his hand without it.

"Queer!" he mumbled, twitching his bushy eyebrows up and down, a mannerism of his. "Now where did I put it? Memory isn't what it used to be. Too bad! Too bad!"

I concluded he had misplaced the snuff-box. "Never mind, Hyde. It'll turn up."

His head came up with a jerk. "Eh? Oh, yes, to be sure. The snuff-box. I hope so. Shouldn't like to lose it. No, indeed! Let me see. Oh, yes, the pistol. Sit down, Peebles."

I did so and he resumed his own chair with an audible creak of old bones. Pitiful, this getting old, I reflected from the comparative immaturity of sixty-nine. My eye fell on the letter he had slid over the object beneath it. As a rule I am not curious about other people's affairs, but I must admit that the incident bothered me. Why should Hyde have been in such haste to conceal the thing from me?

He quickly recaptured my attention by placing the revolver on the desk in front of me. The other matter went clear out of my head. In fact, it was all I could do to keep from leaping to my feet, seizing the revolver, and telling Hyde to name his price. Instead, I casually picked it up, aware that he was watching me slyly.

"Careful, Peebles. It's loaded."

The revolver was a long-barreled Colts forty-five of a type in general use thirty years ago. On the butt was a mounting of filigree gold of crude workmanship. It was this unusual feature that had set my elderly heart thumping like a mill-race. I squinted along the barrel, peered into it, examined the trigger, and ran my fingers lovingly over the filigree. There was some rust on the steel, but oil had been applied recently and the weapon seemed serviceable.

I paused on the verge of breaking the gun. It was too much to expect that the revolver was what I had been looking for, yet I feared to shatter my trembling hope that it might be. Hyde was watching me with his secret smile. I broke the gun. Six shells, one of them exploded, fell into my hand. I caught my breath. My hands began to tremble. Sweat dampened my forehead. I bent lower over the pistol to hide my agitation. When I looked up into Hyde's secret smile I knew I should have to pay for my prize.

"Well?" he asked blandly.

"Do you suppose it is authentic?" I parried casually.

He gave his sly chuckle. "You see the mounting. And the bullets—are they not gold?"

"Oh, yes," I admitted, with the same casual air. "But it wouldn't be difficult to mount gold on a pistol butt. As for the gold bullets—" I shrugged significantly. "If I bought it I should naturally want to feel certain that the pistol had belonged to Alex Peterson."

His smile broadened. "Peterson's initials are on the butt."

So they were. I had not noticed them.

"Couldn't any one have put them there?"

"My dear Peebles!" Hyde exclaimed. "If you don't think the gun belonged to Peterson don't buy it."

He had me there. As a matter of fact I was sure the gun was Peterson's, although I could not prove it was, any more than he could. A thrill of pleasure ran through me. Ever since I began collecting pistols I have wanted to get hold of one of Peterson's gold-mounted revolvers. I had commissioned several dealers—Hyde among them—to be on the lookout for me, but I never had quite expected to realize my ambition. And yet here I was with one of the famous guns in my hand.

There is in me a deep and abiding love for Californian history and tradition. California is, I firmly believe, richer in romance and historical glamour than any other state in the Union. Collecting pistols is a queer way of expressing one's affection for anything, yet it happens to be mine. I have tried to make the California section of

my collection representative of every phase in the development of the state. I have pistols that Cabrillo brought
with him when he entered San Diego Bay in 1542; pistols
that belonged to Galvez and Rivera and Portola when they
set out to colonize California for Spain; pistols used in
the defense of the missions and in the revolutions against
Spain and Mexico; derringers and revolvers carried by the
forty-niners and half the soldiers, highwaymen, and fron-
tiersmen who had made history in the state. To complete
my California collection—although Lucy insists it can not
be complete without an automatic or two from the armor-
ies of the Los Angeles underworld—I wanted one of Alex
Peterson's gold-mounted Colts.

Peterson's fame was mainly local, but I was interested
in him because he was typical of a phase of the West which
is gone forever. I supposed he was dead, but he wouldn't
be an old man if he were alive; no older than I, in fact. He
had had his day in the nineties, but he was a young man at
the time. Probably more legend than act clung to his name,
but this deepened my interest in him. I don't know that he
ever did anything especially remarkable, although his rise
above Skull Valley's lurid horizon must have been as spec-
tacular (and probably as short-lived) as that of the town
of Torridity itself. At least, he lived bravely, extravagantly,
recklessly; recklessly enough, indeed, to have stamped the
imprint of his personality upon the gold-mad town and
kept green its memory long after it had become one of
that abandoned company of ghost cities which haunt the
desolate places of the West.

Peterson, it seems, was an inveterate gambler. He would
take a chance on anything and he would back his judgment with his last dollar. There is a story to the effect
that once he played poker for a human life, but that must
be nonsense. He came to Torridity with nothing but his
guns, grew wealthy, and lost everything he had at poker;

or so the story goes. "Ten-to-One" appears to have been the sobriquet he became known by. But I think he was remembered for his prodigal extravagances as much as for anything else. Raw gold was a medium of exchange in the mining camps in those days and Peterson's swashbuckling temperament ran to, among other things, gold bullets and gold-mounted guns.

And I had one of those guns and five of those bullets in my hands!

"Well, do you want it?" Hyde asked blandly.

I wasn't going to be caught too easily. "Where did you get it?"

Hyde blew his nose. "That," he said delicately, "doesn't matter."

"Oh, yes, it does. If there's a story in it I shall want that, too." Every relic has its story and I always insist on it being thrown in with the price.

"The story," Hyde said smoothly, "is not included in the price. The price is one thousand dollars."

I laughed, wrote him a check for five hundred, and tossed it over. "There isn't more than a hundred and fifty dollars' worth of gold in the bullets and the filigree."

He picked up the check, precisely tore it into fragments, and dropped the pieces into his wastepaper basket. Then he held out his hand.

"The pistol, Peebles."

"See here, Hyde!"

"My dear Peebles! I said a thousand dollars!"

"You didn't pay more than two hundred for the thing," I stormed.

"A hundred seventy-five. Let me have it, please."

"Six hundred," I bid.

"The pistol."

"Seven."

"Let me have it."

"Eight hundred, you pirate," I roared, "and not a cent more!"

"I'll trouble you for the pistol, Peebles."

I capitulated, of course, and wrote him a check. If he'd wanted two thousand I believe I would have put my conscience in my pocket and paid it.

"You'll bargain with St. Peter if he'll listen to you," I growled. "Now give me the story."

He gave me his secret smile instead. "The story is not included in the price. Nor is it for sale. Here is your receipt."

And talk as I would I could not get him to change his mind.

He fumbled for his snuff-box, failed to find it, and mumbled something about having misplaced it. I returned the cartridges to the revolver, leaving the empty shell under the hammer. Hyde then wrapped my treasure up while I speculated about the tale I hadn't got. My eye fell on the letter which concealed the article beneath it and I wondered if by some strange chance there was a connection between Peterson's revolver and the subject of Hyde's conversation with Hammond. But I soon shook the notion out of my head. I am always imagining mysteries where none exist. The only difference between nine and sixty-nine is a matter of years and with the parcel under my arm I left the shop as happy as a boy with the newest thing in mechanical toys.

But if I could have suddenly known exactly what it was I had bought, or if I could have got a glimpse of the significance of what Hyde had refused to tell me, I should have plunged back into his cavernous shop, taken him by the throat, and shaken him until the story dripped word by word from between his teeth. I might then have been able to avert the tragedy that was to blast the lives of those dearest to me.

2
Over the Wire

I had several things to do in town so instead of going straight home I dined at Galli's with my old friend Captain Deacon, our chief of police. Deacon had done more than his share towards making the department as efficient as any in the state and I respect his keen driving brain, although I sometimes deplore his lack of finesse, his mechanical evaluation of the human elements.

The meal over and my business attended to, I drove slowly home. There was no moon, but the sky was powdered with stardust. So near seemed the window of heaven that I fancied I might lift it and look within. We have many such nights in San Felipe. Nevertheless, I was thankful for the eucalyptus log Mrs. Moffit had got crackling in my den. Our valley nights in the spring have an edge to them.

It was just ten minutes past nine. I was to remember the time.

Polyandria reclined on the hearth. She got lazily up, stretched herself fore and aft and came purring towards me. I picked her up and she made herself comfortable on my shoulder. Polyandria is a gold-brown Angora, a magnificent animal, and I suppose I am absurdly fond of her. When I got her two years ago Lucy suggested the name "Polyandria." It had a classical ring and I gobbled avidly at it. The mischief in Lucy's eyes should have warned me, but not until several months later when I heard her calling Polyandria "Many Husbands" did I realize that the two names were synonymous. Lucy is embarrassingly candid at times.

"No more complaints, Polyandria?" I inquired.

"Brrr," she whispered in my ear.

Luther MacNair, a retired private detective of considerable reputation, had recently come to Magnolia Avenue. It turned out that he has a passion for growing tomatoes. Polyandria got among the vines—so he said—and some little damage was done. I insisted on paying MacNair's estimate of the damage, but he was quite nasty about it.

Lucy danced in just then. She is always dancing in upon me. I can describe her entrances and exits in no other way. Lucy is mercurial. She is here and there and everywhere—but in the place I am seeking her.

"Look at me instead of Many Husbands, Uncle John. Am I all right?"

I frowned. "How should I know whether you are all right? Ask Jerry."

"He's busy with his father. That horrid old mine again. He telephoned me during dinner. Something has happened."

"What?"

"He didn't say. Do you like my new dress?"

Women are meant to be admired, I suppose, and I did my duty. It isn't difficult to admire Lucy. She is lovely enough to set even my elderly heart to thumping. The gold chiffon gown she wore had come from the modiste the day before. She stood in it as straight as a slender sword and never, I thought, had anything so well become her sleek dark hair—shingled, of course—and luminous dark eyes.

"You'll do," I said. "Where are you going?"

"To the Chesters. I am singing there. Jerry will come for me after his father has done with him, I suppose. I wish Mr. Ogden would let him reopen that old mine. Jerry believes he can make it pay. I don't know why Mr. Ogden is so stupid."

"He should know best."

"You old people always know best! Jerry is a qualified engineer. His opinion should be as sound as his father's."

"Sounder," I said ironically.

"Sounder, of course," Lucy agreed gravely. "This is a more enlightened age."

"Experience counts for nothing then," I cried bitterly. "When I was your age—"

"You dear Uncle John! That's so long ago you've forgotten. What were you doing all afternoon?"

"Well, I bought a pistol."

"Goodness! Another?"

"It's a pistol I have been trying to get for a long while, my dear." I didn't dare tell her what it had cost me. "It belonged to a man named Peterson who lived in the mining town of Torridity down in Skull Valley."

"Torridity! Why, that's where Mr. Ogden's mine is. Isn't it strange that he won't let Jerry open it up?"

I chuckled. "You'd better be off, my dear. You don't know any more about mines than you do about pistols."

She kissed me again and fled. I heard the whirr of the starter and then the diminishing purr of the engine as the car swept down the avenue. Lucy has an excellent voice and she is doing extremely well with her concert singing. She had some thought of grand opera, but I believe Jerry has talked her out of it.

Now that Lucy had spoken of it I recalled that the mine Jerry wanted to operate—some feeling about it had risen between father and son—was in or near Torridity. The coincidence was interesting. I was getting up to unwrap my purchase when Mrs. Moffit came in.

Without Mrs. Moffit life would be more of a labyrinth than it is and I an infant in the middle of it. She determines the strength of my coffee, the weight of my underwear, my allowance of cigars, and my weekly consumption of spinach. When I sneeze she lemonades me, when I cough she olive oils me, and when I am out late she sits up for me. Mrs. Moffit is comfortably round and many-skirted, and she has no sympathy whatever with the tendency of the modern age to undress itself. Lucy says she has a John Peebles complex.

"How's your head, Mr. Peebles?" she inquired solicitously.

"Head?" I murmured.

Mrs. Moffit looked disappointed. "You had a headache when you got up this morning, hadn't you? I suppose it was that pie last night. I was bringing you a powder." Mrs. Moffit has a powder for everything.

"Ah, yes," I said. "Well, it's all right now and it wasn't the pie." I am very fond of Mrs. Moffit's pies.

She shook her head disapprovingly. "You always say that. Mr. Ogden phoned a while back. He said I was to ask you to call him up as soon as you came in. He seemed terrible upset about something. I didn't know you were home until Miss Lucy told me just now."

She put another log in the grate and poked the fire into a crackling fury that made Polyandria and me push back.

"This is California, Mrs. Moffit," I protested.

"And mighty cold it can get when it wants."

"Don't be disloyal," I chided.

She looked at me darkly. "You can't believe everything those chamber of commerces say."

I sighed as she left me, but I wouldn't be without her for—well, a good deal.

I crossed to the telephone wondering what was the matter with Andrew. Nothing serious, I felt sure, in spite of what Mrs. Moffit had said. Instead of taking the instrument up at once I unwrapped the Peterson revolver and ran my fingers caressingly over the barrel and gold-mounted butt. It occurred to me that I had better remove the powder from the cartridges before I put the pistol among my collection in the great glass case that occupies one side of the room. I was on the point of breaking the weapon when the telephone whirred sharply.

As I picked up the instrument my eye fell on the clock on the mantel. It was exactly nine-thirty.

"Hello," I called.

"Is that you, John? This is Andrew." The voice might have been any one's but his, so strained and unnatural did it sound.

"What is it, Andrew?"

"I want to see you. . . . Come over . . . right away. You hear me? Right—"

The voice had stopped. Then I heard what might have been a gasp. A queer, strangled sort of gasp. Silence again. I could hear the ticking of my watch, feel the quickened beat of my pulses. Now came a dull thud and a rattle.

"Andrew!" I shouted. "What's wrong, man?"

Did I hear a faint groan?

"Andrew! Andrew!" I shook the instrument. "Speak to me!"

Silence again.

Muscle-bound, I stood with the receiver to my ear. The wire was silent, but the silence was audible. It seemed to beat upon my eardrums like hammers. Andrew . . . something had happened. . . .

I threw off the shackles that bound me, flung myself through the French window near my desk, and plunged into the maze of shrubbery outside. Beyond the shrubbery is the high, tile-capped cement wall which surrounds the Ogden place. A gate pierces the wall and I burst through it. Some three acres in extent, the Ogden grounds are laid out in a happy bewilderment of subtropical flora; in their center stands the lovely shapeless house Ogden built twenty years ago. Lights in several windows twinkled through the quivering foliage.

The moon had not yet risen, but my feet quickly found the familiar winding path and I raced through the scented gloom. Suddenly, I heard the pound of feet on the cinder walk ahead and as I neared the walk Jerry Ogden's white flannels flashed past into the drive.

"Jerry!" I called. "Jerry! Jerry!"

Instead of replying, he went on like the wind and I stopped, dumbfounded. He had seemed to drop something as he passed, but the gloom was too deep for me to be sure of this.

"Jerry!" I shouted. "Haven't you dropped something? What's wrong?"

The shadows of the place swallowed him before I could tell whether he had gone on to the garage, which lies on the other side of the house, or down to the avenue, and I stood with a queer coldness tightening about my heart. The reflection that Andrew might be ill and that Jerry had gone for a doctor did not comfort me. Doctors have telephones. . . . Off again at top speed, I did not stop until I had climbed over the iron grille which embraces a tiny balcony just big enough to stand on outside the library window. The doors of the window were ajar, but drawn draperies concealed the room. I was sweating with dread. For the moment I couldn't have parted the curtains to see what Andrew's boy had fled from to save my soul.

Desperately beating my weakness back, I compelled myself to open the window, to part the curtains, to look in. The life forces within me seemed to come to an abrupt stop. I felt as if a pit had opened at my feet. It took all the resources of body and spirit to drive me into the room.

Andrew Ogden sat at his desk, head down upon it. The light of a reading lamp fell upon his neck where a cross of metal burned dully.

3
Gold Bullets

I have seen a good bit of death in my time, but never had it seemed so dreadful as it did at this moment. In the nine years I had known Andrew I had become deeply attached to him—he was perhaps the closest friend I had—and coming upon him struck down like this . . . I could feel the dagger twisting in my own heart. The springs of emotion released themselves and horror and rage and grief had their way with me.

Blinded with tears, I bent over him. He was done for, of course, but the body still was warm. It couldn't have been otherwise since I had spoken to him less than five minutes ago. Five minutes! And now he was gone! I am a methodical man and I looked at my watch. It was twenty-seven minutes to ten. I had answered his call at exactly nine-thirty. It had taken me perhaps two minutes to come from my den. This precision in the matter of time was to prove useful later on.

The head rested on the right cheek. The telephone instrument lay on its side in the center of the desk. Andrew's right hand was near it; his left was closed lightly over the receiver at the end of the desk. Later, when my emotion had subsided, I was to give these details much thought. I recognized the dagger. The blade was sunk to the hilt, but

I knew it to be short and heavy. The hilt was of dull chased silver. A fine tourmaline sparkled in the top of it. The dagger implied certain things which I tried unavailingly to thrust out of my mind.

I pulled myself together. There were things to be done. I must call the police and question Ogden's servants. Of the latter there were three: Hubbard and his wife, and Stimson, the gardener. Henceforth, a single purpose must govern my actions: the establishing of the identity of the man who had left this room within the last five minutes. Nothing else counted—I stopped. Was this true? It wasn't, I knew. Something else counted very much indeed. I could not evade the point. It clung to my mind with the tenacity of a leech. An uprush of horror forced it into words.

"Jerry!" I whispered. "Why didn't you stop!"

Sick at heart, I pulled a bell cord in the corner nearest the desk. The tread of feet was quickly audible. I tried the hall door. It was locked, but the key was in the lock and I turned it. Hubbard came up as I swung the door open.

"You rang, sir?" he inquired.

I looked at him in silence for a moment. Hubbard is a large, bulbous person with a pasty face and a deferential manner. He reminds me of a plump mushroom and I dislike his poor imitation of the English butler manner, but I have found no other fault in him. Certainly he and his wife manage the Ogden house capably enough.

"Is there anything wrong, sir?"

"Yes," I said. "Your master."

His eyes went over my shoulder; then he fell back with a cry. "Good God, sir! He's not—he's not *dead?*"

Still watching him, I let him into the room.

"Who did it, sir? When did it—happen?"

"Within the past five minutes. I don't know who did it. Where is Mr. Jerry?"

"He was here with Mr. Ogden all evening. I passed the door about half an hour ago and they were still talking. Mr. Ogden said they weren't to be disturbed."

"Sure it was half an hour?"

"Perhaps thirty-five minutes, sir. The hall clock had struck nine shortly before."

"Where were you during the past half hour?"

"In the kitchen."

"Alone?"

"Why, no, sir. With Mrs. Hubbard. Surely you don't think—"

"Answer my questions, Hubbard. Were you with Mrs. Hubbard all evening?"

"Almost, sir. I went upstairs for a little while about an hour ago. I was on my way back to the kitchen when I passed the library door half an hour ago."

"Where is Stimson?"

"He was with Mrs. Hubbard and me up to a few minutes ago, sir. He had dropped in for a glass of milk and a piece of Mrs. Hubbard's apple pie, which he's very partial to."

"What do you mean by 'a few minutes ago'?"

"Ten or fifteen minutes, I should say, sir. In fact, it had just turned half past nine when he left. The hall clock struck and we compared our watches with it. He said he was going for a bit of a stroll."

I stepped into the hall and glanced at the clock. Its dial showed nine thirty-eight. My own watch was just twenty seconds behind it. Andrew had telephoned me at nine-thirty. At that moment Stimson left the Hubbards and a few seconds later Andrew was killed. Assuming that Hubbard was telling the truth, Stimson could not have got to the library window, entered the room, and killed Ogden in the brief space of time at his disposal. Nor could the

Hubbards. The library door was locked on the inside so entrance couldn't have been effected from the hall.

"You had better tell your wife," I said. "And get hold of Stimson."

"Here is my wife now, sir."

Mrs. Hubbard had come up noiselessly. She is a tall, thin woman with more of the refining graces than are common among those in her station of life. I always suspected she had been fitted for better things than Hubbard had been able to give her.

"What is it, Alfred?" she whispered.

"The master," Hubbard gasped. "Mr. Peebles found him—like this."

Mrs. Hubbard's eyes flew to the desk. She gave a sharp cry and fell back against the wall, clutching at her throat. Her cheeks became bloodless and this condition together with the prominent bony structure of her face and her sandy-colored hair gave her a look of death afoot. I thought she was going to fall and I took her arm. Her eyes clung to mine with the effect of physical contact. I could not evade them.

"This is dreadful, sir," she whispered. "We've been here twenty years. . . . Herbert and I. . . ."

"Twenty years," I echoed. "That is a long time."

Her eyes dropped from mine and I felt distinct relief. She began to weep.

"You'd better take your wife up to her room, Hubbard," I said. "The police will want to talk to both of you. See if you can find Stimson; then come back here."

I watched them slowly mount the stairs, two elderly people with the debility of age come suddenly upon them. I felt pretty old myself. Twenty years they had been with Andrew. No wonder they were broken up! I went to the hall telephone and called Deacon.

"You'd better come over to the Ogden house right away," I told him.

"What's wrong, John?"

"Ogden—he's dead! It looks like—" I could not pronounce the word.

He gave a sharp cry. And then: "I'll be right over, John."

Deacon is a square-built man. Square of face, square of shoulder, square of heart and mind. Honesty shines in his sea-blue eyes like a light in a window and you feel that here is a man on whom you can stake your life. Never have I known personal feeling to swing him from the path of duty as he saw it by so much as the breadth of a gnat's tail. "Honest Henry" we call him in San Felipe.

Yet I dreaded his appearance.

He is as inexorable as time itself. If a man has the appearance of guilt he investigates him with meticulous honesty, locks him up if the evidence warrants it, and frees him if it doesn't. There is no framing of evidence, no pushing of doubtful suspects for personal glory. Nor will Deacon tolerate anything of the sort among his men. In "open-and-shut" cases such methods are admirable; but when things are not what they seem and facts contradict themselves, the subtle approach and the comprehension and evaluation of human motives are, in my opinion, more likely to get at the truth. Deacon laughs at me of course.

For this reason I dreaded his appearance.

The serious implications of the evidence had not escaped my mind for an instant since I had come into the room. I had seen Jerry flying down the drive a minute or so after his father had been stabbed to death. I had called and instead of answering me he had gone on faster than ever. That was a fact. But so was my faith in his innocence a fact; that is, it was a fact to me. I knew that Jerry couldn't have killed his father. Deacon liked the boy too, but his concrete mind would ignore the human element and consider only evidence that could be demonstrated.

I decided not to tell him what I had seen. He must dig up his own evidence. Perhaps it wasn't Jerry I had seen after all. No, this wouldn't do. He was in my home every day in various kinds of attire and his flannels were as familiar to me as were my own garments. Besides, an eye for detail has become second nature with me. I then tried to comfort myself with the thought that Jerry would return and explain his precipitous flight. He would, of course! But what was the young fool up to?

The dagger in Andrew's neck belonged to Jerry. He had brought it up from South America with him. Its place was among other trophies of his in a glass-topped table cabinet which stood behind the desk and against the north wall near the window. The cabinet is never locked, there being nothing of great value in it. I saw some old coins, stamps and medallions, a few semi-precious stones, most of them uncut, some pieces of carved jade that weren't bad, several little idols of ebony and ivory, and various other odds and ends. So far as I could see there were no fingerprints on the glass.

My eyes went sadly around the large, square room. I had spent many happy hours here and a good deal of the stuff about me had treasured associations in my memory. Andrew hadn't collected extensively but he had loved old things and I had helped him to get much of what was in the room. I have a sense for old art. The andirons were Cellini bronze; so was the inkstand on the desk. I was with him when he had bought them in Los Angeles. He had got the Turkish rug in New York upon my telegraphed advice. The two etchings on the walls were there at my suggestion. I had helped him with most of the books. There were hundreds of them for Andrew had loved books, although it is my opinion that he first bought them to fill a void in his

life and that his love of books had come out of his contact
with them. It is so with books, you know.

I went back to Andrew. By resting my cheek on the desk I
could see into his face without lifting his head. I had known
Andrew as a man endowed with a fine collection of the
"civic virtues." I mean that he was conscientious and eminently respectable, restrained and judicial and successful, a
pillar of the church and a member of the chamber of com-
merce. There are hundreds of Andrew Ogdens in the land.

But from time to time I had felt that this conventional
being wasn't the real Andrew Ogden; that behind it lived
and longed an audacious personality he had never revealed
to me but which, somehow, I had sensed and loved. And
now as I looked at his face in death this strange impression was borne in upon me stronger than ever. I seemed
to see in it a passionate anger, a look of restraint flung
to the winds, something reckless, adventurous, irresistibly
audacious. Perhaps I was wrong. Lucy says I become more
susceptible to impressions as I grow older.

Hubbard came in just then.

"I didn't see Stimson around, sir."

"Never mind. He'll turn up." I thought for a moment.
"Has Mr. Ogden had any visitors lately, Hubbard? Strang-
ers, I mean."

"Why, yes, sir, he has. A man and a woman. And a
queer-looking pair they were. I was going to speak to you
about them."

"Queer looking!" I exclaimed. "Who were they? When
did they come?"

"I don't know the woman's name, sir. She was here
three or four days ago. Let me see. This is Friday. Yes, it
was Monday afternoon. She didn't come to the door. The
master was in the grounds and he met her coming up the
drive. They talked for a minute or two, then he brought
her in here. She must have stayed an hour."

"Queer looking, you said, Hubbard?"

"To be sure, sir. She was one of those tall, angular, elderly females that seem to be all sinew and bone and tight-shut mouth. You know the kind, sir. No emotion, unless they keep it in their insides."

"Usually they do, Hubbard. How was she dressed?"

"That was the queer part of her. She had on a black hat, a long black coat, and a long black dress. I couldn't help noticing the get-up of her, sir. Particularly her dress, the women being what they are nowadays for showing their legs. Not a bit of color to her, sir. Even her eyes were black. Black as coal."

Queer type for Ogden to be interested in, I thought.

"She sounds like a crank of some sort, Hubbard. What about the other person?"

"Well, sir, he was just as queer, in his way. He came this afternoon. I heard a banging on the front door—not the knocker—the banging of a man's hard fist. The look of him gave me a turn when I opened the door. I almost shut it in his face. He was a little crab-apple of a chap, in overalls and a torn coat, and all stooped and puckered. Eighty, if he was a day, a shock of hair as white as a clean napkin all over his head and neck, a stubble of whisker, a leathery skin like an old brown shoe, China-blue eyes all red around the rims, and an eight-sided glass stuck in his eye—that's him, sir."

"An eight-sided glass!" I echoed. "You mean a lens of some sort?"

"Yes, sir. And it was on one end of a wire. The other end of the wire was fastened to his shirt with a safety pin.

"'I'm lookin' for Andry Ogden,' he shouted in a cackling voice.

"I know my place, Mr. Peebles, and I felt sure the master wouldn't want such a looking fellow in his house, so I said Mr. Ogden was out, and I started to shut the door.

"'No, he ain't,' the old man shrilled at me. 'I'm agoin' to see him!' And before I could prevent him he hopped into the hall, shook his fist in my face, and screamed:

"'Tell yer boss ol' Furie is here!'

"He was chewing tobacco—an abominable habit, sir—and he actually threatened to—to inundate me if I didn't. Luckily, Mr. Ogden looked into the hall just then and asked him what he wanted.

"'A word with ye in private,' the old man cackled.

"And do you know, sir, after thinking a moment, Mr. Ogden brought him in here and shut the door! I was stunned. Mr. Ogden has always been so particular about suspicious-looking characters. Furie was his name. It certainly suited him."

"Did Mr. Ogden seem surprised at seeing the man?" I asked.

"He did, sir. Dumbfounded, I might say. At first I thought he hadn't caught what Furie said, Mr. Ogden being a trifle deaf in his left ear, as you know, sir; and then I heard him muttering the man's name over and over. 'Furie, Furie, Furie.' Just like that."

"And you never saw this man before, Hubbard?"

"Never, sir."

"What time did he go?"

"About six, I believe. Mr. Ogden then called in Mr. Jerry and instructed me not to have them disturbed. I spoke of dinner, but he said dinner must wait. He was quite sharp about it. The meal hasn't been served, sir."

I nodded. "When did you last see Mr. Jerry?" I asked casually.

"When Mr. Ogden called me in, sir. At six."

"How was he dressed?" I went on, in the same tone.

"In his flannels, sir."

I shut my eyes for an instant.

"Hubbard," I resumed quietly, "did you chance to overhear any of the conversation between Furie and Mr. Ogden?"

The man drew himself up. "I don't overhear conversations, sir."

I smiled. "Of course not. But this is no time for for-
mality. Did you overhear anything?"

Hubbard flushed. "Well, sir, I did, but it was quite un-
intentional on my part. I was passing along the hall and
I heard Mr. Ogden utter two words in angry tones. He
shouted them and they quite startled me. I heard nothing
else, sir."

"What were those words, Hubbard?"

"'Gold bullets,' sir."

I started so violently that Hubbard looked at me in
surprise. It took me a moment to reassemble my scattered
wits. Could it be possible that the Peterson revolver was
in some way connected with Furie's interview with Ogden?
Coincidence is more active in life than we are inclined
to admit, but gold bullets are uncommon articles and to
assume there was no connection between my gold bullets
and the two words Hubbard had overheard would be assuming a good deal. Going to the hearth, I stood gazing
absently into the embers in the grate.

What a strange concurrence of events! First, Hyde's refusal to tell me anything about the revolver; then, Andrew's telephone call, Jerry's white-flanneled figure flying
down the drive, Andrew stabbed to death at the telephone;
and finally, this thing Hubbard had told me. Were these
events links of a chain that ran back into the limbo of
Ogden's past? And Jerry? For a moment my faith in him
was shaken. Could he have had words with his father about
the reopening of that Skull Valley mine? Sometimes hot
words . . . led to hot deeds. . . .

"Jerry, lad!" I cried in the depths of my heart. "Why didn't you stop!"

Dreadful as my announcement to Lucy must be, would the truth compel me to make it inconceivably more so? My agony of heart became unendurable. Then I took fresh hold on myself and my faith was renewed. Jerry had not killed his father. I was again as positive of this as I was of my own existence.

A heavy pounding sounded at the front door. Hubbard hurried into the hall. He reappeared with Henry Deacon, Dr. Oakley, a local surgeon, and Thompson, a sergeant of detectives.

4
Where is Jerry?

Deacon greeted me briefly and went slowly towards the figure at the desk. He stood looking down at it, his square face white and his sea-blue eyes humid with emotion.

"This is terrible," I heard him whisper. "Andrew! Andrew!"

My own eyes filled with tears. They had known each other well. I think they had been drawn together by some common quality of character.

The dagger was carefully removed—there were no fingerprints on it—and the body was carried to a couch near the hall door. Dr. Oakley began his examination. He was a little dapper person and he went about his task with the precision of a well-oiled machine. Deacon turned to me.

"Well, John, what about it?" His sea-blue eyes were dry now.

I had been dreading the question and as I met his steady gaze I dreaded it more. Involve Jerry I would not. The boy would turn up with some reasonable explanation of his flight and I must leave the way open for him. I detailed my purchase of the revolver and Hyde's secrecy about it, I described the telephone call and how I had found Andrew, I repeated Mrs. Moffit's message and touched briefly on what Hubbard had told me. Of Jerry I said nothing. Henry listened with eyes like points of ice. When I had done he looked at me in silence for a moment.

"Did you see any one as you came over, John?"

Henry is devilishly clever at getting down to essentials. He could not possibly know that I had seen Jerry or any one else, yet I felt as if he were looking into my mind. I suppose I am a poor liar. My voice was steady as I replied.

"I saw no one."

He believed me, of course, but he continued to gaze steadily at me. This unflinching look of Henry's is a mannerism—he means nothing by it—but I could feel myself coloring. A cough at the door relieved the situation.

Stimson, the gardener, stood there with Hubbard. It was Stimson who had coughed. His eyes were riveted upon me and there was in them something I didn't like. Stimson has been with Ogdens' less than a year and I haven't seen much of him. For some obscure reason he irritates me, although I have nothing against the man. He does his work well enough. But now I distinctly felt hostility in his attitude, in the veiled insolent look in his eyes, in the set of his head, in the nonchalant pose of his body. It grew upon me. I was suddenly vaguely conscious of disaster. Stimson moved into the room moistening his lips. He was going to speak. It came upon me overwhelmingly that I should prevent him from speaking and I blurted out:

"Hubbard had better tell you his story, Henry."

Deacon glanced at me sharply. Then: "Go ahead, Hubbard."

Hubbard proceeded to enlarge upon what I had already told Deacon.

"You didn't get the name of that woman in black?" Deacon rapped out when Hubbard had finished.

"I didn't, sir."

Deacon turned to me. "Hubbard tells us Ogden shouted the two words 'gold bullets.' The bullets in this Peterson revolver you bought are gold. Do you suspect a connection?"

My conscience was clear in this respect, at least. "I don't know any more than you do, Henry."

Dr. Oakley spoke just then. "He's been dead an hour or so, Deacon. He was attacked from behind as he was telephoning and he fell forward over the desk. He died instantly."

There was nothing new in this. Deacon looked at his watch.

"Ten-twenty-five," he muttered. "What time did you find him, John?"

"Nine-thirty-three."

At this Stimson again moved forward; his hostile eyes were still upon me. He was going to speak. That sense of disaster came over me again. My fear of what he was going to say was none the less real because I hadn't the slightest idea of what was in his mind. I was on the point of heading him off when the dull thud, thud, of the front door knocker reverberated through the hall. Coming like that, it startled all of us. We looked at one another with tense faces. Again it beat upon the taut stillness of that chamber of death. Hubbard hurried into the hall.

Stimson held his tongue. We waited.

The front door opened. Hubbard's voice, deferential and explanatory, came to us. Another's broke in upon it, hard and rasping in tone, and familiar to me. My eyes sprang to Deacon's in astonishment. I saw him stiffen; a look of irritation crossed his honest face. I love a contest and in spite of my astonishment and heaviness of heart I half smiled. But what had brought Luther MacNair here?

"Good evening, gentlemen."

MacNair had preceded Hubbard into the room and he stood looking at us with that cold, disconcerting stare which was to become so familiar to me in the next few days. He was a tall, lean man with a swarthy skin and a thin face as keen as a razor blade. His eyes were dark and hard, with nothing friendly or human about them. As they fell on me an ironic gleam came into them and I supposed he was thinking of the mess Polyandria had made of his tomato vines. A year or two my junior, he had retired from professional life six months ago and taken up residence in San Felipe. He brought with him a handsome reputation as a man-tracker. Ruthless in his methods and diabolically clever, he was said to be less a personality than a machine. The events of the next few days were to confirm this description of his character.

"Hello, MacNair," Henry said curtly. "I didn't expect to see you here. You know Peebles?"

"Slightly," MacNair admitted in his humorless voice. "He has something unusual in cats."

"Mr. MacNair goes in for tomatoes, Henry," I ventured. Deacon detests them as much as I do.

"I called to see Ogden," MacNair went on. "This man," nodding at Hubbard, "tells me he has been murdered."

Deacon indicated the figure on the couch. "Pretty late for calling, isn't it?"

MacNair glanced at the body. There was no pity in his face.

"I am here at Ogden's invitation," he said. "When I got home a few minutes ago I found this card under my door. I saw the light so I came over." MacNair gave Deacon one of Andrew Ogden's personal cards.

Henry studied the back of it, then he passed the card on to me. His eyes were as deeply astonished as he ever permitted them to become. On the back of the card Andrew had written:

> Mr. MacNair: You were out when I called. There is a matter I wish to discuss with you. Will you drop in as soon as you return? This is important.
>
>   A. O.

Astounded, I returned the card to MacNair. Ogden had telephoned me—he had summoned Luther MacNair. On what common ground had the three of us stood?

"Have you any idea what Ogden wanted?" Deacon asked.

"Specifically, no."

"You mean he may have wanted to see you in a professional way?"

"Yes. But I retired six months ago."

"A man is never retired until he's dead," Henry said grimly. "You have a strong record, MacNair."

"Your appreciation is touching."

Henry looked at the body. "I am sorry you weren't home," he grieved. "Andrew might have been with us now."

"You'll get your man easily enough."

"Ah! the solution is already apparent to you," Henry flashed at him. "I envy you your penetration."

"Dear, dear! I was trying my hand at a compliment."

"You were never known for your compliments, Mac-Nair."

"I suppose not. It's a grim business, this man-catching. But I'm through with it." A mirthless grin twisted his thin lips. "A man with twenty-three hangings and fourteen electrocutions to his credit has no business being interested in anybody's murder but his own. You'll find me at 2341 Magnolia if you want me. Good night, Deacon. Regards to Polyandria, Peebles."

"Amiable fellow," Deacon growled when he had gone. Then he laughed. "He's got a great record, though."

I nodded, shuddering at MacNair's twenty-three hangings and fourteen electrocutions. Some day I suppose we will stop breaking men's necks and cindering their bodies.

Deacon went to the glass-topped cabinet behind the desk and lifted the lid.

"That dagger is kept here, isn't it, Hubbard?"

"As a rule, sir."

"It belongs to Mr. Jerry, doesn't it?"

"Yes, sir."

Deacon dropped his head. I knew what his next question would be. It was the one I had feared more than any other he was likely to ask. Stimson was watching me with a leer in his eyes. Deacon raised his head.

"Where is Mr. Jerry, Hubbard?"

My heart seemed to be pounding in my throat. Why hadn't the young fool stopped when I called? . . . Hubbard's voice appeared to come from a distance.

"I—I believe he is out, sir."

"Where has he gone?"

"I don't know, sir. As I told you, I heard Mr. Jerry and Mr. Ogden talking in the library a few minutes after nine. That is all I know, sir."

"You heard Mr. Jerry's voice distinctly?"

"Yes, sir."

"And you didn't see Mr. Ogden after six o'clock?"

Hubbard moistened his lips. "Not—not alive, sir."

Again there was silence. I managed to get myself in hand. Deacon was thinking. Presently he said:

"I suppose it was you who left Mr. Ogden's card at Mr. MacNair's?"

"No, sir. *I* left it there."

Stimson, the gardener, had answered the last question. He came forward, his hands thrust into the pockets of his khaki breeches, his eyes challenging mine.

"You are the gardener, aren't you?" Deacon asked.

"Uh-huh."

"What time did Mr. Ogden give you this card?"

"Around six, I guess. That Furie feller had just gone down the drive. I was watering them hydrangea bushes out there and Mr. Ogden stuck his head out of the window. He called me, gave me the card, and told me where to leave it. There was nobody home, so I shoved it under the door."

Deacon nodded. "You went at once."

"Uh-huh."

"Did you come back to your work out there?"

"Nope. I'd about finished when Mr. Ogden called me. I went to the kitchen for my supper."

"Your rooms are over the garage, aren't they?"

"Uh-huh."

"Is Mr. Jerry's car in the garage?"

"No, it ain't. But it was there round nine o'clock—just before I dropped in on the Hubbards!"

"Did you see or hear the car go?"

"Nope." Stimson leered at me, then he leaned confidentially towards Deacon. "I'd like a word with you alone, Chief."

Henry eyed him coldly for a moment. "Come this way."

He lead Stimson through a door in the north wall of the library. This door gives entrance to a little den which Jerry Ogden has taken for his own purposes. Beyond a couple of guns, a jumble of fishing tackle, and a few odds and ends of furniture—usually littered with books and magazines and pipes, old sweaters and hats and various articles of outing toggery—there isn't much in it. I watched Deacon shut the door behind them with deep misgivings for I suspected what Stimson was going to tell him.

Hubbard looked at me uneasily and Thompson, the detective, paused in his systematic examination of the room to give me an appraising stare. Oakley had drawn a rug over the figure on the couch. Heavy of heart, I began to pace up and down the room. The place stifled me, the odor of death was in my nostrils. Unable to stand it any longer, I mumbled something about going out for a breath of air and made for the hall door.

The crisp night air revived me, and with no definite objective in view I proceeded slowly down the drive and along the winding path which leads into my own preserves. Coming to the gate, I opened it. The light still burned in my den. A longing for my fireplace overcame me and I went on through the gate. After all, there is no place like one's own snuggery when the earth is rocking beneath one's feet.

Brooding over the tragedy, I passed through the French window. Lucy was sitting in the arm chair in front of the fire, which had burned down to a handful of embers. Her face was buried in her arms, but when I whispered her name she looked up at me. I saw that she knew what had happened. The white misery of her face wrung my heart. Lucy is always so gay and buoyant. What was I going to say to her? She came towards me and put her soft arms around my neck.

"I've just heard about Uncle Andrew," she said gently. Lucy has called Ogden that for years.

"You got away early." I could think of nothing else to say.

"Yes. Jerry didn't come so I drove home alone."

I sank heavily into the chair and Lucy perched on the arm.

"How did you know?" I muttered.

"Mrs. Moffit told me. Mrs. Hubbard was over. It's dreadful! I can't believe it. Poor Uncle Andrew! I can't believe he's gone!"

She began to weep softly, her head on my shoulder, and I let her grief have its way. Soon her dark eyes were fixed on mine again and I knew what was coming.

"Where is Jerry, Uncle John?"

What was I to say to her? I tried to avoid her eyes but their expression was imperative and they transfixed me.

"Where is he, Uncle John?"

"I don't know where he is," I cried desperately.

"You don't know!" she echoed in bewilderment. Her strong little hand came down hard upon my shoulder. "You must know! Has—has something happened to *him,* too?"

Hysterical, she slid to her feet and stood facing me, eyes wide with terror. "What is it? Where is he? I must go to him!"

I caught her firmly by the wrists. "See here, Lucy! Nothing has happened to Jerry. Nothing has happened him, I tell you! He isn't home, that's all. He left the house a little while before . . . it happened. Pull yourself together and go to your room. I'll tell you about it afterwards. I must go back now."

She shut her eyes for an instant; opening them, she gazed at me steadily but with an expression I couldn't fathom.

"I'm sorry, Uncle John. You frightened me the way you looked. I thought something had happened to Jerry. I'll—I'll be all right now."

I stood up, looking at her. "You'll go to your room, Lucy?"

Her eyes swam in a sea of tears. "Of course I will, Uncle John."

She clutched my hand for an instant; then she kissed me on the lips and, turning, went out of the room. I wanted to go after her and take her into my arms and comfort her. Lucy is very dear to me.

Suddenly, I remembered it had been my impression that Jerry had dropped something as he fled down the drive. If my impression was correct I had better find whatever it was he had dropped before Deacon or any of his men came upon it. With this thought in mind I hurried through the window, crossed the garden, and passed into the Ogden grounds. Making my way to where I believed the object had seemed to fall, I dropped onto my knees and crept and pawed around the cinder walk. Without result, however, and I decided to risk a match.

Shielding the flame, I poked into the grass at the side of the walk. A couple of snails crackled beneath my knees—how I loathe the things—and then my pains were rewarded by the glint of metal. I pounced on it and found Jerry's keys. Six or eight on a ring. Undoubtedly they were his. I had often seen them in his hands. Yes, it was just as well that I and not Deacon had found them. Grunting a little for my poor knees, I got up.

"Hand it over, John."

My heart stood still and my old legs trembled until I thought they were going to jackknife beneath me. I turned slowly, the keys behind my back. The darkness did not prevent me from feeling the frigid blueness of Deacon's eyes.

"Hello, Henry," I said unsteadily. "I was looking for something."

"You found it, too," he returned dryly. "Hand it over."

"See here, Henry!" I began indignantly.

"It's no use, John." His voice was weary. "I know what you think of the boy. I like him myself, too; but I thought a good deal more of the father than I do of the son, and if Jerry killed Andrew he's going to pay for it!"

"Killed Andrew! You are crazy!"

He laughed shortly. "I don't know so much about that. Stimson came out around nine-thirty. He saw Jerry rush down here in his white flannels, he heard you call after him, he heard you shout to Jerry that he had dropped something. Jerry's car was in the garage at nine. It isn't there now. When you saw him he was on his way to the garage."

I had expected this would be Stimson's testimony, but Deacon's phrasing gave it a deadly ring that staggered me and I lost my head a little.

"Henry," I shouted, "you may go to the devil."

He looked at me sorrowfully; then his face hardened. "I'll have to take it from you, then." And with this his powerful arms shot out at me.

I fell back, bringing my hand forward so that I might hurl the keys far into the trees and shrubbery behind me. The unexpected happened, then. As my hand shot backward five warm fingers closed upon it and the keys were whipped out of my grasp. Deacon gave a roar of anger, swept me aside, and sprang past me. Spinning round, I was just in time to see Lucy vanish into the darkness of the trees, Lucy, whom I had supposed was in bed by this!

I set off after them. The deep gloom hid Deacon from me, but I could hear him crashing through accumulations of dead leaves. Lucy had gone like the wind and Deacon, who is a decade or so younger than I, also soon left me behind. The gate opened, slammed shut, opened again. I went headlong over a vine. Dazed by the fall, I did not move for a moment; then I climbed slowly to my feet. The French window of my den slammed to and I started on again. I was just in time to bump into Deacon as he was making for the back door.

"See here, Henry."

My conciliatory tone stopped him.

"Well?"

"Leave her alone," I pleaded. "She's dreadfully upset about this. I am, too. We didn't know what we were doing. You and I have got to work together."

"Come to your senses, eh? Well, what was it you picked up."

I took a deep breath. "A bunch of keys."

"Jerry's keys?"

I nodded and sat down heavily upon the step. There was silence for a moment. We did not look at each other.

"I must have them," Henry said, at length.

But his voice was gentler. Something in my being quickened to something in his and the bonds of our friendship tightened.

"I'll get them for you," I promised, a trifle doubtfully, for Lucy has a mind of her own.

His hand fell on my shoulder. "I've got to act as I see fit, John. It looks as if the young fellow did it. Unless he can tell a straight yarn I shall arrest him as soon as I find him." His hand tightened. "I'm sorry, John. She's a fine girl—Lucy. I'd give everything I have to make it otherwise."

I nodded for I knew he meant what he said. "It looks bad," I admitted, "but you don't know the boy as I do, Henry. He *couldn't* have done it. I'll show you before I'm through."

"I hope you will, John."

He left me, then. Desolate of spirit I sat where I was for a little while, sorrowing for the friend who had gone. Then I got up and tried the French window.

5

Enter Luther MacNair

It was bolted and the curtains were drawn, but I saw the dark blur of Lucy's head against the back of my armchair.

"Lucy!"

She did not move and I rapped on the glass.

"Lucy! This is Uncle John!"

There was no response at first; then her head inclined towards the window.

"I am alone. Let me in."

She got up slowly and came to the window.

"Has he gone?" Her voice was muffled.

"Yes. Open the window."

"I won't give them up!" she declared hysterically.

"Now, now, dear. Just let me in and we'll talk it over."

She unlocked the window and I entered. The tragedy in her face swept away the remnants of my self-control and I took her into my arms. We must have wept together. But when I had dropped into my chair and Lucy had curled up in my lap, I felt better.

"Now, dear," I said briskly, "we are going to face this thing with clear brains and brave hearts. Where are those keys?"

"I won't give them up!" she stormed.

"But you must! Deacon knows you have them. You won't help Jerry by keeping them back. And—we've got to have Deacon's cooperation."

"But I followed you, Uncle John. I heard what Captain Deacon said to you. I didn't understand it at all—you haven't told me anything, yet—but he thinks Jerry killed his father. He said Stimson saw Jerry running along the walk—that *you* saw him—called to him—just after—"

She broke off, shuddering, and began to weep again.

I took her firmly by the shoulders.

"Now see here, Lucy! Crying won't get Jerry out of this mess. You must buck up and show us the kind of stuff you are made of!"

And buck up she did, forthwith, drying her eyes on a spider's web of a handkerchief that wouldn't have stopped my ear.

"You've never been in love, Uncle John." She gave me a wintry smile.

"For which I am heartily thankful," I assured her. "As for Jerry, nothing has happened to him yet, and if we keep our heads, nothing will. Give me those keys."

They were under the cushion of my chair and after much wriggling we dug them out.

"You don't believe Jerry did it, Uncle John?"

"Of course not."

"So it couldn't have been Jerry you and Stimson saw running along the walk?"

This was a question! "Are you going to be reasonable, my dear?"

"Yes, Uncle John."

Her dark eyes said so, too, but I was dubious. Lucy and logic are ever at odds.

"These are the facts, then."

Whereupon I told her everything I knew. When I had done she thought for a minute or so; then she said:

"Neither you nor Stimson saw Jerry's face or heard his voice."

"We didn't," I admitted. "At least, I didn't. But I saw Jerry's white trousers, the white sweater with the roll collar you gave him last Christmas, and the pulled-down Panama hat he bought last week. And these are his keys. Moreover, Hubbard heard Jerry's voice in the library twenty minutes before—"

Lucy put her fingers on my lips. "It was somebody else you saw in Jerry's clothes, Uncle John."

I had given this possibility some thought, but I knew if I hadn't been very fond of Jerry I wouldn't have wasted my time on it. For that matter, had the person I had seen on the walk been some one I did not care for I would have taken his guilt for granted. And now, against my will, cankering doubt attacked my faith in Jerry. For after all, my defense of him was backed by faith and nothing else. And faith wasn't fact, however I might argue the point. Had Jerry, lad of impulse that he was, in a moment of furious anger—? I shuddered and put the thought away and confessed myself as illogical as Lucy.

"That would imply willingness on Jerry's part to let some one else have them," I observed, "and he was wearing them when Hubbard saw him at six o'clock."

This opened wider fields of speculation and we fell silent. Suddenly Lucy took my face between her hands; her eyes were alight.

"What is it, dear?"

"Mr. MacNair!"

"Eh?"

"Luther MacNair, the detective, Uncle John! You must get him to take the case for Jerry."

"MacNair!" I cried, aghast.

"Why not? You told me he is known all over the country. You said he solved nearly every case he undertook."

I had told Lucy something of the sort a few days ago, but now I was thinking of MacNair's twenty-three hangings and fourteen electrocutions. The cankering doubt of Jerry returned. If, in a frenzy of rage, he had struck his father down, MacNair would fix the crime upon him as surely as night follows day. On the other hand, if Jerry were innocent—he *must* be!—MacNair was the very man to prove it. I swung like a pendulum between these extremes, cheered by the one, devastated by the other.

"MacNair has retired," I objected. "He'd probably refuse to help us."

"But he mightn't," Lucy pleaded. "We could ask him."

Her eloquent eyes pinned me down. How could I tell her of that cankering doubt? How could I tell her of that procession of dead men and of my unholy fear that Mac-Nair might add Jerry to its tragic number? Indecision held me in torment and then my faith renewed itself and courage illuminated the blackness of my soul.

"Very well," I said. "We'll ask him."

Lucy flung her soft arms around my neck and kissed me. "You dear!" she cried, mussing my thinning silver hair and tweaking my white mustache. "Come on! We'll go right away."

"My dear child! The man will have been in his bed for hours. Look at the time! Twelve o'clock! Off to bed with you." I am prone to forget that Lucy is of the night-owl age.

She slipped to her feet and stood facing me pityingly, hands on her slender hips. *"You'd* make a fine detective! Don't you know they always get on the ground at once? If you don't come with me this minute, Uncle John, I'll go alone!"

That settled it, of course. Grumbling, I got my hat and we set off. MacNair's house is a shabby old stucco place set in a lovely garden two blocks below ours. He was having a sun porch built on to it and other alterations made and we had to pick our way through a jumble of builders' materials. A side window was lighted. Lucy rang the bell; rang it again, and soon we heard footsteps in the hall. A light snapped on over our heads, the door was flung open and Luther MacNair stood before us in a wine-colored dressing gown. By the look on his face he was none too pleased to see us.

"Hello, there," he growled, "I was just going to bed."

"I am sorry to disturb you at this hour," I said apologetically. "But the reason of our call is rather serious. This is my niece, Lucy. Mr. MacNair, Lucy." MacNair, I imagine, was the first detective Lucy had met outside the pages of fiction and she widened her eyes becomingly at him. "We are dreadfully upset about this tragic affair at the Ogdens'. The police seem to think Ogden's son, Jerry, had something to do with it."

"Indeed!"

"Yes. My niece and young Jerry are greatly attached to each other. As a matter of fact, they are engaged—"

"Yes, yes!" he interrupted irritably. "But what's it got to do with me?"

"Your reputation followed you here, Mr. MacNair," I said humbly. "We came to consult you."

"To consult me! I told you and Deacon I was out of this sort of thing."

"To be sure," I stammered. "But I thought—the matter is so urgent—we hoped you might be persuaded—"

"Won't you take hold of it for us, Mr. MacNair?" Lucy broke in pleadingly, her dark eyes more eloquent than I had ever seen them. "There's no one else we can turn to. Mr. Ogden sent for you—he must have had faith in you. If—if it's a question of money—that can be arranged."

MacNair turned his disconcerting stare on the girl. Lucy can be fetching when she wants and his harsh mouth relaxed a little.

"Money!" he said sharply. "I have all the money I need."

He seemed to think rapidly for a moment. I got the impression that he wasn't interested in the monetary aspect.

"Come inside," he said curtly.

We followed him into a library and he offered us chairs in front of a fireplace with a red ember or two still glowing in the grate. Paper, sticks and a log soon started a crackling blaze and MacNair drew up a third chair. The reflection from the fire softened his lean, hard face: the swarthy skin, the high cheek bones and slit of a mouth, the deep, penetrating eyes. As I studied the man, neither liking nor disliking him, it came over me that we had come to the right place. If any man on earth could put his finger on Ogden's murderer it was Luther MacNair.

"Tell me what you know." His voice had a rasping edge to it.

While I was talking he asked me one or two pertinent questions, but for the most part he remained silent until I had done.

"Hyde refused to tell you where he got the pistol?" MacNair growled.

"Yes."

"And Hubbard heard Ogden shout 'gold bullets' while this man Furie was in the library. Furie, eh? Good name, that."

"Are you inclined to connect Furie with the murder?" I asked quickly.

"I am inclined to consider him. That woman in black, too. And Nathan Hyde, perhaps. Don't misunderstand me. I am not saying any of them did it. They have merely entered the case—that's all."

"You are going to help us then?"

He flashed his disconcerting stare at me. Out of the corner of my eye I saw Lucy turn rigid in her chair and her white face lengthen a little.

"I suppose I shall have to," he grumbled. "It's about as odd a thing as I ever tackled."

Lucy gave a sob of relief, but she was too overcome to do more than whisper some incoherent expression of her gratitude. MacNair paid not the slightest attention to her emotion.

"I want it clearly understood," he went on, "that I play no favors. If I take the case I look for Ogden's murderer. When I find him I shall turn him over to the police, no matter who he may be. Is that understood?"

I nodded, shuddering a little and avoiding Lucy's eyes. Apparently he took it for granted that he would be successful in his quest; but his tone was not boastful and it came upon me again that if MacNair could not put his finger on the man who had killed my friend no one could. But I was not to easily forget that procession of unhappy dead.

"We are not afraid, Mr. MacNair," Lucy assured him bravely.

"Do you believe from what I have told you that Jerry Ogden killed his father?" Lucy winced at my question, but it had to be asked.

"Why shouldn't I?" he returned with such brutal directness that Lucy gave a cry of pain. "Hubbard heard him talking to his father shortly after nine. You and Stimson saw him running as if for his life two minutes after the thing was done. He hasn't turned up since. His car is gone. You picked up his keys. What more do you want? If it had been any one else you had seen racing along that walk you'd have known who killed Ogden."

"I *feel* that Jerry didn't do it," I said doggedly.

"You *feel!*" MacNair mocked. "Got any evidence?"

"I have my faith in him."

"Faith!" MacNair's laugh was the most devastatingly ironic sound I ever heard come from human lips.

"Have you no faith in human nature?" I demanded.

Again he laughed. "I have faith in my own good brain and my own two hands. The only other thing I have faith in is the certainty that human nature will salt its own beans. I've been catching crooks for thirty-five years. Do you suppose I got them with faith?"

The man's cynicism appalled me.

"What about the possibility that somebody else was wearing Jerry's clothes, that somebody else dropped his keys?" I ventured. "I didn't see Jerry's face, remember." This was Lucy's belief and I was beginning to incline towards it myself.

MacNair laughed. "Why should it be somebody else? Because you want it to be. Well, never mind that." He lighted a cigarette. "See here, Peebles. It looks as if young Ogden killed his father. But I am not starting out on the assumption that he did. I'll draw my conclusions . . . later."

"Fair enough," I agreed.

"We understand each other, then. You have known Ogden for some time, I take it?"

"About nine years."

"Intimately?"

"He was my closest friend."

"Do you know of anything in his life that might suggest a motive for his death?"

I hesitated, thinking of that masklike quality I had sometimes sensed in Andrew.

"You had better be frank with me."

"It's rather hard to explain," I said. "Ogden and I were together a good deal and the engagement of the children brought us closer still. But, well, I always had an idea there was a side of him I hadn't seen. Sometimes I wondered if the Andrew Ogden I knew really was the man himself."

"Nothing definite, eh?"

"Nothing."

"What kind of a lad is young Ogden?"

I smiled at Lucy. "A fine, clean boy. A bit reckless and impulsive, perhaps, but that's all. He favors his father in looks but he has none of that restraint, that secretiveness, I sometimes sensed in Andrew."

"On good terms with his father?"

"Of course. They had their differences, I expect."

"For instance?"

The question came so abruptly that I was startled. So was Lucy, the color flaming into her white cheeks. Both of us were thinking of Jerry's difference of opinion with his father about the mine. Had it resulted in a break between them? Probably not. But even if it had it didn't follow— Of course it didn't! The notion was absurd.

"Come, come!" MacNair rasped irritably. "What is it?"

"Nothing much," I replied calmly. "Ogden owns a mine down in Skull Valley. Near Torridity. The 'Two Brothers,' I believe the mine is called. It hasn't been operated for thirty years and Jerry, who is an engineer, thinks there's pay gold in it. He wanted to reopen the mine, but Andrew wouldn't have it touched. I don't know why. Jerry is a persistent youngster and he kept at his father constantly about it. They hadn't quarreled, so far as I know."

MacNair grunted. "Did you ever hear Ogden mention Furie and this woman who was dressed in black?"

"Never."

"Ever hear him refer to 'gold bullets'?"

"Never."

"Furie and the woman in black will have to be account-ed for. I suppose Deacon will run them down." MacNair stood up. "That'll do, now. I'll see you after breakfast. Better tell Deacon I'm working on the thing. He's a pig-headed devil."

"Don't forget the probability that Ogden's murderer got hold of Jerry's flannels," I reminded him.

He grinned mirthlessly. "It's become a probability, has it? You'd better sleep on what I said about fixing the responsibility. I meant it. If you want me to drop the case say so in the morning."

Lucy answered him. "We are not afraid of the truth, Mr. MacNair."

He nodded. "I shall want to see that Peterson revolver, so don't turn it over to Deacon yet."

With this he let us out into the darkness.

6

Through the Window

It was half-past-two when I got into bed. My body ached with weariness, but I was consumed by that fever of unrest which always comes upon me after great excitement. I have a nervous temperament and the active and sometimes hazardous life which I led before I retired had not hardened my mettle. My mind was going round and round like an endless phonograph record and I felt as if I could never sleep again.

The telephone call . . . Andrew's last words . . . Jerry running like the wind . . . the unforgettable horror of that first moment in Andrew's library . . . Hubbard's story of Furie and the woman in black, and Andrew shouting 'gold bullets' . . . the coming of Deacon and Luther MacNair . . . Stimson's story, my fears for Jerry and Lucy's agony of mind . . . MacNair's pitiless cynicism and the drift of the evidence. God in heaven! To what was it leading? . . . And then all over again until I thought I would go mad.

The hall clock struck three . . . presently three-thirty.

But gradually my overwrought nerves quieted down and I felt sleep stealing upon me.

And then, suddenly, I was wide awake again. Some slight noise must have aroused me, but my first thought was that I had neglected to do something. Ah, yes! I had put Polyandria out and forgotten to let her in again. But a sense of "wrongness" persisted in my mind. Probably it was due to imagination, but I knew I couldn't rest until I had satisfied myself about it. I was on the point of sliding out of bed when a weighty object landed with a thump on my abdomen. Alarmed, I put out my hand, felt silky fur, and laughed.

"Polyandria! Where did *you* come from?"

The question disturbed me. If I had left Polyandria locked out—and I was sure I had—how had she got in? Putting her aside, I got out of bed, slid into my trousers and carpet slippers, and crept into the hall. Halfway along it I stopped. The door of my den was ajar. Inside, a light beam circled the room. Some one with an electric torch was there, some one who had come in through the French window and, incidentally, let Polyandria in with him. And there are those who doubt the intelligence of cats!

It was an awkward situation, you will admit. The rascal was after my pistols and as the revolver I keep for protective purposes was in my desk I didn't yet see what I was going to do about it. If I made my presence known I would either frighten him off—probably with a sackful of my best pistols—or bring him out, automatic in hand, to settle me.

I am not a courageous man. On the other hand he wasn't going to rifle my cabinet while I had breath of life to prevent him. My eyes flew around the shadowy hall in search of a weapon. Ah! Lucy had left her golf clubs by the dining-room door for everybody to trip over. I quietly extracted one of them, the brassie, I believe it was.

Creeping to the door of the den, I peered inside. The man was softly opening and shutting the drawers of my desk and pouring the light beam down into each in turn. This puzzled me for I had expected to see him rifling the cabinet. But when he came to the left-hand bottom drawer and straightened up with something in his hand, I almost shouted out the conclusion that poured through my mind.

"The Peterson revolver! I put it in the drawer before I went to bed." The words "gold bullets" suddenly resounded in my brain. "Good God! Is he—could he be Andrew's murderer?"

The notion was fantastic, but it would not leave me. His back was towards me, the localized light from the torch threw him into deep shadow, and I could make nothing of either his face or figure. In a moment he would be off. How was I to stop him?

A faint sound at my feet drew my eyes down, but I felt rather than saw Polyandria at my ankles. She follows me like a dog and she had come down after me. Stooping, I reached for her, intending to draw her out of what might become the line of fire, but she eluded me and made for the partly open door. Her soft body collided with it and the opening widened. A hinge creaked loudly.

The light went out and the night huddled me into its velvet cloak. I saw nothing, heard nothing, but I pictured my man waiting, pistol trained on the door, finger on trigger, body turned to stone. My blood became ice and fire by turns. This was my chance—I must take it! Sinking to my knees, golf club in hand, I wormed my way into the opening, widening it again. Another creak. I froze against the floor expecting the tearing agony of a bullet. It did not come. The stillness and the blackness pressed upon me like tangible presences.

I was in the room. Silence still. Breathing deeply, I raised myself onto my stood feet, crouched against the wall, stood upright, waited. The next minute was the most nerve-shattering of my life—standing there . . . waiting for him to shoot . . . sweat drenching my garments. Ugh! Facing a firing squad would be something like this. A nice

situation, you will admit, for a man in his sixty-ninth
year!

A rustling sound reached me and I felt rather than saw
the passage of a body towards the window. Ah! he planned
to slip through the window and run for it before I discovered what he was about. Moving away from the wall,
I hung the golf club over my shoulder, hands vised upon
the stick. I must drive it home before he got his gun into
action—or stop a steel-jacketed bullet!

My eyes by this were more accustomed to the darkness
and I saw vaguely against the ebony background a lighter
oblong which I knew to be the window. The oblong
darkened as if a man had passed in front of it. I started
incautiously forward and stumbled over a rug, betraying
my position. Quickly recovering myself, I sensed a leveled
pistol in the man's hand. I say "sensed" because though I
could not see it, nevertheless, I knew it was there. One's
intuitive faculties sometimes are amazingly keen at such
moments.

Leaping forward, I brought the brassie over my shoulder in a sweeping arc. I struck blindly and with small hope
of landing the blow before the man fired. But the darkness
must have confused him as to my exact position for land
it I did—on his shoulder. Evidently the blow numbed his
arm for the pistol dropped, unexploded. The thud of it
was music in my ears.

Letting go of the brassie and forgetting that this was no
job for a man of my years, I flung myself at the fellow. My
hands went to his throat and one of his came to mine. We
hung onto each other like a couple of collies. He could use
only one arm at first, but he was beyond me in strength
and I don't believe I ever encountered such ferocity in a
human being before. He fought silently—both of us did,
for that matter—and with an economy and concentration
of energy that anticipated every move I made. He put into

the struggle a fury, a malignancy, a diabolical cunning of which I was incapable. And this, mark you, with his one hand. Now he brought the other into play and I knew that he was going to be too much for me. His fingers were like talons—they seemed to be cracking the sinews of my throat. His knees hugged mine, his breath scorched my face, his heart seemed to be devouring my heart. Every inch of him was alive and squirming and irresistible.

Breathing became agony, my endurance was leaving me, my head felt as if it were splitting asunder. Just then Polyandria got between our feet. We stumbled over her and crashed to the floor. The man must have trodden or fallen on her tail or toe for she howled and the man grunted as if her claws had got home. He kept his grip on my throat, but I lost mine on his. Moreover, he maneuvered my body and his in such a way that I fell on my face and he came down astride of me. I tried unavailingly to fling him off. Cries for help rose in my throat, but I could not voice them; his grip tightened beyond endurance, a shadow crept over my brain. At last I had come to the end of my life. I surrendered myself to the inevitable.

And then the pressure on my throat suddenly ceased and the man was no longer astride my body. My ears were ringing, but I thought I heard feet in the hall. The door opened, the wall switch clicked, but darkness still permeated the room. There isn't a chandelier in the den and I had turned the current off at the desk lamp and the reading lamp. This prevented me from recognizing the man.

The French window crashed to and then, to my astonishment, I heard Luther MacNair's harsh voice:

"Stop, there! Hands up!"

Some one laughed. And then:

"Back, ye fool, or I'll drill yer! Git inside!"

The voice was deep, throaty, commanding, and I did not recognize it. Somehow it struck me as being disguised.

A shot rang out. Another. I tried to get up, but only succeeded in rolling over. The reading lamp flashed on and I saw Lucy and Mrs. Moffit standing over me. At that moment MacNair burst through the French window. His hat was gone and his face was black with fury and bitter disappointment. Lucy dropped beside me, a cry of grief on her lips.

"Uncle John! Are you hurt? You *are* hurt!" Her soft hands fluttered at my throat; her eyes, deep with tenderness, did much to compensate me for my pain. "We got here just in time!"

"I thought he was gone," my housekeeper moaned. "He looked like poor Moffit lying there all white."

Mrs. Moffit was in her nightgown—Lucy insists she wears two—and her curl papers. She had one slipper on, the other was in her hand. Lucy, also, was in her nightgown, but Lucy's nightgowns and Mrs. Moffit's have little in common.

The effort to swallow pained me dreadfully.

"Get something for his throat!" MacNair snapped.

Mrs. Moffit fled, still carrying her slipper, and Mac-Nair dropped at the other side of me.

"Did you recognize him?"

I swallowed again while Lucy caressed my throat. "No," I whispered. "Did you?"

"I did not," he cried savagely. "It was pitch dark in the shrubbery. I had been in the Ogden grounds about five minutes when I thought I heard some one over here calling for help. The man jumped through the window as I came up—bumped into me and knocked the torch out of my hand. I pretended I had a gun—and he put a couple of shots through my hat. I wish I'd risked it and gone after him."

I couldn't help grinning a little, keen as my disappointment was. This was the very thing to put MacNair on his mettle.

"Good thing—you didn't," I returned faintly. "Two murders—on our hands—then. Pretty nearly—joined Andrew myself."

Lucy shuddered and tears from her swimming eyes wet my cheeks.

"What did he look like?" MacNair demanded impatiently.

I shut my eyes and tried to assemble my impressions of the man. They were pitifully few. He had left me with nothing more definite than an impression of tensile strength and animal ferocity.

"He fought like a tiger—and he was as hard to hold—as a steel spring," I said, with difficulty. "That's—all."

"Haven't you any idea what he looked like? Whether he was tall or short, young or old, stout or thin?"

I shut my eyes again and tried to form some sort of a mental picture. "I don't think he was stout," I mumbled. "He may have been fairly tall—but I'm not sure. I can't tell about his age, either. The room was black as a cave. When he shouted at you—he said 'ye' and 'git.' His voice struck me as being disguised. Didn't you get anything?"

MacNair shook his head. "He collided with me before I saw him. His body was scarcely more than a shadow to me. It's damnable!" he fumed, springing to his feet. "He may have had something to do with that affair at Ogden's!"

"I believe he had."

"What!"

"He was after the Peterson revolver."

"How do you know?"

I explained.

"Good God, what a chance we've lost! It may have been Ogden's murderer." MacNair started for the window, but stopped. "It's too late now. How did he know the revolver was here? What did he want with it?"

I shook my head feebly. "I didn't tell any one I had it. Hyde may have." And then: "'Gold bullets,' perhaps." The words had come to my lips of their own accord.

MacNair looked at me, his dark eyes brilliant with expression. "'Gold bullets,'" he echoed.

"It wasn't Jerry," I added dryly.

"How do you know—you say the voice was disguised?" This stumped me. "I *know* it wasn't," I insisted.

MacNair laughed ironically. "Where is the revolver?"

"I think I am lying on it," I said. A metallic object was pressing into the small of my back. "Here it is." Feeling better, I sat up. "The rascal had it leveled on me when I hit him with the golf club. He dropped it and used his own gun on you."

MacNair looked the pistol over. "Queer, he should have known you had it."

I nodded. "It's just another of the many queernesses we have to explain. I'm glad you happened along. You'd better stay for breakfast. If it hadn't been for Lucy"—patting her hand and being kissed in return—"and you and Mrs. Moffit I'd be past caring about breakfasts."

"No, thanks," he declined. "It's nearly dawn. I want to have a look around the Ogden grounds before Deacon and his men mess things up. That was my object in getting there at this ungodly hour."

"You don't waste time," I said, admiringly.

He laughed grimly, but he seemed pleased.

"'Evidence evaporates. Get on the job early,' is one of the maxims of my profession. There's another I'm fond of, too. 'Stick to your job until it's finished.'" He grinned mirthlessly. "There, Peebles! I've taught you how to be a successful detective in two lessons. Write 'em down."

His cynicism chilled me. He was less a creature of warm flesh and blood than a cunning contrivance of wheels and pulleys and cogs and levers. Again I had the thought that if any man on earth could put his hand on Andrew Ogden's murderer it was Luther MacNair.

They helped me into a chair. The window, I saw, had been neatly cut with a diamond near the bolt. Mrs. Moffit appeared properly skirted and carrying water, hot and cold, and a dish of warm olive oil.

"I'll do it," Lucy offered, when I had drunk.

"Miss Lucy," my housekeeper whispered, raising her eyebrows towards MacNair who was inspecting the gold bullets he had ejected from the Peterson revolver, "you are in your nighty."

"Of course I am. Uncle John is in his pyjamas."

Mrs. Moffit pressed her lips together. "Mr. Peebles has his trousers on," she said stiffly.

"Lucy," I interrupted dryly, "you might get me my dressing-gown."

She gave me a little gay-sad smile and tripped out of the room. Lucy insists Mrs. Moffit is so modest that she bathes herself in the dark.

I called Polyandria. She sprang onto my knees and while Mrs. Moffit pursued her ministrations I turned her upside down and examined her claws. On the middle claw of the right front foot I found what I was looking for. Mrs. Moffit was persuaded to cease her attentions long enough to pass me a lens which I keep on my desk and I bent it on the claw. For a minute or so I meditated on what I saw, and on one or two other matters that had come into my head. When I finally looked up MacNair was watching me ironically.

"Well?" he queried.

I chuckled. "There's a drop of blood on one of Polyandria's claws. She got between that rascal's legs and mine and tripped us. He came down on her toes or tail and she scratched him. You had better look for a man with a scratch, MacNair."

"Not bad," he said curtly, and I felt proud of my observation. "Another demonstration of my contention that one should get on the job early. A few minutes later you wouldn't have found it." He pushed Mrs. Moffit aside and peered through the lens. "The scratch will be on an exposed part of the man's body," he went on, "or his garments would have cleansed the claw as the cat drew it back."

"An excellent point!" I remarked. "It hadn't occurred to me. Our task is again simplified: we look for a man with a scratch on an exposed part of his body."

"Hardly as simple as that," MacNair drawled.

"What do you mean?" I exclaimed, struck by his tone.

"I mean if we were to find a man with a scratch on, say, his wrist, it wouldn't necessarily follow that he'd killed Andrew Ogden."

"He'd have to tell a pretty strong story to convince me that he hadn't," I said warmly.

At this, MacNair pulled up his right sleeve and revealed to my astonished eyes a red welt two inches long on the underside of his wrist.

"What do you say to that?" he chuckled.

"Good Lord!" I exclaimed. "What a remarkable coincidence! How did you get it?"

"Coming through the window just now. You must trim that briar rose of yours, Peebles."

"Oh," I said in abashed tones. "I'm sorry. I've always been skeptical of the value of circumstantial evidence, too."

"But you shouldn't be," he informed me bluntly. "It's generally dependable, and usually it's all we have to go on. Direct evidence—an actual witness to a crime—is a rare bird. Unfortunately, circumstantial evidence, like the Bible, is subject to human interpretation. That is to say, we don't always make due allowance for all the facts. Coincidence is the biggest maggot in the circumstantial cheese, for coincidence plays a larger part in human affairs

than we are prone to admit. Make allowances for coincidence and you'll get along nicely with circumstantial evidence. I shall still look for a man with a scratch, Peebles.
And I shouldn't be surprised if it is on his wrist."

Lucy came in just then, partly dressed, and carrying my
gown. She can be quick enough when she likes. I told her
what we had found and she bent excitedly over the lens.

"I'm proud of you, dear," she whispered with that tender, sad look in her eyes. Then, gayly: "He'll make a splendid Dr. Watson, won't he, Mr. MacNair?"

"I don't suppose he'll do any worse than most of 'em,
MacNair admitted sourly.

He tore a scrap of blotting paper from my desk pad,
absorbed the drop of blood, and placed the scrap in an
envelope, which he pocketed. Polyandria accepted these
attentions as matter-of-factly as she did her morning cream.

When I had dismissed Mrs. Moffit—no easy matter,
I can tell you—and Lucy had helped me into my dressing-gown, I picked up the gold-mounted revolver. Mac-
Nair had reloaded it and I ejected the cartridges into my
palm. It was my intention to put them away in my desk
until I had time to extract the powder from them, as I am
averse to keeping more than one loaded weapon in the
house, but MacNair objected.

"I wanted a pistol expert to go over the revolver and
the cartridges. You'd better let me have them just as they
are. An expert may be able to give us some hint as to where
they came from. Never mind reloading the revolver—the
cartridges will do loose in my pocket.

"How stupid of me!" I cried. "I never thought of getting an expert to look at them."

As I handed him the revolver and the cartridges one of
the latter caught my eye and I drew it sharply back.

"Hello!" I exclaimed. "This cartridge has been tampered with."

7

Out of Torridity

I held the cartridge up so that MacNair could see it. There were deep scores in the gold bullet and the edge of the discolored brass shell was nicked and cut as if a knife blade had been thrust in between it and the bullet.

These defacements must have been there when I inspected the cartridge in Hyde's shop, but I suppose I was too excited over my find to attach any significance to them and I probably gave them no more than a passing glance. But the events of the night had opened my mind to the importance of the apparently trivial, and I was curious about the cartridge.

"I didn't notice the marks," MacNair said. He seemed annoyed at himself.

I chuckled. "'Even Homer nods.'"

His face did not change. Later, I was to decide that his ironic cast of countenance was an expression of his philosophy of life; and that he never permitted either victory or defeat to change it lest his fellowmen forget that he invariably held their opinions in contempt.

I dug the bullet out with a jackknife and looked for the powder. There was none. Instead, I saw what was evidently a wad of paper and I poked at it with a pin, as excited as a boy with his first air-gun. It came out reluctantly.

"A message, Uncle John!" Lucy cried ecstatically. Mac-
Nair said nothing.

When I had got the scrap of paper spread out on the
desk it looked as if Lucy were right. It was dirty and brittle and had been torn off the top edge of a newspaper—a
very old newspaper—and there was writing in indelible
pencil on it; scarcely legible writing for the wad had been
folded so tightly that some of the words were obliterated.
A date line was partly decipherable and, to my astonishment, I made out:

TORRIDITY . . . . . . Monday, July . . . . . . 1896.

"Torridity!" I gasped.
"Eighteen ninety-six," MacNair muttered.
"The writing, Uncle John—-read it!" Lucy whispered.
And with the aid of the lens I did so, amazement going
through me like fire in a hayfield.

"'. . . . . . done for, Alex. Dillon got me . .
. . . . skunk, but I . . . . . . a bullet . . . . . .
him, somewhere. Good-b. . . . . . . old scout.
You did . . . . . best for me. I've . . . . . . a
bad devil.
                                        "Jerry!"

"Jerry!" Lucy echoed.
There was silence for a moment. Lucy's hands fluttered onto my arm and stayed there. MacNair stared at
me, a blazing intentness in his eyes. The look overcame his
habitual cynical expression as nearly as any I ever saw in
them.

"No wonder your man wanted the gun," MacNair said
harshly.

I nodded. "I suppose so. And yet—if this note from
the dead was written in 1896, and it hasn't been disturbed

since it was put into the cartridge, how could the man have known it was there?"

MacNair shrugged. "Ask me another."

Lucy still clung to my arm. "This 'Jerry,' Uncle John, it isn't . . . it couldn't be . . ."

"Our Jerry? Hardly! This note was written years ago—probably in 1896, by the look of it—and the writing certainly isn't his." I considered the scrap of paper for a moment. "This Alex must be—"

"Peterson himself," MacNair supplied.

"And 'Jerry'?"

"A friend or a relation. Maybe a brother. Ever hear of any one by the name of 'Jerry' being connected with Peterson?"

"No. Peterson would have been forgotten long ago if it hadn't been for his gold-mounted guns and his willingness to gamble on anything. I wonder who Dillon is—or was."

"The Lord knows! 'Jerry' says he put a bullet into him—a gold bullet, presumably, as one of these shells is empty. And then he scrawled this note and shoved it into the cartridge we found it in. I wonder why he didn't put it into the empty."

"If this happened in 1896 the gun hasn't been used for thirty years."

MacNair nodded. "We must find out where Hyde got it." He put the scrap of paper under the lens. "Do you know what became of Alex Peterson?"

"I don't. He may be alive for all I know."

"You said he was an inveterate gambler. It seems to me I remember hearing something about a 'poker game that cracked the town.' In connection with Peterson, I mean. Do you know anything about it?"

"A 'poker game that cracked the town,'" I muttered. "Yes, the phrase is familiar, but I don't know where I heard it. It must be a part of the Peterson legend. Peterson is supposed to have once played poker for a human life."

"I've heard that, too."

"It's nonsense, of course. The West is full of these wild yarns."

He pondered for a moment. "I suppose we may safely assume that this gun belonged to Alex Peterson; that he was friendly with or related to a man called 'Jerry'; that a man named Dillon shot this 'Jerry' and left him dying; that 'Jerry' wounded Dillon, presumably with a gold bullet; and that 'Jerry,' dying, wrote this note."

"Do you connect this, and the attempt to steal the pistol, with the murder of Andrew Ogden?" I inquired slyly.

"I wouldn't go that far, yet. Of course, the motive for Andrew Ogden's death may be rooted in something that happened thirty years ago. So may the motive for stealing the pistol."

"In that case," said I, triumphantly, "Jerry Ogden *couldn't* have had a hand in his father's death!"

"Nothing of the sort!" MacNair snapped irritably. "Hubbard heard Ogden shout 'gold bullets' at this man Furie—these bullets are gold—but it doesn't necessarily follow there is a connection, although I admit one is suggested, gold bullets being uncommon articles. But even if there is, what of it? Jerry's motive for killing his father might have come out of something that happened before he was born. Something to do with that mine, for instance. I have a healthy respect for facts, Peebles, facts hard and square and solid, and we have no facts that warrant your conclusion. On the other hand we have facts that indicate young Ogden's guilt."

I realized that I had spoken too soon, but a curious idea had come into my head. "What if this man Dillon who killed 'Jerry' should also have killed Andrew Ogden?"

MacNair's ironical expression sharpened. "Why?" he demanded.

I smiled sadly. "Just a vagrant thought. You don't believe in inspirations, of course. If Dillon knew of the note in this pistol he would have good reason for trying to get it. And if Ogden also had come into possession of the dangerous information it contained—dangerous to Dillon, I mean—you see my drift?"

MacNair shrugged. "Pure speculation, Peebles. You are constantly evading the main issue."

"All right. By the way, what about the sameness of these names? The two Jerrys, I mean. Coincidence, do you suppose?"

"I don't know. Likely enough. Coincidence accounts for a good deal in life. . . . But here comes the sun. I'll leave the pistol and the cartridges for Deacon. See you later."

I picked up the telephone and called Henry. There was no word of Jerry and my heart sank. Henry said he was coming to the Ogden house at once and he promised to drop in on me first. I put the instrument down and looked into Lucy's tragic eyes. She tried to speak but her lips were trembling and the words wouldn't come. I was no better off myself. Turning, she fled from the room.

Horribly depressed, I sat at my desk and tried to evaluate properly the little we knew. I didn't make much headway for I was too heartsick to think. So low did my spirits sink, that if it hadn't been for Lucy I would have wished I might follow Andrew. But soon the morning sun got into my bones and I felt better. My brain began to function and presently I was considering the affair pro and con. A fact here and a fact there. What was it MacNair had said about facts? Sound stuff, at any rate. A competent man, MacNair. I couldn't have got a better.

At length I fished a little red-backed notebook out of my desk. None of its pages had been written on. I have

used many such notebooks in my time. Opening it at the
front page I began to write, carefully numbering each paragraph as I went on. When I had written down what was in
my mind I put the notebook away in the desk feeling that
I had accomplished something after all.

Mrs. Moffit put her head in just then.

"Breakfast is ready, Mr. Peebles," she announced.

8

Twenty-Six Poker Chips

Deacon arrived just then and we discussed the note and the incident that led to its discovery over a couple of poached eggs. His amazement was as great as my own, but, like MacNair, he made it clear that a voice echoing out of the comparative antiquity of 1896 wasn't going to modify his theories to any extent, although he admitted that the pistol might have a place in the Ogden puzzle. My odd fancy that the man Dillon mentioned in the note might have killed Andrew didn't impress him.

"One theory is as good as another," he said. "But thirty years is a long time. Dillon may be dead. He might have died as a result of the bullet this 'Jerry' says he put into him. On the other hand 'Jerry' mightn't have died at all. He was able to write the note and seal it up in a cartridge—the Lord knows why! Or again the note might not have been written in 1896. Still again, the whole thing may be a fake. We'll see Hyde, of course."

This was stretching it a bit too far. "Look here, Henry! Have you forgotten that Hubbard heard Andrew shout 'gold bullets' while he was talking with Furie?"

"I haven't, John. Have you forgotten that you and Stimson saw young Jerry running along the walk a minute or so after his father was stabbed? Does it mean nothing to you that his car is gone, that he hasn't turned up, that we have telephoned his friends, his professional associates, and everybody else who might know anything about him, without hearing a word of the lad?"

It meant a good deal to me, but I didn't say so. There was silence for a moment.

"You don't mind my having MacNair on the job?" I asked.

Henry laughed. "Of course not. MacNair's a good man, if he does know it. He's welcome to any evidence we find." His hand fell on my shoulder. "I'm sorry, John," he said huskily. "It looks bad. You are a darn' fine fellow to have for a friend."

He left me, then, taking the pistol and the note with him and I went to my room and dressed. Coming out, I ran into Mrs. Moffit. She looked ill and I didn't wonder.

"How is your neck?" she inquired.

"My neck is doing nicely," I said firmly, for I saw she had designs on it again. "You are not looking well yourself. Why don't you get a colored woman in for a day or two?"

She sighed. "I'll be all right when I've had a cup of tea. It does pick me up. You must let me rub your neck to-night." She turned away with that resigned air which always infuriates me. Why will women martyr themselves!

Mrs. Moffit is never very well and I have suggested domestic help to her at least once a week ever since she came to me, but she scouts the idea. Her trouble is an internal something or other of mysterious origin and perambulating habits. "First it's here and then it's there; now it's up and now it's down," she explained to me when I engaged her. But she steadfastly refuses to have it removed. I don't believe any living woman gets as much enjoyment out of her something or other as Mrs. Moffit gets out of hers. She has tried New Thought, Divine Healing, Episcopalianism, Spinal Manipulation, Disciples of the Fiery Ring, Physical Culture, Olive Oil, and the New Psychology—everything in fact but simple surgery. Recently she embraced Cosmic Indulgence, which comes, I believe, from Los Angeles. Mrs. Moffit always tries to convert me to her latest faith and I try to understand, but so far I haven't made much progress with Cosmic Indulgence.

As I entered the Ogden library I saw that Andrew's body had been removed. Deacon and MacNair were sitting at the desk, talking. Henry gave me a quizzical look, but MacNair remained as disconcertingly ironical of expression as ever. On the desk were a deck of playing cards, a lead bullet, a piece of gold-bearing quartz, a small black-bound notebook, and three stacks of red poker chips.

"Where did you get these?" I demanded in amazement.

"The chips, the cards, and the notebook were in that safe over there," Deacon replied. "I found the combination in the desk." He nodded towards a small wall safe, the door of which was open. A panel was hinged to conceal it when the safe was shut. "The quartz and the bullet," he went on, "were in here." He touched the righthand top drawer of the desk.

The cards and the chips astonished me. "Henry," I said, "do you happen to recall Andrew's attitude towards cards?"

"Of course I do. He detested them. He wouldn't have them in the house. That's what made me leave them out."

"Religious scruples?" MacNair drawled.

"No," I replied. "He was a churchman, but he wasn't narrow or dogmatic. He simply detested cards and gambling of any form. He wouldn't even discuss them, let alone have them in the house. Jerry had to do his card playing outside. Yet Deacon finds both cards and poker chips in his *safe!*"

MacNair grinned ironically. "These church pillars! Know anything about gold quartz?" he asked suddenly.

"No," I said curtly, resenting his thrust at Andrew's religious activities. I picked up the specimen. "It looks rich."

"Rich!" MacNair grunted. "It's rotten with gold. I happen to know something about gold-bearing ore. That bit'll run ten, twenty, thirty thousand to the ton. There probably isn't a great deal of it."

I whistled. "Sounds like a big strike."

He nodded. "But here's the queerest thing of the lot." MacNair slid the black notebook towards me.

I took it up, prepared for anything but what I was to find. The book looked old. Only the first two pages had been written on; the rest of them were blank. At the top of the first page a name was penned in slightly faded ink. The dashing handwriting was Andrew Ogden's.

"Dillon!" I whispered, my eyes on the name. "James Dillon!" The writing danced tauntingly before my eyes and melted into an unintelligible mass which, for an instant, seemed to become the color of blood.

"The plot thickens," MacNair said acidly.

Beneath the name was a list of entries. The upper entries, like the name, were slightly faded; the lower ones were black. As my eye ran down the entries I felt as if I were descending a ladder inside the edifice of Andrew Ogden's life. I began to dread what I might find at the bottom of that edifice.

"There are twenty-six entries," I said unsteadily. "Each one is for five thousand dollars."

"And each one is dated the first day of January of its respective year," Henry added tonelessly. "The last entry is dated the first of the present year."

His troubled eyes met mine and I remembered that Andrew had been his friend also.

"Ogden has paid Dillon five thousand a year for twenty-six years," MacNair drawled.

"You infer?" I cried heatedly.

He shrugged. "Only one thing can be inferred."

"I'll bet every dollar I have Andrew Ogden lived clean and died clean!" I shouted.

MacNair laughed. "I told you we would be treading on somebody's toes."

I cooled down. "Very well. The assumption is that Ogden paid Dillon five thousand a year for twenty-six years. Dillon killed the 'Jerry' who wrote that note, and since Dillon has been receiving payments up to the first of the present year he didn't die as a result of the bullet 'Jerry' put into him. I again offer the theory that Dillon killed Andrew Ogden."

"Why?" MacNair asked.

"I don't know."

"Of course you don't! You theorize without facts. If Dillon was blackmailing Ogden why on earth should he kill him?"

"For the same reason that he killed 'Jerry,' perhaps. Or possibly Ogden refused to pay more blackmail and Dillon killed him for that reason."

"'Possibly' and 'perhaps,'" MacNair echoed raspingly. "If Ogden refused to pay more blackmail Dillon would expose him, not kill him. Else why should Ogden have submitted to blackmail?"

This was logical.

"You are forgetting young Jerry," Deacon reminded me. "You and Stimson saw him tearing along the walk last night. That fact has got to be overcome before we can assume Dillon or any one else killed Ogden, and I don't see any way of overcoming it. A fact is a fact."

"Insisting something is a fact doesn't make it one," I retorted bitterly. "It wasn't Jerry we saw. It was some one else. Some one in his flannels."

"'Insisting something is a fact doesn't make it one,'" Deacon quoted me gently. "Where is Jerry, John?"

"God knows!" I said wearily. "But he'll turn up."

MacNair gestured impatiently. "Jerry is the likeliest candidate so far. But leave Peebles to his sentimentalities for the moment, Deacon, and consider Dillon. The latter may or may not have killed Ogden, but I venture to say he could throw a good deal of light on the affair. Very well. Who is Dillon? He has been blackmailing Ogden for twenty-six years. But—is 'James Dillon' this man's right name? Blackmailers usually submerge their own personalities."

"You mean this man may have been drawing his five thousand a year under a name not his own?" I inquired.

"Yes."

"And that 'James Dillon' may be the 'operating name' of some one known to us?" I went on shrewdly.

"Exactly. Furie, the woman in black, Hubbard, Stimson, Nathan Hyde. Perhaps Deacon here. Even your estimable self."

"Why not Luther MacNair?" I asked ironically.

"Certainly, if you wish."

"At least you leave out our Jerry."

"Hmn! you return to the bone of contention. Yes, I eliminate young Ogden as a possible 'James Dillon,' but not as the slayer of his father. Dillon may have killed the unknown 'Jerry' and blackmailed Ogden all these years; but it doesn't also follow that he *killed* Ogden, though he may know why Ogden was killed."

"You accused me of theorizing without facts," I said derisively, "but you are doing a good bit of it yourself."

"No. I'm not theorizing; I'm speculating. When I theorize I base my theory on fact. You don't. In face of evidence to the contrary you say Jerry Ogden couldn't have killed his father. You call your assertion theory when it is nothing but speculation for you have no basis of fact. When I say Dillon blackmailed Ogden I state a theory. Its basis of fact is this record of Ogden's payments to him. Again, you

say you believe Dillon killed Ogden and call your belief a
theory. But your only basis of fact is your faith in the boy,
which isn't a fact at all. Is the difference clear?"

"Quite," I said dryly, for I knew he was right. "In a
word my theories are not theories at all?"

"Yes."

"And if I offer the suggestion that Ogden's murderer
stole Jerry's flannels I speculate, eh?"

"Exactly. You have no basis of fact."

"Well, I'm of the opinion that he did, MacNair. And I
still believe Dillon killed Ogden. Moreover," I looked at
him shrewdly, "I am inclined to think you agree with me
on both points, your silly facts to the contrary."

"Jerry, or Dillon, or the devil himself, I'll see that he
gets a rope around his neck," Henry cut in bluntly.

During this fine-spun argument I had been arranging
the poker chips into stacks of five. I had five stacks and
one over.

"Hello," I cried. "There are exactly twenty-six poker
chips here. Ogden made twenty-six payments to Dillon.
Queer, isn't it?"

"I noticed that before you came in," MacNair grinned.
"I suppose it's going pretty far, but I wonder if there's any
connection between the chips and the payments. This is
speculation, though. Let's see if we can get a fact out of it
and turn it into theory. You might ring for Hubbard."

I did so. MacNair took a sheet of letter paper and one
of the poker chips. Folding the chip inside the sheet, he
placed both in an envelope, which he sealed. Then he flattened the envelope on the desk, picked it up, and ran his
fingers over it. The imprint of the chip inside was visible
on the envelope. Hubbard came in just then.

"You rang, sir?" he inquired of me.

"Yes," MacNair replied. "You have been here a good
while, Hubbard?"

"About twenty years, sir."

"How did Mr. Ogden get his mail?"

"The mail carrier leaves it in the box inside the drive-way gate twice a day, sir. I brought it up to Mr. Ogden."

"Always?"

"Almost always, sir."

"Was there usually very much of it?"

"Not a great deal, sir."

"Come here, Hubbard."

The man came to the edge of the desk, ill at ease, and MacNair presented him with the envelope in which he had sealed the poker chip.

"Did you ever notice in Mr. Ogden's mail letters that *felt* like that envelope?"

Hubbard ran his fingers over it. "Why, yes, sir. A number of times."

"Tell us about them."

"Well, sir, I began to notice them three or four years after I came here, though they may have been coming in before then. I couldn't help noticing them on account of the chip inside."

"You knew it was a chip, eh?"

"Yes, sir. They kept coming in and after a while I began to expect them. You know how anything unusual sticks in your mind, sir. But I don't believe they came oftener than once a year and it seems to me they always arrived during the first week in January."

"Splendid, Hubbard. And how did you know poker chips were in the envelopes?"

"I chanced to be in the room when Mr. Ogden opened one of the envelopes, sir. The chip fell out."

"Did Mr. Ogden make any comment?"

"No, sir. He wasn't the commenting kind, but his face became bitter and hard and hurt as if he were remembering some dreadful thing. He didn't look like the Mr. Ogden I knew, sir."

"That will do, Hubbard."

The man withdrew and MacNair laughed. "There you are: a beautiful demonstration of speculation turned into theory."

"Your theory being, I suppose, that our blackmailer has a sense of humor?" I queried.

"Exactly. He received his yearly blackmail and acknowledged it with a poker chip."

"But why a poker chip?" Deacon exploded.

"I've exhausted my facts," MacNair drawled.

"Then speculate!" Deacon rapped out. "What's in your head?"

MacNair gave his disconcerting laugh. "I'll leave speculation to Peebles. He's got more imagination than I."

"Yes, thank God!" I cried. "And more faith in honest flesh and blood!"

But I couldn't bring my eyes to meet the mockery in MacNair's. He was impressed by my insistence on Jerry's innocence and Dillon's guilt, but there was something else in his head, and I thought I knew what it was, if Deacon didn't. My surmise left me sick of the bewilderment of life. It was nonsense, of course, but it stuck in my mind like a leech on a sick man's brow and I wished MacNair and his clockwork logic in Hades.

"What about this lead bullet, the cards, and the quartz?" I went on.

"Poker chips imply cards, don't they? As for the quartz and the bullet, I don't know. They may have nothing to do with the case, though the lead bullet looks as if it had plowed through somebody's breast bone. Speculate, Peebles."

The bullet was flattened, but whether it had snuffed out a human life as MacNair suggested I had no means of knowing. Just then I didn't greatly care.

"See here, Henry," I cried suddenly, "have you had Jerry's clothing checked over?"

He nodded. "Thompson went through it with Hubbard. Jerry's khaki hiking clothing is missing."

"He couldn't have been wearing both khaki and flannels," I burst forth triumphantly.

"Not unless he had one on over the other," Deacon said. "And that isn't likely. He may have had the khaki stuff in his car."

I felt I had gained a point.

Henry got up. "I'm going into town," he announced briefly.

I watched him pass out with a feeling of uneasiness.

I was desperately afraid of his tenacity of purpose. Turning to MacNair, I said:

"Do you still believe Jerry Ogden killed his father?"

"My dear Watson! Haven't I made it clear to you that I never theorize without a basis of fact?"

"Speculate, then!" I snapped.

He shook his head in mock gravity. "I never speculate on my chances of hanging a man."

I lost my temper. "MacNair, you are intolerable!" I raged. "You know this boy's innocence is everything in the world to me! You know my niece is breaking her heart over him! If you have got on to anything—one way or the other—tell me what it is! I don't believe there's an ounce of pity in you! I don't believe it matters to you whether young Jerry is guilty or not!"

"Frankly," he said coolly, "it doesn't. So long as I hang the man—or woman—who killed Ogden I don't care whether it's your Jerry, Furie, the woman in black, Hubbard, Deacon, John Peebles, or his cat, Polyandria. Now leave me in peace. I want to go over Ogden's stuff alone."

Turning his back on me, he opened the left-hand top drawer of the desk and began to systematically examine its contents. His ruthlessness lashed my grieving spirit and at that moment I detested him; but my admiration for his capabilities cooled me down and I turned away, wishing him no greater evil than that Polyandria would get into the remainder of his tomato vines.

If my role was to be that of Watson I was determined that it should be an active one. And so I began a close inspection of the library, commencing with the cabinet from which the dagger had been taken. It told me nothing and I proceeded to the bookcases, to the various articles of furniture, to the window, and finally onto the little railed balcony outside. Here I came upon something that moved me deeply.

It was a dusting of gray white powder in size and form vaguely suggestive of the sole of a man's shoe. There had been no wind during the past twenty-four hours, the balcony was sheltered, and I knew that the powder might have been deposited the night before. Dipping the tip of my finger into the powder, I put it to my tongue.

"Cement," I muttered. "MacNair!" I called.

"What is it?" he cried impatiently.

"Your deductive powers are required. Bring an envelope with you."

He came with marked irritation, but when I pointed to the powder his mood soon changed. Frowning, he dropped onto his knees and tasted the powder.

"Cement," he mused. "Hmn! Looks as if some one who had stepped in cement had stood here." He grinned dryly. "Not bad, Watson; not bad."

Puzzled and thoughtful, I got up and watched him brush the powder into the envelope. He went carefully over the rest of the balcony, scrutinized the iron grille, and peered down into the adjacent shrubbery.

"Nothing else here," he muttered. "Good work, Peebles!"

We reentered the library.

"Have you finished?"

"Yes. I didn't find anything. We might as well go."

I followed him out into the hot sunlight. There is nothing as honest as sunlight.

9

Raw Gold

I did not feel equal to facing Lucy in my present state of mind, so I lunched with MacNair in town. It was a dull sort of meal. MacNair was introspective, and repellent in manner, and I was in no mood for conversation. We were sipping our coffee when my companion said abruptly:

"You cannot definitely recall any single detail of the person of that man you fought with this morning?"

I shook my head. "I wish I could. He was as strong and hard to hold as a wild cat—that's all. The room was pitch dark. I couldn't see a thing. His voice, I told you, seemed disguised."

MacNair nodded. "Well, it's too bad! I wish you could have given me something definite."

"Those two bullet holes in your hat are pretty definite," I smiled.

"So far as we know," MacNair went on, "Hyde was the only one who knew you had that pistol. How old is he?"

"About eighty."

"Hmn! He wouldn't be likely to fight like a wild cat."

"No. Although he is a man of unusual vitality."

"Indeed. Well, let's see what he's got to say for himself."

We found Hyde in his office at the rear of his gloomy shop. As he rose to greet us the contrast between the shabby interior and the polished elegance of his spats and morning coat struck me more forcibly than ever. He shook hands with me and as I introduced him to MacNair I reflected on the strength of his grip. Again I thought of Lucy's "reincarnated buccaneer," but I also thought of him as having been a sly old buccaneer who'd rather scuttle a ship than board one.

"Dreadful affair up your way last night," he condoled, as we sat down. "Captain Deacon was in before lunch."

"I lost the best friend any man ever had," I said soberly.

"Too bad," he grieved, shaking his gaunt old head. "Too bad!" He seemed to be addressing himself rather than us. "Yes, indeed! A dreadful business!" His eagle eyes, I saw, to my amazement, were moist and he actually blew his nose. I had never suspected him of sentiment. "I suppose the boy Jerry hasn't turned up, yet? Deacon said something about him."

"No," I replied briefly. "Mr. MacNair is looking after our interests. That pistol you sold me yesterday afternoon figures in the case. I wish you'd tell us what you know about it."

"Ah, the pistol," he said suavely. "No, I don't know anything about it. I saw it was one of Alex Peterson's and I bought it on your account. Deacon was inquiring about it."

"Whom did you buy it from?" MacNair rapped out. MacNair had been studying the old pirate; their eyes clashed. Hyde pretended to think.

"Let me see, now. Ah, yes! An old man, he was, to be sure. I don't know his name. I never saw him before."

"What did he look like?"

"Hmn. He was quite old, I should say, and of less than the middle height. That's about all I remember of him. Dear me! this memory of mine!" Hyde took off his gold-rimmed glasses and began to polish them. "A bad business, getting old, eh, what, Peebles?"

MacNair ignored this pretense. "Had he a wizened-up little face the color of saddle leather, red-rimmed eyes, a shock of unkempt white hair, an eyeglass on a wire and the look of a man who has, let us say, prospected for gold all his life?"

I thought Hyde was going to lose his temper, but he gave us his sly smile instead, although the glasses shook in his hand. MacNair's question didn't surprise me. I had already concluded that Hyde had got the Peterson pistol from Furie.

"You are quite well informed," Hyde said smoothly. "Why come to me?"

He put on his glasses and felt in the tail of his coat. For a moment he fumbled there, MacNair and I watching him narrowly. "Dear me!" I heard him mutter. "Now where did I put it?" His hand came away empty and I guessed he had been after his Louis snuff-box.

"You were going to say, Mr. MacNair?" he inquired blandly.

"That the name of the man you bought the pistol from is 'Furie'!" MacNair rapped out.

Hyde chuckled. "Perhaps it was. You hit him off pretty well, I must say. A queer chap, Furie. Indeed, yes! I should say he'd been blowing about the deserts half a century or more."

"Did he tell you where he found the revolver?"

"No, he didn't."

"Did you ask him?"

"My dear sir! I don't ask questions."

"You never saw him before?"

"Never."

"Have you any idea where the revolver came from?"

"Not the slightest."

I think he realized that we didn't believe him for he leaned forward with a confiding air, as if he had decided he'd have to tell us something, and tapped the desk with his bony fingers.

"Here's a tip that'll stir you up, gentlemen. I didn't tell this even to Deacon."

"Well?" MacNair snapped.

"I could have sold that pistol again after Peebles bought it. Probably for a good deal more."

"To whom?"

"To Andrew Ogden," said Nathan Hyde. "He telephoned me about it at six o'clock last night."

MacNair wasn't surprised. Neither was I, for that matter, but the announcement depressed me horribly for it looked like a confirmation of certain conclusions reason was forcing upon me. The small silence that followed gave me time to collect myself.

"What did Ogden say?" MacNair inquired.

The dealer chuckled slyly. "He asked me what I'd done with the Alex Peterson revolver Furie had sold me. I said it had gone and I thought he'd jump out of the telephone at me. Yes, indeed! 'Who's got it?' he barked. I told him and he cooled down. 'Peebles, eh? That's all right.' And then he hung up."

MacNair looked at me. "That was why Ogden telephoned you."

I nodded unhappily, overwhelmed by a sense of failure. My feeling was illogical, of course, but I couldn't help it. If I had gone to Andrew at once he probably would have been alive at this moment.

"Did you tell any one else that Peebles had bought the revolver?" MacNair inquired of Hyde.

"Dear me, no! Why should I have?"

"Hmn!" said MacNair. "Well, every man to his taste. Some go in for pistols, some for pottery, some for pictures. My hobby is swords."

This was news to me. MacNair's tastes, I thought, ran solely to tomatoes.

Hyde smiled and rubbed his hands. "Ah, to be sure. I have a very fine Japanese sword guard by Masamune in the shop. Perhaps you'd like to see it."

"I should," said MacNair.

Hyde excused himself. The moment he was gone Mac-Nair stiffened in his chair and listened attentively. Then, quick as a cat and bent double, he slid over to Hyde's shabby desk, leaned across it, and, to my amazement, opened the top drawer. The lower part of the partition that separated the office from the shop was of wood so Hyde could not see what he was up to. MacNair stared down into the drawer for a moment, then he slipped quietly back to his chair.

Before I could demand the reason of this extraordinary conduct Hyde reappeared with the sword, a fairly good example of Japanese art.

"A beautiful bit of workmanship, Mr. MacNair," the dealer said smoothly, indicating the sword guard. "Observe it. Take it in your hand. Have you ever seen a finer?"

"Hmn!" MacNair responded dryly. "Not bad. How much?"

Hyde's eagle eyes narrowed a trifle. "Ah, yes. The figure is just twelve hundred."

MacNair laughed ironically. "Cheap at half price." He returned the sword. "If you haven't sold it in, say, two months from now, I'll give you five hundred."

"My dear Mr. MacNair," Hyde protested, "I couldn't take a penny less than twelve hundred."

"Well, put it away and we'll talk about it a couple of months hence. I shall have some funds coming in then."

Hyde coughed. "Er, I might consider a thousand."

"Not to-day. My finances are low just now. . . . Do you know anything more about this Peterson pistol?"

The old pirate shrugged. "What else could I know? I buy my pieces and hold my tongue. That is business." He followed us to the door. "You may lose a fine bargain, Mr. MacNair. Well, I shall expect you in two months."

We left him then.

"A beautiful liar!" MacNair said harshly, as we crossed the street.

"I didn't know you were interested in Japanese swordcraft."

"I'm not," he grunted. "I wanted to get him out of the office."

"What was in the drawer?"

"What do you suppose?"

"I haven't the slightest idea," I said irritably.

He gave his harsh laugh again. "Cultivate observation, Watson. It's an admirable quality. If you had been watching him closely as we entered the office you would have seen him snap that drawer shut. I concluded there was something in it that he didn't want us to see, so I determined to find out what it was."

"Curious," I remarked, "but when I dropped in on Hyde yesterday afternoon he flipped a letter over some object on his desk before I could see what it was. Hammond, one of our lawyers, was with him at the time and both of them seemed startled at my appearance. Well, what did you find?"

"A bit of rich gold quartz like that piece Deacon came upon in Ogden's desk."

"You don't say!" I exclaimed. "I'll bet that was what Hyde covered up yesterday afternoon. Gold quartz, eh! Do you connect it with Furie?"

"Hubbard's description of Furie suggested an old desert rat and a connection is inferable, of course. How far it goes I don't know."

"That would bring Hyde into the case," I muttered. "Hammond, too, maybe. By the way, Hammond was a prospector in his younger days." And I told MacNair what I knew of him.

"Interesting," he muttered. "But it by no means eliminates young Ogden," he reminded me, pointedly. "However, we have two possible lines of inquiry open before us. Blackmail is one of them; the gold-hunting instinct is the other. One of them should lead us to Ogden's murderer. They may converge before we find him."

"Hello," I cried, suddenly. "There goes Hammond, now."

The lawyer was coming along the other side of the busy street at a brisk walk. He did not see us. Turning, we followed him with our eyes. He came to Hyde's shop, and entering it, disappeared from our sight.

10

The House of Ogden

The inquest was held that afternoon. Stimson, Hubbard, and I, were the principal witnesses. I told my story truthfully, since I couldn't very well do otherwise, but I was careful to make it clear that I had neither seen Terry's face nor heard his voice on the walk. Stimson, it developed, hadn't either. The Peterson revolver, my experience of the early morning, and the curious discoveries Deacon had made among Ogden's effects were not introduced as evidence. Nor did Luther MacNair present any of those theories he had already indicated to Deacon and me. The jury found that Andrew had died of a dagger thrust in the back of his neck, inflicted, in its opinion, by Gerald Ogden, the victim's son. The verdict added nothing to my peace of mind, although I knew it couldn't very well have been different.

It was late afternoon when I swung the car into Magnolia Avenue, MacNair beside me. His harsh mouth had relaxed a little and he seemed well satisfied with his day's work, but his arrogant spirit oppressed me. I suppose my state of grief and bewilderment and dread made me acutely sensitive to the rigid contours of his personality. Deacon had promised to meet us at the Ogden home. As I turned into the familiar driveway my grief quickened a little for I loved the place next to my own. We found Deacon in the library. He gave us a grave nod.

"Any word of Jerry?" I asked.

"None, John."

My faith in the lad still held its head high, but I sat down, shaken. A new fear seized upon me. Had Jerry, like Andrew, been done away with? The thought harrowed me and I was glad when Deacon said:

"You saw Hyde?"

Nodding, MacNair lighted a cigarette. Henry's honest face was troubled and I decided he had something on his mind.

"Anything new?" I inquired.

He considered us thoughtfully for a moment. "Yes. About this woman in black. Her name is Lundy. Mrs. Joe Lundy. Andrew gave her a check the other day."

"A check?" I echoed.

"A check," Henry said slowly, "for a thousand dollars."

"Good Lord! Whatever for?"

Deacon shook his head. "I don't know."

"Ogden seems to have been liberal with his cash," Mac-Nair drawled with an inference that angered me. "How did you get on to it?"

"My man Thompson found his check book in the pocket of a suit upstairs. One of the stubs was made out to a Mrs. Joe Lundy for a thousand dollars. We got in touch with Ogden's bank, the First National. The check was cashed the day before yesterday. Mrs. Lundy is this woman in black. The teller remembered her by the odd clothing she wore."

The information bewildered me. What possible connection could this strange figure, Mrs. Lundy, have with the tragedy of the night before? That she had some connection with it, I was convinced. Deacon must have sensed my thoughts.

"She can't be this 'James Dillon,'" he said sharply.

"It was no woman that fought me this morning," I declared vigorously.

"You don't know whether it was or not," MacNair interrupted.

"He was in trousers and a coat. I know that much."

"A woman may wear anything, nowadays."

"He had fingers of steel."

"Occasionally women have fingers of steel."

"Well," I retorted triumphantly, "if it was a woman you can eliminate young Jerry."

"I didn't say it was Mrs. Lundy you fought with!" Mac-Nair snapped. "I simply said you don't know. And you don't. Neither do I."

No man, even at sixty-nine, is going to admit he might have been bested in physical combat by an elderly woman and I should have given him his answer if Deacon hadn't spoken again.

"Never mind Mrs. Lundy just now," he growled. "She doesn't fit—yet. I found something else." He opened a drawer in the desk. "This. It was wrapped in oiled paper on the shelf in Andrew's bedroom closet."

At what he had brought forth I cried out in astonishment. Even MacNair was affected. The harsh contours of his face seemed to stand out like the lines of a charcoal drawing. Deacon's square jaw relaxed a little and he smiled wearily.

"Alex Peterson's gun," I whispered.

"Alex Peterson's *other* gun," Deacon replied.

The Colt was a replica of the one I had bought from Nathan Hyde to the last detail of gold filigree on the butt. I ejected the cartridges into my palm. There were six of them and the bullets were gold!

"Alex Peterson would have *two* guns," MacNair said crisply. "Those highflyers always had. I thought we should be turning it up."

I scarcely heard what he said. Deacon's discovery had
astonished me less than it had shocked my moral sense,
for all day the trend of the evidence had been towards the
conclusion implied by the finding of the pistol in Ogden's
room. The universe was falling in ruin about my ears.
Those solid, tangible things to which a man anchors his
life were rocking and rivening beneath my feet. My faith
in Andrew was one of them. Was I to find him unworthy?
MacNair's rasping voice steadied me.

"You have given us another fact to build a theory on,
Deacon," he was saying. "A fact hard and square, fast and
real. Nothing like these grim realities, eh? You have swallowed your dose already. Peebles is having a hard time
with his, but he'll get it down."

"The theory?" Henry demanded bluntly.

MacNair's cynical laugh infuriated me, but I held my
tongue. Facts, not emotion, were going to solve our problem.

"Very well," MacNair began. "Consider the facts. This
man Furie calls on Hyde yesterday afternoon. Hubbard
overhears Ogden shout the two words 'gold bullets.' Furie
leaves. Ogden telephones Peebles and is stabbed as he sits
at the instrument. Incidentally, Ogden has a card left at
my house asking me to call and see him at once. Peebles has told us that he sometimes thought of the Andrew
Ogden he knew as not being the man himself. Hubbard
and his wife had a similar feeling. For years Ogden was
a leading citizen, a developer of the town, a pillar of the
church, a business man of wide interests. But—were these
qualities representative of the man's real self?

"During the afternoon Peebles buys a gold-mounted
pistol from Nathan Hyde. Early this morning Peebles
house is entered by a man who is after the pistol. One of
the gold bullet-loaded cartridges of the pistol is found to
contain a message from a man named 'Jerry.' The message

was written in 1896 and it accuses one James Dillon of murder. Later on, we find evidence that leads us to believe Ogden has been paying Dillon blackmail for twenty-six years. Ogden and Dillon are bound up together, then. It also turns out that Ogden desperately wanted this gold-mounted pistol himself. Hyde, it appears, bought it from this man Furie who called on Ogden. We also find in Ogden's safe twenty-six poker chips and a deck of cards. Ogden was known to be prejudiced against card-playing.

"Why should Ogden have been paying Dillon blackmail for twenty-six years? Why should Ogden want this gold-mounted pistol? Our feeling that he was not the man the community supposed him to be, becomes certainty. And now we have your discovery, Deacon, of this other gold-mounted pistol in Ogden's room. It is one of the most interesting bits of evidence we have yet turned up and I am inclined to think we may hazard a theory."

He paused, a sardonic gleam in his eyes. I guessed what theory he was going to propound. A bitter pill it would be, but I supposed I would have to swallow it.

"I venture to say," he went on, "that Alex Peterson, swashbuckler and gambler, and Andrew Ogden, our late exemplary citizen, and builder of San Felipe, were one and the same man."

Again he paused. His eyes challenged mine, but to sorrow I could find nothing to contradict in his statement. Neither could Deacon, apparently.

"I suggest, furthermore," MacNair continued raspingly, "that Dillon blackmailed Ogden because of something happened when Ogden was Alex Peterson; that the man 'Jerry' was a close relation—a brother, perhaps—or close friend of Peterson's (so close, in fact, that Ogden called his own son after him); and that the poker chips and the deck of cards symbolize the indiscretion for which Ogden was blackmailed."

I could find no fault with his argument, try as I would.

"Sounds reasonable," Deacon growled.

MacNair bowed ironically. "By the way," he resumed, "I wonder if either of you have forgotten the so-called legend of the 'poker game that cracked the town'?"

I jumped at this. "You mean that fool yarn about Peterson playing poker for a human life?" I stormed. "Surely you don't expect us to swallow that, too?"

"My dear Watson! I was merely dropping a seed into the ground made fertile by our recent discoveries. *If* that poker game should prove to be a fact and not a legend I suggest that it *might* have had something to do with Ogden's death."

"It isn't a fact," I said doggedly. But I wasn't so sure, for he had carried me along with the sweep of his logic and I was no longer certain of anything. "What about those pieces of quartz?" I demanded. "There should be motive enough for you."

"I was coming to them. One specimen was in Ogden's desk; the other was in Hyde's. They look alike. Curious, that. I believe Furie could tell us something about them. At any rate, they bring Hyde into the affair this lawyer, Roy Hammond, too, perhaps. For all I know to the contrary Hyde may be Dillon, but as I said this morning it doesn't follow because Dillon blackmailed Ogden that he also killed him. On the other hand I don't say he didn't. But to return to the quartz. You told me something about this 'Two Brothers' mine of Ogden's. Down in Skull Valley, isn't it? I wonder why Ogden called it the 'Two Brothers.' Perhaps he bought it under that name. You said young Jerry wanted to open the mine and that Ogden refused to let him touch it. Interesting situation, don't you think?"

"You are trying to build their difference of opinion into a motive!" I charged. "The cost of mining gold has gone down steadily for years. Jerry is an engineer and he thought the mine could be made to pay. His father didn't!"

MacNair grinned. "Don't fume so, Peebles. It's bad for a man of your age. I am inclined to think there's more to it than that. As you say, the cost of mining gold has gone down, but for this reason Ogden should have let his son open the mine unless he had a *better* reason for keeping it closed. There's the point. He doesn't seem to have given the boy the *real* reason. And that is what I am after. You follow me?"

Henry nodded. "It looks that way to me."

"Now take these specimens of gold-bearing ore," Mac-Nair went on. "Suppose they came from the 'Two Brothers'—perhaps from a new vein Ogden didn't know of—"

"That won't do," I objected. "The mine is closed. Now I come to think of it Jerry told me half the mountainside slid down in front of it years ago."

"There may be an exposed vein somewhere. Let us assume Jerry found it. Naturally, he would want to exploit his discovery. His father refuses to let him touch it and gives him no adequate reason for doing so. They become angry. Anger turns to rage and, well—there you are."

"Yes!" I exploded. "Nowhere at all. In the first place, if these two specimens came from a new vein in the 'Two Brothers,' Hyde, also, knows of that vein; in the second place, you yourself expressed the opinion that Furie was an old prospector and that he knew something about the specimens, too; in the third place, you haven't got rid of Dillon yet. I don't see why the greed motive shouldn't be as strongly operative in one man as in another."

"Neither do I," he said dryly, "but unfortunately for your argument, which expresses my point of view so far as it goes, the other evidence implicates young Ogden and not Hyde or Furie. However, I wasn't theorizing. I was

trying to get at a motive by speculation. You still confuse
the two. As for Dillon, I'll show you him dead or alive
before I'm done. There's Mrs. Lundy, too. As Deacon said,
she doesn't fit—yet. But she will. Ogden didn't give her a
thousand dollars for nothing."

His arguments were sound, but I didn't see any reason
for telling him so. Anyhow, before I could reply Deacon
spoke.

"There's sense in what he says, John. You might as well
admit it. I'm sorry, but I can't get it out of my head that
the boy did it. He may have come to blows with Andrew
about the mine."

"He wouldn't have stabbed his father in the back while
he sat at the telephone!" I retorted indignantly. "Get your
hands on James Dillon and you'll have Ogden's murderer,
Henry. And don't forget that Polyandria marked your man."

Deacon got up to go. "I haven't forgotten anything,
John. I wish to God I could forget some things." And with
this he went out.

There was nothing else to be done, and so we followed
him. I put the car in the garage and MacNair, at my invitation, came into the house with me. Mrs. Moffit had got
a fire crackling in the den and he put his back to the blaze
while I, excusing myself, sat down at the desk and began
to pencil in the little red notebook which had been the
recipient of my confidences that morning. MacNair
watched me, his ironic look tempered by amusement.

"Clews?" he inquired when I had done.

"In a way," I admitted, with a sheepish chuckle, dropping the book back in the drawer. "The Dr. Watsons are
usually as useless as one's appendix and often as trouble-
some and I have always wanted to improve the role."

His dark eyes sparkled. "And this is your first opportunity?"

"Yes. I thought I might be able to supplement your conclusions with one or two of my own."

"Good idea! Two heads are better than one. Well, I must be off."

"No, indeed!" I exclaimed, standing up. "My housekeeper fries an excellent chicken and you must have dinner with us."

He laughed. "You tempt me. I have an indifferent cook."

"Mine is the best in San Felipe," I bragged. "You will stay?"

"Thanks. I will."

"Splendid! Excuse me while I speak to Mrs. Moffit. . . ."

The meal wasn't especially lively, although both Mrs. and Lucy did their best, and I must admit MacNair was interesting in his cold-blooded way. But his twisted outlook and his ironical philosophy of life took from our intercourse that spontaneity which always graces my table. I suppose the trapping of one's fellow beings discourages the social instinct. He and I had a pleasant hour in my den, though, and I found him able to tell me a good many things about small firearms. The evening was eminently satisfactory to me.

When he had gone I put another log on the fire and settled down for an hour or so of meditation. Scarcely had I done so than Lucy came in.

"Has that dreadful man gone, Uncle John?"

I chuckled. "You wanted him, too, my dear."

She nodded. "I'm not sorry. If any one can help us it is he. But—oh, dear! he isn't human."

Dropping onto a stool at my feet, she leaned her dark head against my knees. My fingers were soon stroking her sleek black hair. A common sadness of spirit suffused us and neither of us spoke for a little while.

"There's no word?" Lucy whispered presently.

"None," I said, huskily, and she pressed her head hard against my knee.

When she looked up I tried to avoid her eyes, but there must have been some magnetic quality in the look she turned on me for I felt my eyes drawn down to hers. Her expression tore my heart and I had to blow my nose violently before I felt equal to recounting what had transpired during the day. I went at it haltingly, for I am a poor hand at telling a tale; but when it was done both of us felt better.

"You still believe in him, Uncle John?"

"My dear child! Of course I believe in him!"

"And—you don't think—anything—dreadful could have happened to him?"

I sensed the terror leaping in her breast, but I kept my voice steady.

"Certainly not! He'll turn up in a day or two." She nestled softly against me then. In her tender moments Lucy is inexpressibly dear to me.

11
Lucy Makes Up Her Mind

I must admit I am getting on for the sort of thing that begun at breakfast the next morning. Nothing like it had come my way in ten years or more and it surprises me that I carried on to the end as well as I did. Probably my pride in the audacious, lawless thing Lucy did re-kindled the fires of my vanished youth, for I have the timid man's admiration of daring. How intensely vivid a woman's love for a man may become! The miracle of it leaves me a little breathless even now.

The horn of MacNair's car, as arrogant as the man himself, gave tongue in front of the house just as I was going to shave and I hurried out in my slippers.

"I am going to Los Angeles," he announced curtly.

"Have you got word of something?" I asked eagerly.

His face was inscrutable. "I don't know, yet. It may not amount to anything."

"Well, silence is the prerogative of the Holmes tribe. You have a fine car, MacNair. Just ten miles over the five thousand mark," I observed, with a glance at the speedometer.

He nodded. "It's fairly speedy. I expect to be back to-morrow."

The engine gave a throaty purr and the roadster slid from under my hand. At breakfast, half an hour later, Lucy had little to say. Shadows encircled her eyes and my heart ached for her. We had got to the toast and coffee stage when the telephone rang. It was Sunday, Mrs. Moffit's day off, and Lucy answered the call. Mrs. Moffit had got our breakfast ready and gone to her Cosmic Indulgence circle, which meets every Sunday morning at eight. After the service she was going to her Cousin Agatha's. We didn't expect her back until evening.

"Somebody wants to speak to Captain Deacon," Lucy announced from the door of my den.

"He's not here. Why didn't you-—" I stopped. Her eyes were fixed on me piteously. "What's the matter, child?"

"I don't know—oh, nothing," she whispered. "I didn't— tell him. I thought it might be—I thought something might have happened—he seems excited—"

"Nonsense!" I cried, but my old heart thumped a bit. "Deacon must be dropping in here. Wait, I'll speak to him."

A sense of disaster weighed upon me as I took up the instrument. "Hello."

"That you, chief?" some one demanded crisply. I have been told that my voice over the wire resembles Deacon's. Before I could make my identity known the voice ran on: "Some'dy just phoned in they seen Jerry Ogden driving along the Peskella road to Skull Valley night before last!"

I almost dropped the instrument. "This is Peebles. Captain Deacon isn't here yet."

"Oh, ain't he!" The voice cooled down. "I thought you was him."

The floor was rocking beneath me. Jerry . . . Skull Valley . . . night before last.

"If you'll leave a message—" I began in a voice strangely unlike my own.

"Tell him to call headquarters. He said he might stop at your place first. Don't forget!" The receiver clicked down.

I stared into the mouthpiece numb with horror. Jerry . . . Skull Valley . . . Torridity. Torridity and Andrew's death had come to form a sort of unholy unity. Jerry had gone there. But why? And why hadn't he returned?

"Good God!" I muttered. "Unless he can explain himself Deacon will bring him back under warrant!" A horrible fear that Jerry mightn't be able to explain his flight to Deacon's satisfaction, although he would to mine, overwhelmed me.

"What is it, Uncle John?"

I put the telephone down slowly. How was I to keep it from Lucy? But when I looked into her eyes I knew there would be no keeping it from Lucy.

"It was headquarters. Deacon is dropping in here. They—they want him to call up."

"There's something else, Uncle John. Something about Jerry. What is it?"

"Steady, old girl," I pleaded, dropping an arm over her shoulder. "Somebody saw Jerry driving along the Peskella road towards Skull Valley the night before last."

"Skull Valley—Torridity," she whispered.

I nodded. "Probably."

"I thought he might have gone there. Deacon is coming here, you say. You won't tell him?"

"I shall have to, Lucy. If I don't, they'll call him at the Ogdens'."

"Yes, of course! Oh, dear! what are we to do?"

She clasped her hands desperately. "What *can* we do?"

"Jerry will explain," I mumbled. "Why shouldn't he explain? Don't we know he's done nothing to be afraid of?"

She turned on me fiercely. "Of course we do! And of course he'll explain, but will Deacon accept his explanation? If Jerry were to come back now and give himself up Deacon probably would. But Deacon believes Jerry did it and if he finds him out there he'll think he's hiding—don't

you see? He'll arrest him—handcuff him—put him in jail.
I know he will! Oh, dear God! what can we do?"

This was my own view of the matter. If we could have
warned Jerry that Deacon was on his trail the boy could
then have anticipated arrest by giving himself up to the
police. But there was no way of warning him. What the
devil was he doing out there? A thought struck me.

"If Jerry has been in Skull Valley since the night before last he may not know—about his father. The town is
abandoned. There are no telephones, no newspapers, no
means of communication. That's why he hasn't turned up
and why Deacon hasn't been able to find him."

"Of course that's why, Uncle John," the girl cried fren-
ziedly, "but if Deacon finds him out there—in that dreadful place—he won't believe anything Jerry tells him! You
know he won't!"

This was true. "There's no way of warning him," I
groaned. . . . "Here's Deacon, now."

A car had stopped in front of the house. Lucy's face
whitened; she looked as if she were going to fall. And then
a queer, excited look leaped into her eyes and she slipped
into the hall. Her cheeks were burning when she returned.

"It is Deacon and he's alone!" She caught me fiercely by
the coat lapels. "Let me handle him, Uncle John! Please!"

"Handle him! My dear child! What do you mean?"

She shook me almost furiously; her intense expression
alarmed me a little.

"I've got an idea! It's Jerry's only chance! You must let
me try it! You will, won't you? Promise me you will, Uncle
John!"

"Why, why—good Heavens, girl, don't shake me! What
can you do with Deacon? Oh, very well! What do you want
me to do? He's here now."

Deacon's two short rings pealed forth.

"Nothing! Just stay here and don't interfere. Don't interfere whatever I do! Promise!"

Her intensity disturbed me. "But see here, Lucy— Oh, very well," I promised, for she was starting to shake me again. "Provided you don't hurt him."

She was off in a flash, shutting the door behind her. Another two rings on the bell, then the front door opened.

"Hello, Miss Lucy," Henry greeted her. "Is Uncle John up, yet?"

Lucy laughed. "Hours ago, Captain Deacon. We were just looking at Polyandria's new babies. You must see them."

Polyandria's excursions into maternity are more frequent than I like, but I wasn't aware that she had recently taken one of them and you may imagine my bewilderment.

"I want to," Deacon exclaimed heartily. "Where are they?"

"Down here," Lucy rippled.

Henry has a warm spot in his heart for Polyandria and I wasn't surprised to hear him follow Lucy down the hall. What she was going to do with him I hadn't the slightest idea. I felt uneasy for at times Lucy exhibits an extraordinary talent for the unexpected. The wisest course for me to follow would be to shut my ears and bury my nose in my little red notebook, but I have found my curiosity invaluable in days gone by and I stuck my ear to the door instead.

"In here, Captain Deacon," Lucy said pleasantly.

"I don't see them, Miss Lucy."

"Over there in the corner. Go right in."

A door slammed, a key turned, and my heart climbed into my throat. Only one door in the house slams like that. A massive piece of finely paneled English oak, it had been imported by a local millionaire whose home had been dismantled after his death. I had picked the door up cheap at Hyde's and hung it in the entrance of a little storeroom near the patio where the morning sun would bring out the rich grain of the ripe old English wood. A few trunks occupy the room and one small window, not large enough for a man to pass through, lights it.

Lucy came racing down the hall. "Uncle John!" she panted.

"Are you mad!" I cried, flinging open the door of my den. "Let him out at once!"

"I won't!" she blazed at me and with so scorching a light in her eyes that I fell back.

"What do you expect to gain by it?" I cried. "You'll only antagonize him! Let him out! Be sensible, child!"

She beat on my chest with her fists. "You promised you wouldn't interfere! Don't you dare!" And then, for Lucy is an excellent actress, pleading followed frenzy. "It's Jerry's only chance, Uncle John! Please! Please. Please!"

"His only chance! Nonsense! You are making things worse for him. Do as I tell you!"

She stamped her foot at me. "How stupid you are, Uncle John! Don't you see? If I get to Jerry *first* and he gives himself up it'll make all the difference. They'll *have* to believe his story! The evidence is against him—we know it is—his best way of fighting it is by coming back of his own free will. Deacon cannot accuse him of hiding in Torridity, then, can he? You must see it as I do!"

Her meaning was clear enough, although I hadn't yet fully realized her intention.

"My dear child! Do you suppose after you have gone to the length of imprisoning Deacon that the act of surrender will help Jerry?"

"Don't 'dear child' me, Uncle John! Why shouldn't it? What I do isn't Jerry's fault. I act on my own authority.

Captain Deacon will be furious, but you must smooth him over!"

"You have a high regard for my diplomatic abilities," I said grimly. "Give me that key!"

"I will not! You have my opinion—I have yours. I still think I'm right." Her face fell into lines of supplication again. "Don't let him out, Uncle John! Good-by!"

"Good-by," I echoed. Her intention became apparent to me. "Lucy!" I roared, and made a dive at her.

Evading me easily, for the girl is like quicksilver, she went off through the front door, slamming it shut behind her. I was after her as fast as my old legs would carry me, but by the time I got out into the garden she was climbing into Deacon's police car. Deacon's car! What madness wasn't she capable of! Deacon must have left the key in the ignition for as I ran down the walk shouting to her the car throbbed in its vitals and slid away from the curb. One glimpse of her inspired face I had, and then, with a toss of her head, she was off.

"You promised, Uncle John!"

Her voice, high and clear, blew back to me. The car rocketed down the avenue, rounded a curve at fearful speed, and vanished.

Sick at heart I tumbled onto a cement bench near by. Deacon, my friend, was pounding on my old English door and Lucy, my niece, was on her way to Skull Valley, that pit of desolation on the other side of the Skeleton Mountains. A nice state of affairs, you will admit! What was I going to do about it?

Skull Valley! If you want a trenchant simile for blistering heat and pitiless cold, for nature vicious, abandoned, and forgotten of God, there it is. The name is a symbol. Gold is the valley's heart, borax and salt its wind-blown beard, poisoned waters its blood, and lizard, sidewinder,

and vulture the furtive tenants of its evil house. Good
water may be beyond the next butte. If it isn't, you'll find
madness and, an hour or so further on, death, for Skull
Valley is the devil's cemetery and the bleached bones of
man and beast its tombstones. At noon in the summer
the heat may crack your skull; at night in the winter the
shrilling winds will lance your lungs. There are roads, of
course, and nowadays you can drive across the valley in an
hour or two. If you lose the road, God help you! A few of
the mines are running; many of them are not. Here and
there an abandoned mining camp rattles its bare bones in
the wind blasts. Torridity is one.

And to Torridity, sixty miles away, Lucy was driving
like the wind, bareheaded and without even a canteen of
water! Incredible youth! I loved her for it!

What was I going to do, you ask? Well, I might smash in
my English door—Lucy had taken the key with her—and
let Deacon out. He would stop Lucy by telephone and she
would never forgive me. Or I might leave Deacon where
he was and take after Lucy. The first was what I ought to
do, and the second was what I was going to do, call me
a romantic old ass if you will. I offer in extenuation of
my elderly madness: First, the fact that Lucy's argument
had impressed me. It seemed vitally necessary to Jerry's
well-being that he give himself up before he was arrested.
(Of course, I wasn't naive enough to imagine Lucy's daring
was likely to be quite as effective as she supposed.) Second, the pitch of admiration to which Lucy's audacity had
fired me. I hadn't the heart to spoil her splendid gesture.
And if she had the courage to take the law into her own
hands, so had I, the habits of a lifetime to the contrary.
Yes, even though it cost me Henry's friendship! And, third,
she wasn't going down into that devil's cemetery alone.
Not while John Peebles had breath of life to go with her!

Slipping quietly into the house, I listened for a moment to the terrific uproar Deacon was making behind the oak door. Fortunately, the room was remote from the avenue or he would have been heard. I made my way out to the garage, feeling uncomfortable about leaving him behind. There never had been a wrong word between us. Filling a couple of water canteens at a faucet, I took them into my car with me.

Two mountain ranges lay between me and my destination. The first forty miles of road would be paved or good dirt, the next twenty would fall by degrees from poor to dreadful. Lucy, I reflected as I swung into the avenue, had ten minutes start of me and a faster car. She would make for Pitchfork Canyon, the only possible approach to Torridity from the west, and I hoped to reach her before she began the descent. That road down into the Skull is a madman's nightmare and I didn't fancy her making it alone. It meant furious driving, something I am averse to.

As soon as I was clear of the city I opened the throttle and prayed that I wouldn't meet a traffic officer.

The San Felipe Valley was drenched in sunlight and the sweet scent of orange blossoms hung like incense. I love our inland California valleys at every season of the year, but in the spring there is a tenderness, a vitality, an odorous freshness in the air, that sets me longing to take the world into my arms. This morning I had little time for sentimentalizing, however, and when, some short while later, the rhythmic throb of the engine fell steeply into silence, I had even less. I got out and looked in the tank. It was empty! The nearest filling station was seven miles behind me!

Raging at my carelessness, I flung my coat into the car and set off down the scorching road. . . . No one gave me a lift. When I finally got my hand on the wheel again Lucy was some three hours ahead of me. Likely enough she was at Torridity.

12

The City of Silence

As you probably know, Skull Valley lies between the Skeleton Mountains and the Red Gold Range. From the west you descend into it by Shinbone Canyon and on the east you ascend from it by the Devil's Mouth. Eighty years ago a band of emigrants drove their covered wagons through the Devil's Mouth, then unnamed. Most of them died of heat and thirst in the inferno below; of the survivors that staggered up Shinbone Canyon three months later half were mad and naked in their madness.

Nowadays a road of sorts spans the valley from Shinbone to the Devil's Mouth and if you want a taste of the grim terror of the place you may cross it by car. But Torridity is ten miles south of the road which spans the valley and the intervening stretch of desert is impassable to any car born of Detroit. Another road, a miserable affair, leads into the valley by way of Pitchfork Canyon, passes through Torridity, and joins the main road at Devil's Mouth on the east. This is the only road into the town from the west. I supposed Jerry and Lucy had taken it and I purposed following it myself.

It was just one o'clock when I reached the summit of the Skeletons. Time was precious—my fears for Lucy had increased with every mile I had come—but nothing on earth could have driven me down Pitchfork until my eyes had had their desire of that sardonic masterpiece below. I had been to the summit several times and descended both Shinbone and Pitchfork, but never before had the valley gripped my soul with so violent a sense of unholy horror and sleek and tawny beauty.

The valley blazed with light and color. Waves of lavender and rose and emerald green washed buttes and dunes of brown and rose and pale gold and a hundred sunrises dissolved in the sapphire dew of a hundred mornings. But as I looked upon this bewitching opalescence it seemed to me that something alive and watchful lurked beneath it. Something sleek as seal skin, vital as a young tiger, alluring as a perfumed goddess. Vaporous arms reached out to me and tried to cloud my senses—and I knew that its beauty masked a spirit as venomous as Satan and that it would spit me on its griddle if I didn't look out.

My eyes leaped to the saffron flanks of the Red Gold Range, then fell again into the rainbow sea below. A last look and I started down the Pitchfork. The road had been blasted out of the side of the canyon forty years ago to become a veritable golden highway, for millions in silver and gold and borax from the valley mines had been mule-teamed around its hairpin curves. But with the closing down of the Torridity mining properties in the middle nineties the road had fallen into disuse.

The sloping walls of the canyon were a desolation of loose and tumbled rocks, volcanic in their origin and many-colored as Joseph's coat. Some of them were as big as houses; others clung together in fantastic edifices that mocked the laws of God; still others had the shape of living things: animals, human beings, and weirdly distorted trees. Over all brooded so profound a melancholy that my soul was hounded into the darkest recess of my being.

Little repair work had been done on the road of recent years and the spring freshets had made a ruin of it. Below me fell a thousand-foot drop and as I crawled around the sharp hairpin curves which constituted most of the descent I looked at death a score of times. Back wheels on the edge of nothing—car slipping, sliding—clinging to the wheel asweat with terror—the specter of death moving upon me. . . . And then the danger was over and I was into another as bad. Nor did I for a moment forget that the next bend might show me Deacon's car upside down and Lucy's broken body. Now and then I caught a glimpse of tawny desert. Heat beat upon my face in waves, stifling me, for the canyon drew like a chimney flue.

In two hours I reached the bottom. The opalescent beauty of the desert had vanished. Grim and terrible, it seemed to say, "I've got you, fool!" And I wondered if it hadn't. But the trail to Torridity, wretched as it was, lay before me, and I was cheered. Ah! there were car tracks. Several of them. My heart gave a bound. Lucy was ahead of me. I would be with her in half an hour!

The trail was vile, but I got along fairly well. Gullies, buttes, and small outcroppings of rock marred the flatness of the desert plain. Beyond a few bristling cacti and a mournful Joshua tree or two there was no sign of life. The empty desolation oppressed my spirit and again I was seized by that profound melancholy I had felt in the canyon. It grew upon me. I could not shake it off. The air seemed charged with sinister potency. Was I driving upon disaster?

Out of a sky as hard as a metal bell poured a ferocious, blinding heat that made me thankful for my water canteens. A light, hot wind blew and a faint moaning sound was in the air. Here and there a spurt of dust arose and a pebble spun crazily. Perhaps I was running into one of those shrilling windstorms for which the valley is notorious. They come in a twinkling, sometimes last for days, and cease as suddenly as they begin. Disturbed, I widened

the throttle and bumped on faster, momentarily expecting
the day to become night. Nothing happened. Yet I felt it
was coming. The smell of it hung in the burning air.

Just then Torridity lifted its sun-bleached bones into
view and I blared on my horn. In the heydey of its glory
it had been a typical western mining town of some fifteen hundred population, its buildings the usual jumble of
saloons, dance halls, dives, pool rooms, stores, and miners' shanties. The present hopeless desolation of the town
shocked me. I have been in a few "ghost cities" of the West,
but none of them had seemed quite so abandoned of God
and man as this one did. Where was it gone, that carousing
mob which had rioted through its doors, reckless, lustful,
drunk, sober, hands ready to guns, scoundrels, wantons,
gentlemen, scum? I shuddered. The place was a tomb.

And here it was that the candle of my friend's life had
burned with such hectic brilliance that its reflection shone
up through the dust of thirty years. What tragedy had
dimmed its light? Dimmed it, perhaps, that it might burn
the more steadily in our San Felipe Valley? I had quietened
the horn and now, in the crooked main street, I stopped
the car and with head bared listened reverently. I don't
know whether I listened for the voices of the living or the
dead. The wind moaned a little. Sand sifted and blew. A
window rattled. A door creaked. That was all.

Again I sounded the horn.

"Lucy!" I shouted. "Lucy! Lucy!" And then: "Jerry,
where are you? Lucy! Lucy! Jerry!"

No response. I got out of the car. North, south, and
east the view was distant; west, it ended against the barren
flanks of the Skeletons which rose immediately behind the
town. But nowhere was there sign of human life. Here and
there on the rutted street were the faint imprints of car
tires. I tried to follow them, but the ground was unyielding
and the trail soon ended. At any rate, they had been here.

Getting in the car, I drove up and down the street, blaring my horn and calling the children by name. Without avail.

It was close on four o'clock. Lucy, I reasoned after some thought, had got here about noon. She had found Jerry and they had left together at once. But as I hadn't met them on their way back it followed that they had taken the trail across the valley and joined the main road at Devil's Mouth on the east. They had then started back across the valley, along the main road, and by this time were probably approaching Shinbone Canyon on the west. Another couple of hours should see them back in San Felipe.

Instead of following them I would remain overnight in Torridity and improve my opportunity by nosing around Andrew's old haunts. Evidence of some sort was in my mind, but of what nature and how I was to find it, I hadn't the slightest idea. If I *had* known I wouldn't have planned so casually, I can tell you!

The sun was waning, but the street was still as hot as a boiler pit and I looked about for a temporary garage. Near where I had stopped were the wide-open doors of a livery stable. They hinted of cooler regions beyond and I drove through them into the semi-darkness of the building. Stopping the engine, I tackled a pile of sandwiches and a bag of fruit I had bought at a stand near the filling station and washed them down with draughts of water from one of the canteens. Refreshed, I went out again and made my way up the street, looking to right and left.

I had gone some fifty yards or so when I began to wonder if I were as completely alone as I had supposed. Whence came the thought I hadn't the slightest idea, for there was neither sight nor sound of any living being, although I knew that a city population could hide in the several hundred buildings that comprised the place without my being aware of it. The odd feeling grew upon me and I wished I had brought a revolver.

Stopping in front of the largest building in the town, a sort of dance hall, saloon, and hotel, evidently, I concluded that it was as good a place as any to begin my investigations. The building was square and solid-looking; its windows were broken and the front doors stood open, held so by drifts of sand. A flimsy porch fronted it. Most of the name on the face of the building was obliterated, but what was left had a familiar look.

There were three words in the name and the last word seemed to be "Place." I also made out a "J," and "L," and a "D." The rest of it suddenly flashed upon me. "Joe Lundy's Place"—that was it.

"'Joe Lundy's Place,'" I muttered. "'Joe—' Good Heavens!" I shouted. "Joe Lundy—that woman in black—the woman Andrew gave the check to!"

It couldn't be coincidence, of course. The woman in black was or had been the wife of a man who had kept this resort thirty years ago! And Andrew Ogden had given her a check for a thousand dollars! But why? And why had the woman dressed in the garb of yesterday? And why had the swashbuckling Alex Peterson become the staid and respectable Andrew Ogden? And why had Dillon blackmailed him? And who was Dillon? Why—why—why— I could have gone on until my vain questioning toppled my reason.

Sick of mystery and bewilderment, I entered the resort, prepared for anything now. It must have been a pretentious place in its day. A dance floor, warped and sprung, occupied the middle of the building. At the upper end was a small stage. Along one side ran a bar with a mahogany top and a tarnished brass rail, an expanse of mirrors, and armies of bottles—dead soldiers, I suspected. A stair led to a wide gallery which ran around the hall. Doors and booths flanked the gallery.

Broken bottles littered the sandy floor; tables and chairs lay in confusion. Several of the mirrors were cracked into the pattern of a spider's web, evidently by bullets, and again I thought of the boisterous mob that had rollicked through the place. I heard the whirr of the roulette wheel, the click of poker chips, the rattle of dice, the clink of glasses, the shrill glee of the women, the swish of milling bodies. And I thought of Alex Peterson swaggering, no, stalking among a pay-night crowd, his gold-mounted guns on his hips.

"Andrew! Andrew!" I groaned. "What manner of man were you?"

In the dining room cheap cutlery and heavy crockery lay on the tables as if they had been placed there the day before yesterday. A lizard squatted in a sugar bowl, a tarantula glowered in a soup dish. Sand everywhere. . . . Cues stood in their racks and lay athwart the poolroom tables. A piece of chalk neatly capped a pool ball. In the card room the roulette wheel waited. I spun it. Poker chips . . . cards. Black jack. A faro layout. Poker dice. A man's hat hung on a wall. Upstairs in the bedrooms were pillows and blankets. A flimsy red dress hung in a closet . . . and slippers to match. Names were scrawled on the walls. And so it had stood for thirty years.

The pathos of it touched me and I went slowly down the stair, reflecting sadly on the impermanence of human achievement.

And yet, this wholesale abandonment to the contrary, I hadn't been able to rid myself of the feeling that I was not as completely alone as I seemed. Whence came the feeling I still knew not, for I had come upon no sign of recent human presence in the resort. But it lay in my breast as heavy as lead. Coming behind the bar where I had not yet been, I tripped over a bundle of soft stuff lying in the shadowy passage between the bar and the wall, and almost went headlong.

I picked up the bundle and found myself staring at Jerry's white flannels!

My amazement turned to dismay. Belief in Jerry's innocence was as firmly fixed in my mind as was my certainty
of Dillon's guilt. But I also knew what conclusion Deacon's tenacious mind would have drawn if he instead of
I had found the bundle! Emerging from behind the bar, I
loosened the bundle of clothing and went carefully over
each article. The white shirt, the cream flannel trousers,
the canvas shoes, the white woolen sweater. Undeniably
they were Jerry's. His initials, worked by Lucy, were inside
the collar of the sweater. A pocket contained a packet of
his favorite cigarettes.

It was evident that the flannels had been planted. And
by Dillon, I supposed. Dillon, then, as well as Jerry, had
been in Torridity within the past forty hours. For all I
knew to the contrary he was here now. Perhaps it was his
presence that had affected me with that odd sense of not
being alone in the place.

The thought excited me and when the graveyard quietness of the resort was suddenly punctuated by the throb
of an automobile engine Dillon's name sprang, burning,
to my lips. Was I coming to grips with him again? Why
hadn't I brought a revolver! As I sprang, electrified, to my
feet a sage green roadster flew past the open door and my
conclusions collapsed. The car was Jerry's, and Lucy and
the boy were in it, their heads together.

My old legs had carried me in half a dozen bounds
almost to the door when I tripped over a beer bottle. Up
again, I stumbled outside. The roadster was a hundred
yards down the street, bound for the open desert and, I
supposed, the Devil's Mouth.

"Lucy!" I roared. "Lucy! Jerry! Stop there! Where are
you going? Lucy! Jerry!"

They did not hear me.

Shouting their names, I tore down the street. Still they
did not hear me, and the roadster passed entirely beyond

the range of my voice. Plunging into the livery stable, I climbed unsteadily into the sedan, determined to catch them if I burned out the engine. The sun had gone to my head and my heart, not as good as it used to be, was thundering unmercifully against my ribs. A swallow of water revived me and I started the engine. The car slid forward with a springless thud, thud, that sent me tumbling out again.

The tires were flat. They had been cut by some sharp instrument.

I sank limply onto the running-board. You can hardly blame me for harboring the thought that Jerry and Lucy had seen me after all.

But I didn't harbor it long.

I knew my Lucy better than that. And Jerry was a fine manly young fellow with the instincts of a gentleman and a deep affection for me. No, they had neither seen nor heard me just now, or, incredible as it seemed, when I first had come into the town. But where had they been that the blaring of my car horn had not reached them? The Two Brothers Mine? Likely enough, since Jerry was so taken up with it. Probably he had camped there, and there Lucy had found him. And where were they off to now? San Felipe, without a shadow of doubt. On Lucy's account Jerry had insisted on the longer route across the valley and back again over the main road, instead of the shorter but more dangerous one by way of pitchfork Canyon. They would be in San Felipe before midnight. Yes, I knew my Lucy!

But not so well as I thought, it was to turn out.

And what of the man who had slashed my tires? Dillon, undoubtedly. Knowing that Jerry was in Torridity, he had come to plant the flannels; not too obviously, but where they were likely to be found. The children, I decided, didn't know he was here and he may not have seen Lucy arrive, although he probably had seen her depart with Jerry. He certainly knew I was here, for he had gone to the trouble of slashing my tires to insure my remaining. The latter conclusion disturbed me. Why in the name of common sense hadn't I brought a pistol?

I don't know what made me think of Furie just then. He had slipped completely out of my mind. MacNair had assumed, and rightly, I thought, that Furie knew something about the Two Brothers mine; perhaps, indeed, had brought Ogden the bit of quartz we found in his desk. Moreover, Hubbard's description of him strongly suggested the old desert-rat type found in such localities as this. Mightn't Furie be a relic of Torridity's vanished prosperity bound to the abandoned town by an abnormal development of that home instinct which is in all of us? The thought intrigued me, but it opened up fresh possibilities. Was it Furie's presence I had sensed in the town instead of Dillon's? Was it, indeed, Furie who had slashed my tires? And had Dillon, after planting the flannels, taken himself off?

My head ached with this play and counterplay of supposition—speculation, MacNair would have called it—and I peeled an orange. Jerry and Lucy were gone. Dillon and Furie might or might not be here. What was I to do? The orange refreshed me and I began to wonder about the Two Brothers mine. MacNair had connected Furie and the quartz specimens with it and I had concluded Lucy had found Jerry there. Yes, undoubtedly the Two Brothers should be my next objective. After swallowing a sandwich and washing it down with draughts of warm water I set off up the street towards the flank of mountain behind the town. Jerry had told me that several abandoned mining properties were close to the town and I supposed one of them was the Two Brothers. On the outskirts, to which I soon came, my feet found an indistinct trail of sorts and I let them carry me along it.

The sun was declining towards the Skeletons, but the wind blew hot as a dragon's breath and in its teeth whistled that eerie sound I had heard as I drove towards Torridity. Louder, now, and more a swish than a moan, it seemed pregnant with menace. I thought it hissed at me, "Go back, you fool!" A thin sand haze hung in the air. The grit of it stung my throat. A windstorm impended, I felt sure, and common sense urged me to go back; but just then I saw at the base of the mountain the buildings of an abandoned mining property and I forgot my danger in the excitement of discovery. Heading into the bite of the wind, I quickly identified the property as the Two Brothers by the huge mass of splintered rock and bowlders heaped up in front of what had been the entrance to the main bore.

It took me half an hour or so to explore the various aspects of the property. The boiler plant, the rock crusher, the ten-stamp mill, cabin, kitchen, bunkhouse, and "tailings" dump. In ruin and a-creak in the burning wind, the buildings were a sorry mess, but the machinery was in fair condition. A few spare parts and a gallon or two of oil would soon have it spinning again. Great bowlders were strewn about the property; several of them had crashed through the roofs of some of the buildings and lay inside. The landslide must have been a terrific affair. From the "tailings" dump I followed the ore-cart rails up to the great pile of debris which blocked the entrance. To remove it would be a sizable job, but I couldn't think of any reason why Andrew shouldn't have let Jerry tackle it, if he wanted to.

In a barn-like structure which must have been used as a stable was the police car Lucy had commandeered. It cheered me mightily, for the barren results of my exploration of the other buildings had disappointed me. Just what I had expected to find I don't know. Leaving the car where it was, for the time being, I started back along the flank of the mountain.

The sun was lower. A magenta hue was creeping over the landscape and imparting to the sand haze its blue-red hue. The wind had quickened; its eerie note shrilled a little. Seen through this deepening color veil the mountain looked altogether different and as I proceeded I got a fresh perspective of its flank. Thus it happened that before I had gone a hundred yards beyond the limits of Two Brothers property I came upon a narrow gash slashed deep into the flinty mountainside which I hadn't seen as I came up. A vague trail led into the gash and the imprint of shoes showed in a sprinkling of sand at my feet.

"Some one has been through here," I muttered.

It certainly looked like it. Striking into the gash, I found myself between towering walls of reddish rock which gradually widened into a sizable canyon that cut into the heart of the Skeletons. I had gone some two hundred yards when I noticed a "V"-shaped joint in the steep south slope of the canyon. The slope was about five hundred feet high at this point. As I approached the joint I saw that it was really a cavern-like slash in the rock wall.

I had come within thirty feet of the slash when a rifle cracked and a bullet flattened against the rock twelve inches above my head!

13
The House of Fear

When a rifle bullet whines in one's ears there is nothing to do but stand where one is, and this I did. My eyes sprang up the opposite slope which ascended gradually and I saw not far above me a small wooden shanty from which, I concluded, had come the shot. There was no cover nearer than the cavern-like slash and I wondered if I were to be dropped dead as I stood.

Presumably not, since a second shot didn't come. The slash offered sanctuary. Only thirty feet away! Could I make it? Once inside it I'd be safe enough and when it was dark I could get away. I suppose it was an idiotic thing to do, sixty-nine not being as smart on its legs as it might be, but I suddenly hurled myself towards the slash. Before I had covered a third of the distance the rifle cracked again and my hat leaped and fell over my face. Losing my balance, I reeled back against the cliff, my heart thumping like a two-cylinder engine.

It seemed likely that a third shot would put an end to the foremost collector of pistols in San Felipe County and I stayed where I was. A minute or so passed. The sun was beginning to set beyond the crest of the Skeletons. It grew perceptibly darker. What were the man's intentions? So far as I could see no one was coming down the slope. Perhaps he merely intended to keep me out of the slash. Holding

my breath, I edged experimentally away from the slash.
Nothing happened and I dashed the sweat from my forehead. Apparently I might take myself off, but I mustn't go
into the slash.

Why?

It didn't take me long to speculate about it, as MacNair
would say, you may be sure. If the slash was not a new opening into the complicated workings of the Two Brothers mine,
what was it? And if the marksman on the hillside was not
guarding a recently exposed ledge of gold-bearing ore somewhere within the bowels of the mine, what was he doing?

"Who is it?" I muttered. "Furie—Dillon?"

If MacNair was right in his assumption that Furie knew
something about the specimen we had found in Ogden's
desk, and I rather believed he was, it might be Furie.

These thoughts had come in a flash. My immediate
concern was to get away. I could think the thing through
when I was in safer quarters. With my eyes upon the slope
opposite I made my way along the trail, half expecting the
smack of a bullet. But it didn't come and presently I was
out in the desert again.

The sun had gone. A reddish-brown hue had come over
the scene and the atmosphere was like glass washed in the
lees of red wine. Into the shrill cry of the wind had come a
human note as awesome as a voice from a tomb. It seemed
to invest the brooding solitude with an ominous quality
of personality. Little wheels and whirls of sand sprang up,
danced, died. The sand haze nipped my throat, stung my
nostrils, watered my eyes. A curious sense of the desert
holding itself in leash, of malign forces gathering beneath
this outward tranquility, affected me and I hurried over
the vast and empty desolation with dread clutching at my
heart. I began to run.

When I had come within a hundred yards of the nearest
building the wind screamed like a herd of terrified horses.

A dense brown fog rose up from the earth, a hail of sand and gravel smote me back and front, lashing my face and head as with wire whips, and the universe turned black. The ferocity of the wind was beyond conception. It took me into its arms and, spinning me like a top, ran with me screaming down the street. Abruptly it let me go and for a moment I hung in a little pocket in the wind. Geysers of sand sprang up from the earth, ropes of sand fell from the sky, and I saw them driven by the bellows of heaven into the revels of a pit full of fiends let loose.

And then, suddenly, a blast of sand poured into my face, blinding me; the wind picked me up again, spun me, and hurled me against the side of a building. Pinning me there so that I could move neither right nor left, it smote me blow upon blow until I thought my senses would leave me.

Once again the wind picked me up and sent me spinning down the street. Then it smote me sidewise. I pitched through an open door and went headlong.

At sixty-nine one's bones are as tender as an aching tooth, and I was glad to remain still for a minute or two. Where I was I neither knew nor cared. My body felt beaten to a pulp, and my face was stinging and bleeding from tiny cuts inflicted by the gravel-toothed wind. Decidedly I was getting too old for this sort of thing.

The wind yammered and snarled like a regiment of baboons, shaking the building to its foundations. Blasts of it volleyed in through the open door and the broken windows, distributing sand as effectively as if the roof were a gigantic pepperbox. I had heard and read of the sandstorms of Skull Valley scouring the enamel off a car until the metal work shone bare, and grinding the glass of a windshield until it was opaque, and never quite believed it. Now I could have credited anything to them.

The thought of Lucy and Jerry out in it gave me a bad minute or two. But I reflected that Jerry had a sound

head on his shoulders, and if they shut themselves in and
sat tight nothing serious would be likely to happen to
them, provided they had water and the storm didn't last
too long. Knowing Jerry, I didn't worry much about their
water supply, but I wasn't as confident about the duration
of the storm. However, they were young, and youth has a
way of turning its adventures into frolics.

More comfortable in mind and body, I looked about
me. My eyes were inflamed and half blinded by sand, but
I had a sense of space and familiarity, and I decided I had
been tumbled into Lundy's Place. I got some of the sand
out of my eyes and stood up. My head felt twice its normal size and my legs were as weak as straws. When I had
got my bearings I saw vaguely the door through which I
had blown, but the hall was as black as a witch's hat. I
was feeling around for a chair when I stopped sharply, my
body turned to stone.

Ever since I had come into this graveyard town my
senses had been abnormally acute. It was much as if
the suspension of communication with living folks had
sharpened those faculties of intuition which I had always
despised. Before I had seen Jerry and Lucy making off in
Jerry's car I had felt that I was being watched, and even
after they had gone the impression had remained. Now it
was at me again, stronger than ever. I could have sworn
there was some one other than myself in the building.

There came a lull in the roar of the storm, and suddenly, out of the profound silence, a definite indoors sound
broke on my eardrums. It might have been the slur of a
footstep, the scrape of a chair leg, the creak of a staircase;
anything but the storm outside. Of that I felt sure.

But it wasn't the sound that brought me up rigid, heart
pounding in my throat; it was the sense of danger that
came with it. Some one was in the room. He knew I was
here. Why didn't he declare himself? Who was he? The

man who had fired on me in the canyon? No, not Furie—if that were Furie; he could not have got down here before me. Dillon, then? This was more probable and I had been right in my surmise that he was still in the town.

Fear held me as in a vice and I make no bones about admitting it, either. I'll face any man if I can meet him eye to eye; but an unknown, unseen enemy sends the horrors up and down my spine. Moreover, I had no weapon of any sort, whereas Dillon would be armed; nor was I in shape for a hand-to-hand struggle.

Outside, the storm was bellowing again, so I couldn't depend on my ears, but I thought the sound I had heard had come from somewhere near the door. I pondered swiftly, desperately, and decided on a risky experiment. The bar ran along almost the entire east side of the building. Bending double, I picked my way to the lower end of the bar, knelt behind it, and fumbled in my pocket for matches. I was disturbed to find only two. One must be enough. It was a foolish thing that I did then, but I was determined to try and force my unseen enemy to show his intentions. Still crouching low, I struck a match and held it above the bar.

Crack! Crack!

Splinters of glass from the shattered mirror behind me showered upon my back and head. So close to my hand had the slugs passed that the match flame had leaped in their wind. The double flash had told me that my enemy—Dillon, presumably—was posted near the open door. But how long would he stay there?

I am no more cowardly than most men, I hope, and I have been in one or two tight corners in my life, but the wind of death on my flesh had set my nerves a-quiver. Was there nothing I could do but squat here in the dark and wait for a bullet to burst my heart or pierce my brain? My hand feeling about under the bar encountered a heap of empty beer bottles. I could not have expected to accomplish anything by the move, so I suppose it was my excited mental state, as much as a desire to give the man a run for his money, that made me stand noiselessly up, bottle in hand, and hurl it in the direction of the flash.

As the bottle left my hand I dropped behind the bar again. To my joy I heard a grunt, a scorching oath, and the crash of glass.

Crack!

The bar quivered as the slug plowed into it. "He'll be stalking me next," I reflected. "Once he gets to this end of the bar, I'm done. If only I had a pistol!"

The irony of owning several hundreds of them and being unarmed when I needed one had not escaped me.

I thought of the stair and the gallery above. If I could get up there I might have a better chance. The storm favored me; it would cover any noise I might make. Grasping another beer bottle, I crept to the stair and started up it on my toes. Halfway up, the wind dropped for a minute, and at precisely that moment I stumbled over a sprung board. The board creaked.

Crack!

The bottle smashed in my hand. I dropped the fragment remaining. The flash had come from the bottom of the stair. Desperate strength came to me, and I bounded up to the top.

There I listened. He was coming up at a run! I slid around the newel post and fled along the gallery, evading chairs and table legs as by a miracle, until I came nearly to the other end. But now my insurge of strength had evaporated, and I crept to the wall and leaned against it, as weak as a glass of skimmed milk. Almost instantly the scrape of a chair or table leg came to me, in a lull in the wind, and I knew the hunt was on.

Keeping close to the wall, I moved noiselessly down the gallery, and incidentally, entered upon the most terrific half hour of my life.

The gallery, as I have said, ran around the four walls of the hall. It was about twenty feet wide. The staircase I had climbed entered upon the north side of the gallery. At its head I had turned along the east side. Now I came to the end, and turned onto the south side. Dillon was somewhere behind me.

But where? Still following me? Or was he waiting near the head of the stairs for me to circle the gallery and run into his arms? Again I stood still and listened intently. The scream of the wind had dropped to a mutter. I was sweating profusely. I dared not go on; I was afraid to remain still.

Halfway up the west side of the gallery I stopped once more and crouched against the wall, desperate as a hunted beast. I was at the end of my endurance. I prayed that something, anything, might happen, and happen quickly.

Upon that prayer, a beam of light shot out of the darkness in my rear. I cast one backward look, my eyes dazzled by the brilliant glare which had its source not thirty feet away. He had kept the torch back until he was sure I was unarmed. Now he knew he had me. I drove myself on again. Life had become a matter of seconds; nothing on earth, it seemed, could help me. Yet the will to live held me to the effort. I'd be game to the last breath.

Just then I pitched headlong over a broken chair, slid along the floor and came to rest within a few feet of the north wall. The lower end of this side of the gallery had been partitioned into alcoves. I squirmed into the further corner of the alcove next to the north wall and stood up, hugging the north wall.

For the moment my pursuer could not see me. The light beam swelled and wavered, seeking trace of me. I heard, or imagined I heard, the approaching tread of the man's feet. Then my hands, reaching out into space, fell upon the back of a chair. On the spur of the moment I picked it up, whirled it around the alcove partition and let go, leaping back into the alcove.

The chair went home. The man cursed and the light beam swept downward; then, spinning like a shooting star, it fell through the well of the hall. A tinkle of glass as it struck the floor was faintly audible, and welcome darkness once more enshrouded me.

As I crouched there against the wall, alert in every mental fiber, I sensed the man's approach, I heard his excited breathing, and I *felt* him, at last, standing in front of the alcove, gun leveled. And as I gathered the last remnants of my strength, preparatory to the final effort for life, the pistol cracked again. I must have been hidden from the man, or he would have got me. As it was, the shot was in my favor, for the flash showed me exactly where he was. Tensing my body, balancing on the balls of my feet, I let myself go.

I struck him like a battering-ram and he staggered to the balcony rail, dropping the pistol. But he recovered in a flash and before I could follow up my advantage he lifted me bodily and flung me against the north wall in the alcove.

My head as well as my body struck the wall, and with the blow I passed into that borderland which lies between sensibility and unconsciousness. Still, as I lay crumpled there. I dimly sensed that my enemy was groping for his pistol. Well, let him find it, and use it, too. The quicker the better. I could not lift a hand to stop him. Death was nothing, just then. If I could have been sure that Lucy and Jerry were to find happiness, I could have died cheerfully.

Dimly these fancies passed through my half-darkened mind. And then I made a curious discovery. My head and shoulders were not piled up in the alcove against the north wall, as I had supposed, but were lying in a room behind the wall. Part of it, at least, had given way or swung in when I was thrown against it, and the upper portion of my body had gone with it. I had previously noticed no door.

I was not much surprised; my state of half mind forbade that. But the discovery did seem to offer a new way, a remote chance, of escape. If I could get behind that wall or door and shut it fast before the man found his pistol— He was still feeling for it. I should have to move quickly.

Where my strength came from I know not, but I suddenly found myself on my elbows wriggling painfully forward into the room behind the wall. Two-thirds of my body were in when I collapsed, exhausted. Again strength was given me, and I got myself completely into the room.

A dozen seconds may have elapsed before I was able grope for the door or section of the wall. Door it proved to be, solid and heavy, and it swung slowly before my feeble effort. It stuck and creaked, creaked alarmingly. I groaned in despair, for my partial success had retired my dazed brain with the will to live.

"Dear God!" I sobbed, "I've *got* to shut it!"

Crack!

The bullet ripped through woodwork and by the flash I got a glimpse of some one leaping into the alcove. Just then the door swung to and a latch clicked. My hand encountered a flat bolt halfway up the door. I drove it home, and sank in a huddle on the floor.

14
Poker Faces

The storm lashed at the building and loose boards rattled like skeletons dancing in a closet. But in one or two intervals of comparative quiet I was vaguely aware of the man investigating the other side of the wall. He would rap on the door with the butt of his pistol, then hurl himself upon it, but without effect. A line of light would then appear at the bottom of the door, presumably from a match, and I supposed he was examining the barrier. I was too ill to care and too dazed to move.

Some time passed and then I heard him no more.

Presently I began to feel better and as my mind cleared I became curious about the place I had fallen into. The room was pitch black. I could see nothing, not even the outline of my hand twelve inches away from my face. I still had a single match. Treasuring it between my fingers, I was loathe to use it.

If I struck the match the flame would burn out and I would have lost my last anchorage in reality. The thought frightened me and I lay on my back desperately clutching the match and staring up into the soft blackness. In a way, I think I feared the light even more than I did the dark. Not the light itself, of course, but what it might reveal, for I had an uncanny sense of some fresh horror awaiting me. This sounds absurd and nightmarish in broad day, but it will indicate to you the abnormal state of my mind and how unfitted I was to pass on the nature of what was to follow.

I tried to rid my mind of its obsession by focusing my attention on the events that had brought me to this graveyard town. The experiment wasn't exactly beneficial. Words and phrases reeled and jigged through my head like imps at a burning. I thought I would go mad. Gold bullets . . . poker chips . . . playing cards . . . the man "Jerry" . . . Andrew Ogden and Alex Peterson the same man . . . blackmail . . . Mrs. Joe Lundy . . . Dillon . . . Furie . . . Jerry flying for his life—but it wasn't Jerry! . . . Nathan Hyde . . . Jerry and Lucy driving into the sandblast. And then: who had fired on me at the mine? Furie—Dillon? Dillon—Furie?

Furie—?

"God help me!" I screamed. "It can't be real! It's a nightmare! I'm asleep! I'll wake up presently! Or else I am going mad!"

I found, then, that the storm had stopped. When, I did not know, for I had lost track of time. The bones of the old building no longer rattled; silence filled the room. But now that I had become aware of it this silence was more devastating to my tortured nerves than the uproar which had preceded it. I wanted to weep, to laugh, to scream, to dash my head against the floor. I felt as if I were standing in the middle of an empty universe.

And then I made a discovery.

With the storm over, the room wasn't as dark as it had been when I fell in through the door. A faint luminosity was observable and I made out the shape of a small window on the north side of the room. Outside the window, which was broken, the luminosity was brighter and I supposed it was starlight. As I continued to stare at the window a paralyzing coldness came over my body.

I was not alone in the room!

Two men were sitting facing each other over a table in front of the window. The outline of their heads and shoulders merged into the shadows which enclosed the frame, but they were unmistakably there. That is, unless I were mad, and I was not at all sure that I was not! They must know I was here. Why didn't they speak, or come to me? They sat perfectly still. Why didn't they move? They sat in darkness. Why didn't they make a light?

Well, I told myself, there was nothing to fear! And with this thought my bound muscles relaxed and I tried to get up; but my head was throbbing dreadfully and as soon as I raised my shoulders I went deathly sick and flopped back. I moved my lips in speech, but no word fell from them, and I hammered on the floor with my fists. There was no response. Again I tried to speak, this time with better success.

"Say, there! I wish you'd help me."

The two men neither spoke nor moved.

That paralyzing coldness began to creep over me again, but I shook it off. Struggling mightily, I managed to get to my haunches, at the same time controlling the nausea which threatened to topple me over. Then I remembered the solitary match in my hand. The very thing to attract their attention!

I drew the match sharply across the floor; but it must have been defective, or else my wobbly hand made a mess of it, for while the phosphorous flared up it did not light the stick, but hissed and sputtered and began to go out. The brief and feeble flame made little impression on the dark face of the room and it didn't reach the men's bodies or heads; but it did slightly illuminate the surface of the table. At what I saw I dropped the match and flopped down on my back again.

"I am mad, or else I am dreaming," I said, quite aloud.

The two men did not speak.

In that moment of light I had seen playing cards and stacks of poker chips on the table. The two men were playing poker *in the dark* and their cards were exposed! It was a showdown.

Crouched against the floor, I fought the horror rising in my breast. I was asleep! That was it, of course. Afterwards, I would laugh at my crazy nightmare! And yet—and yet—I ran my hands over the floor. Sand scoured my finger ends. I felt of my body thin and bony, but real enough. Breathing deeply, I lifted my eyes to the window again. The outlines of the two heads and shoulders were still there.

"Well," I said aloud, "if you want to sit in the dark pretending to play poker, why shouldn't you? It's your business, isn't it? And if you don't choose to take notice of me I can likewise ignore you."

But this nonsense didn't check my rising hysteria, which suddenly got the better of me.

"Who are you?" I shrilled.

Silence still.

"What are you doing there? You can't play poker in the dark! You can't make a fool of *me!*" I pounded on the floor with my fists.

No response.

"For God's sake speak to me!" I screamed. "Who—*who* are you?"

Still that devastating silence.

I got to my hands and knees and crawled towards the table. "Why don't you speak to me?" I begged. "I can't stand it! I'll make you talk! *What* are you?"

Sliding my hand over the edge of the table, I clutched one of the playing cards. That, at least, was real, and I thrust it into a pocket to prove the reality of my experience. Steadying myself with the table, I climbed to my feet. I thought I would fall, but somehow I managed to remain standing.

My trembling hand went out to the arm of the figure on my right. I felt a shirt, gritty with sand. Still half blinded, I could make nothing definite of the man in a visual sense, but there was solid stuff beneath the shirt. I fearfully ran my hand up to the shoulder. No word or movement from the figure.

"Speak to me!" I implored. "A word! Oh, speak!"

Still that dreadful silence. Horror crawled within my breast. My hand crept along the shoulder to the neck, and then to the face.

The flesh was cold!

Something snapped in my brain. All feeling went out of my arms and legs and body and I pitched senseless to the floor.

15
The Desert Rat

It was morning when I came to. A finger of sunlight slanted across my face, blinding me to my surroundings and intensifying an ache already violent at the back of my eyeballs. Still in a dazed condition and uncertain of what had happened to me, I lay quiet and waited for memory to refresh itself of the events of the night.

Recollection came quickly. First, there had been the windstorm, turning calm day into furious night and spinning me into the resort. Then had come my discovery of Dillon in the hall, my ascent of the staircase, and Dillon stalking me in the gallery. Of course it was *Dillon!* The crack of his pistol, the bite of bullet on woodwork— I never would forget these things. They were as vivid to me as fire. A door had opened, then—an unexpected door.

Here I paused.

The sandstorm, my experience with Dillon, the opening of the door, my painful entrance into the room beyond, had been real. No mistake as to that! But the rest of it? The two men playing poker. Playing poker in the dark. Their unmoving stillness. Their silence. Their cold, waxed faces— I shuddered. Then I grinned a little. Nightmare or delirium; nothing more. Yes, I saw exactly where reality ended and illusion began. In the brilliant sunlight of early morning what else could it be but illusion? Reassured and slightly better, I opened my eyes, moved my head out of the sunbeam, and looked around.

I was lying on the floor of one of the rooms off the west balcony, a pillow under my head. A bed, a bureau, and a chair were in the room. The door had been smashed in. Sitting on an empty beer case, a rifle between his knees and a canteen at his side, was the oddest-looking creature I had ever seen.

He was a little wizened-up crab-apple of a man as tough as saddle leather and the color of walnut juice. Snow-white hair thatched his skull and ears and neck, and his face was furrowed like a fresh-plowed field. I could not see his eyes for his head was bent. A faded overall and a dirty blue shirt covered his wisp of a body and his bare feet were thrust into clumsy boots a size or so too large for him. His arms were long like an ape's and enormously strong, I thought, and they terminated in a pair of sinewy hands covered with loose skin pleated like an accordion. If hands can express a quality of character, furtive cunning was the impression his gave me of him. He was fingering a lump of quartz at which he peered through a lens stuck in his eye. I watched him, fascinated.

"Good morning, Furie," I said, at length.

His ancient head flashed up and I put his age at eighty. The small, red-rimmed eyes, China-blue in color and set m a dirty wedge of a face confirmed the impression of him his hands had given me. The glass in his eye, held mono-cle fashion, was eight-sided and I concluded that it a lens from a pair of old-fashioned spectacles. A thin copper wire ran through a hole in the lens and the other end of the wire was secured to his shirt by a safety Pm. As I addressed him the quartz vanished inside his shirt with astonishing swiftness.

"He—he—he!" the old man cackled. "So ye ain't cold yet, huh?"

"I don't know that it isn't your fault I'm not," I observed.

"Huh!" he shrilled, shaking his shaggy head at me. "Hain't I bust in the door an' put yer head on a piller an' gived ye a guzzle o' water?"

"Very kind of you," I admitted, "but I was thinking of *that.*" And I nodded at the rifle leaning against the door jamb. "You tried your hardest to put a bullet an inch or so from my head up at the Two Brothers yesterday afternoon."

"'Twaren't me!" he shrilled.

"Who was it, then?"

"I dunno," he mumbled craftily.

"Furie," I said, "you are a liar. Out with it, now. Why did you fire at me yesterday?"

"Who tol' ye I was Furie?" he countered. "I ain't seen ye before."

"Never mind that now," I said wisely. "Answer my question. Why did you fire at me?"

"There's too many comes a-nosin' round these parts now'days!" he screamed. "That thar mine ain't none o' yer business, nor nob'dy else's! I ain't tellin' nothin'!"

I managed to get to my knees and, by degrees, to my feet. My head spun but I was able to stand erect, and after I had taken a swallow from the canteen I felt better. Dropping onto the bed, I fixed a stern eye on the crafty face in front of me.

"See here, Furie, you called on Nathan Hyde Friday morning."

"I ain't tellin' nothin'!"

"Where did you find that pistol you sold him?"

"Whut d'ye say?" he squealed, shaken.

"I am the man who bought it off Hyde. Where did you find it?"

He began to interlace his bony fingers. "Hain't I said I ain't tellin' nothin'!"

I leaned nearer, pointing my finger at him. "You also called on Andrew Ogden. You took him a specimen of gold quartz—like that piece you thrust in your shirt just now. Where did you get it?"

Something of madness leaped into his eyes. "I ain't tellin'!" he yelped.

"Well, it doesn't matter," I said softly. "You got it from a new vein in the Two Brothers."

He leaped to his feet, speechless and foaming, his walnut shell of a face as yellow as saffron. Quivering, he shook his bony fists in my face, his eyes bloodshot, the eight-sided lens dangling from its wire. Never before had I seen in a human countenance so insane, so blasphemous, an anger. I thought he would do himself an injury. But suddenly the floodgates opened and he poured his pent-up emotions out upon me.

"'Tis my gold, this!" he screamed, prancing up and down, eyepiece rattling on its wire. "Hain't I tramped Skull and Skeleton fifty year alookin' fer it? Hain't I thirsted an' starved? Hain't I burned and sweated and freezed? Hain't I cotched snakebite an' drinked water as stinked an' had the hide sanded offen me? Hain't I seen me eyesight go and me teeth drop out? Hain't I cussed an' scraped an' hunted an'— Hell's Bells! Hain't I weared meself to a passel o' hide an' a rattle o' bones? *But I found it!*" His voice rose in a scream of triumph. "An' nobody's agoin' to take it away frum me! A-glintin an' a-gleamin' thar in the dark! Rotten with gold! The smell of it! The feel of it! Gold! Thar ain't nothin' like it! Yer dog'll bite ye, yer mule'll kick yer slats in, yer pardner'll slit yer gullet! But gold! Gimme a bucket o' gold an' I'll not call Rockyfeller me uncle!"

Quite mad on the subject of gold, as most of us are mad on the subject of something or other—pistols, perhaps— he raved on in this vein. But he was pitiful, too; as pitiful as an unfed passion for gold can make a man.

"Would Andry Ogden have knowed it ware thar if I hadn't tol' him, I ask ye? But I'm squar' shootin', I is. 'Andry,' sez I, 'the claim is yourn but the findin's mine, so I'll split ye fifty-fifty.' 'Ye will not!' he yells at me. 'How dare ye trespass on my proppity! I'll have the roof o' the jail over yer crack-brained head!' That's a pardner fer ye! Give me gold! Yaller gold! Raw gold with the sun a-glintin' in it! The feel of it, the smell of it—"

I thought it time to stop him. "Furie!"

His flow of eloquence stopped and, munching his jaws at me, he fumbled for his eyepiece. As soon as he had got it in place the cunning look again enlivened his face and I concluded that either he saw but dimly without the lens, or, like the Englishman and his monocle, he derived from it a tonic for his self-possession.

"Huh?" he shrilled.

"What else did you say to Andrew Ogden?"

"He-he-he!" he cackled, crafty again. "I shooked him up!"

"What did you say to him?"

"I ain't tellin'!"

Leaning nearer, I said gravely, "Andrew Ogden is dead."

"Huh!—whut?" He jumped as if a rattler had struck him. "Dead!" he shrilled. "Dead!"

"He was stabbed to death in his library after you left him Friday night."

"Stabbed! Whut! Whut! Andry Ogden!" The old face twitched so violently that the eyepiece fell out again, clawed at it feebly. "Who done it?"

I looked at him accusingly. "The police will be asking *you* that question before long, I'm thinking."

"'Tis a lie!" he screamed. "I left him alive! 'Tis a lie if they say I killed him!"

"Hmn! Well, maybe it is. You can prove it?"

"Prove it!" he mumbled. "Prove it! How in Whoopin' Harry's a old geezer like me to prove anythin'?" Then,

shrewdly, "How'll they prove it agin me when I didn't do
it?"

"Maybe they won't if you tell everything you know."

He looked at me suspiciously. "Are ye one o' them p'lice
slickers?"

I thought, half-smiling. "Well, yes, in a way. You had
better tell me what you and Ogden talked about."

He opened his mouth, then shut it stubbornly, shaking
his shaggy head.

"Nossir! Thar ain't nothin' to tell. An' I ain't agoin' to
tell it, neither. They can't prove Andry Ogden's death agin
me, 'cause I didn't kill him."

I let the point rest. "Ogden's son Jerry was here. Did
you see him?"

"Uh-huh. The girl, too."

"What did they say to you?"

He gave me a sharp look. "Nothin'—much."

"Do you know why Andrew Ogden didn't want the Two
Brothers opened?"

This seemed to amuse him. "He-he-he!" he cackled. "Ye
ain't been in the mine, eh?"

"No. Why?"

"Nothin'. He-he-he! Jes' nothin'!"

"When did you find the canyon entrance to the mine?"

He considered for a moment. "Couple o' months ago.
One o' them earthquarks done it."

"Indeed!" This was illuminating. Two months ago a
mild earthquake had shaken up the central valleys, finding
its greatest intensity in Skull Valley.

"You said you were guarding the mine because people were
hanging around it," I went on. "Who were those people?"

"I dunno."

"What did they look like?"

"Dunno. Both was tall. One of 'em ran to meat. City
hawgs! I shet meself up!" This contemptuously.

"How long have you been in Skull Valley, Furie?"

He shook his head mournfully. "God knows. Forty, fifty, sixty year."

"Ever hear of Alex Peterson in the old days?"

"'Ten-to-One' Peterson!" he shrilled. "Ev'rybody round them parts knowed Ten-to-One thirty year ago."

"You were in Torridity then?"

"Uh-huh." He nodded his white head with pathetic bitterness. "Bin here ever since. Hain't had the brains to git out. But it ain't no use to ax me about them days. The sun ain't left me nuthin' but hide an' hair an' a passel o' bones. It's even b'iled the mem'ries outen me. . . . A dom good job, too!"

The intensity of his bitterness compelled my belief, but I determined to try him with another question or two.

"You've lived here all alone—all this time?" I inquired suggestively.

He nodded mournfully. "Uh-huh. Who'd live in this devil's skillet but a old fool of a desert rat like me?" Then he broke into his cackling laugh again. "He-he-he! When I gits crazy lonely I talks to Bull and Nap."

"Bull and Nap!" I exclaimed. "Who are they?"

His eyes were crafty and he dropped the lids over them. "Nothin'," he mumbled. "Nothin' but foolery' A couple o'—o' hombres I talks to—when I feels sociable."

I thought I understood. Men in desolate places sometimes create personalities, out of their own imaginations. Even a shadow pardner is better than no pardner at all! My heart went out to the old fellow. "Bull" and "Nap"! probably they were as real as flesh and blood to him. Decidedly they were none of my business.

"Did Peterson ever own the Two Brothers?" I went on diffidently, after a small silence.

He shook his head slowly and opened his eyes again. "I dunno. Mebbe. I dunno. Hain't I tol' ye the mem'ries all b'iled outen me?"

I looked at him steadily. "You can call them back if you want to, Furie. Try and remember this: Did you ever hear of a 'poker game that cracked the town'?"

A wild look came into his eyes. "Poker game," he mumbled. And then: "Peterson—Ten-to-One—Lundy—Joe Lundy—" He stopped and rocked to and fro as if he were in pain.

"Yes, Lundy," I cried excitedly. "Joe Lundy! That's it, man! Try and remember!"

His words, the look in his eyes, fired my brain. Had I got hold of a main thread? Was this half-witted desert rat to untangle the snarl of Andrew's life? Crouching on the edge of the bed, I watched him fumble among the threads of his memory.

"Lundy—Peterson—" he was mumbling.

"Yes, yes! Go on!" I implored.

But he sprang to his feet in a sudden access of rage.

"I tell ye I disremember! How's a danged ol' fool like me to be a-tellin' erbout whut happened in them days when he don't git a swill o' decent water to ile the hinges of his memory onct in ten year? Ye can't live in the Skull like I done and remember. Ye don't want ter. The quicker ye fergits the better ye feels! An' I ain't a-goin' ter remember!" he screamed. "An', I ain't a-goin' to answer no more o' yer questions. Andry Ogden and his doin's ain't none o' my business. Nor who killed him! If he's dead the gold is mine—ev'ry two-bit piece of it! Hain't I found it? Hain't I b'iled and freezed and sweated for it? Hain't I . . .?" And he raved on.

Bitterly disappointed, I realized that he wasn't going to tell me anything vital about Andrew; at least, not now. But I hadn't done with him yet and I stopped him sharply.

"Where were you last night?" I demanded sternly, going towards him.

He goggled at me through his eyepiece. "In me shanty by the mine."

"You are lying," I said, although I didn't believe he was. "You were in this building."

"I waren't!" he shrilled. I had dropped my hand on his shoulder, but he flung it off with a sinewy strength that surprised me. Leaping back, he glared at me angrily. "Keep yer hands whur they belongs! I tol' ye I waren't here! Let that be enough!"

I was inclined to believe him. "Is there anybody else in the town?"

"I dunno," he mumbled.

"A man was in this building last night seeking my life," I went on. "He fired at me, stalked me around the gallery. If I hadn't managed to crawl into this room he'd have got me."

So wholesome an effect had the hot morning sunlight had upon me that I no longer doubted *this* was the room into which I had fallen, or that the figures I had seen it were anything else but figments of my disordered imagination.

"It waren't me!" Furie snarled. "Mebbe I kept ye outen the mine, but I didn't chase ye round no gallery!"

"How did you happen to find me here? I bolted the door."

I thought his eyes flickered for an instant, but he spoke readily enough.

"I comes up onct in a while. This morning this yere door was bolted. It waren't never locked before and I looked through a crack. You was lyin' on the floor, so I busts in the door and gives ye a guzzle o' water. An' ye calls me a liar fer doin' it!"

Munching his jaws, he glared at me through his eyepiece and I considered him in silence for a moment. Yes, he was speaking the truth. Dillon was the man who had been after me. This shouldn't have escaped me for a moment. I was on the point of telling Furie that I believed him when the purr of an automobile engine unexpectedly broke upon the graveyard quiet.

"Another o' them city sharps!" Furie screamed.

Nimbly as a cat, he whirled on his heel, made for the stair, and clattered down it at astonishing speed. I ran to the window. A sedan was lumbering slowly down the crooked street. Its hood was scraped to the dully gleaming aluminum and its windshield, ground opaque, had been broken so that the driver could see ahead. The car stopped and a man got out.

It was Deacon.

16

The Golden Wall

One doesn't leave a chief of police locked up in one's house with impunity—even when he happens to be a very good friend—and ever since I had left San Felipe there had lain in the back of my mind the certainty that presently I should have to reckon with Henry. I was determined to accept full responsibility for Lucy's rash act and as I made my way downstairs I wondered what he would say to me.

Furie had vanished. Henry was staring up at the building with a grim look on his honest face. His expression didn't soften when he saw me.

"I was rather looking for you, Henry," I said agreeably, as he came towards me.

"Glad to see me?" he inquired ironically.

"Indeed, yes." I was. "Your car seems to have had a bad time of it. I suppose you were out all night."

He ignored the observation. "What have you got to say for yourself?"

"I've got a good deal to tell you."

"You should have! Where is my car, your niece, and young Ogden?"

Evidently he wasn't going to be generous. "Your car is over at the mine. The children aren't here."

"Children!" The term seemed to amuse him. "Where are they?"

"I don't know."

"Did you see them?"

"Oh, yes. They left the place just after I got here yesterday afternoon. Neither of them saw me. They were gone before I could stop them."

"So." Henry gave a short laugh. "Why did you do this fool thing, John?"

I looked at him seriously. "You know why I did it, Henry. I wanted the boy to have his chance. I felt sure he could explain his absence satisfactorily and I wanted him to give himself up for the sake of appearances. I don't believe he knew his father was dead. Anyhow, your men will have him now."

"Hmn! Maybe. Why did he come to this Godforsaken hole?"

"Something to do with the mine, I fancy."

"You said you saw them go. What did you mean by that?"

I told him.

"I suppose I don't need to point out to *you* the seriousness of what you did."

I nodded humbly. Hardly! Police chiefs aren't to be handled like baggage. But you can clap me in jail if you want to."

He grunted. "Do you imagine you helped the boy's case by locking me up?"

"I rather think so. Jerry has surrendered himself by this time and that was what we wanted. You can't charge the boy with my sins."

"Or your niece's. I suppose not."

"I'd sooner it had been any one else in the world than you, Henry," I assured him earnestly. But I felt I had to back Lucy up. She was risking a good deal for the boy. The responsibility is mine, of course, for not letting you out. . . . Er, how did you get out?"

"Thompson," Henry said briefly.

"I suppose you finished my fine door?"

"Yes. Thompson is pretty good with an ax. He seemed to enjoy the job. You'll be able to use it for kindling."

"Have you got anything to eat with you?" I asked.

"Sandwiches and water," he grunted. "Let's get out of this infernal heat."

The sun was well up in the heavens now and the huddle of buildings seemed to shrink and shrivel beneath the terrific downpour of heat from the blue metal bowl above. As I looked around I was struck by the odd fancy that the Skull was an altar on which were offered up to the sun god the bones of dead ambitions. When Deacon had got his sandwiches and canteens we were glad to go into the resort.

"Whew!" he gasped, wiping the sweat off his forehead. "A week of this would finish me!"

"Furie has had upwards of fifty years of it."

"Furie! Is he here?"

But I was ravenous and parched with thirst and I wouldn't tell him anything until I had devoured half a dozen of his sandwiches and helped myself to his canteen. Henry made a pretty fair showing, himself. The heat had melted some of his grimness.

"Well?" he demanded, when I had done.

I had decided to make a clean breast of everything that had happened to me and I began with that sense of surveillance which had come upon me almost as soon as I had begun to breathe the town's graveyard atmosphere. My feeling didn't impress him much, but the name "Joe Lundy's Place" brought a whistle out of him and when I spoke of finding Jerry's flannels he became all attention.

"Where are they?"

I got the bundle and we went over the various articles together.

"The boy's, of course," Henry said decisively. "He changed here."

"Nonsense!" I retorted angrily. "They were planted."

"By whom?"

"Dillon."

"And who is Dillon?"

I smiled. "You are the detective in charge, Henry."

"Hmn. This is 'Joe Lundy's Place,' you say. That's interesting. Go ahead."

Of the children's departure and my failure to make them hear he knew already, but I repeated what I had told him and added a word or two about my deflated tires.

"It's evident they didn't want you following them," he said bluntly.

"Who?"

"Those 'children,'" he drawled.

This angered me. "Do you actually mean to say you believe Jerry deflated my tires?"

"I'm sorry, John." His face was serious. "You would, too, if it were anybody else but Jerry. You've allowed your affection to blind your usual sound common sense. But go ahead."

Letting the point rest, I passed on to my adventure at the mine.

"At least you cannot accuse Jerry of firing at me," I said caustically. "He was halfway across the valley by then."

Henry grunted something unintelligible.

My return to the village, the swift coming of the sand-storm, my unceremonious entrance into the resort, and my belief that some one else was in the building fetched little response from him. But when I recounted my nerve-racking experience in the resort and my providential fall through the door in the gallery he sat up with a jerk. I paused to give it time to sink in.

"What happened, then?" he asked, a little breathlessly.

It was hard enough to convince him of fact without going into fancy and I decided to say nothing of my nightmare. Henry plays poker himself and I didn't want him to conclude that my nightmare had begun before it actually had.

"Somehow I got the door bolted," I said. "And then I became unconscious."

A humid expression that warmed my heart came into his eyes. Henry and I had loved each other as men occasionally do and I rejoiced that Lucy's rashness hadn't come between us.

"It's a wonder I found you alive, old man," he said huskily.

We blew our noses in unison and I told him of my return to consciousness and of my interview with Furie.

"Furie, eh," he mused, when I had done. "Are you sure he didn't get into this building last night without your seeing him—just before the sandstorm, I mean?"

"He couldn't have," I said positively. "No, I am inclined to believe Furie. And of course it wasn't Jerry," I added challengingly.

"It could have been, at that," Deacon insisted stubbornly. "The sandstorm might have driven them back. But it isn't likely, I'll admit."

"Who was it, then?"

"Furie, probably. He's half crazy, you say, and he regarded you as dangerous to his claim on the mine. Wait a bit," he went on, as I was about to pounce on him. "You were going to ask me why he didn't finish you *after* he broke in the door. Of course I don't know why he didn't A crazy man is a creature of impulse. He is apt to do anything under the sun. After breaking in the door he may have had one of his lucid moments and lost his nerve. Or he may have just changed his mind. Perhaps he decided you weren't as dangerous as he had supposed. I can't tell you why, but that doesn't affect my conclusions."

I chuckled. "You argue plausibly, Henry. But I insist that it wasn't Furie. Do you mean that he killed Andrew?"

"No, I don't. Ogden refused to recognize Furie's claim, they quarreled, and Furie left in a rage. Now if Andrew had been found dead immediately afterwards we would have concluded that Furie had killed him. But he wasn't. And I can't make myself see that half-blind old desert rat, unfamiliar with city life and Ogden's grounds, later on creeping in through the side window, taking the dagger from the cabinet, and stabbing Andrew in the neck. Besides," and he looked at me sadly, "the principal evidence points elsewhere. As for Dillon, he blackmailed Andrew, certainly. But as MacNair said, it doesn't follow that he killed him. Why should he have? No, I am beginning to believe that this new ledge in the Two Brothers is at the root of the thing. Jerry quarreled with his father over it and Furie attacked you because of it."

"You are very tenacious," I said. "Has it occurred to you that since Jerry was seen driving along the Peskella road Friday night he *couldn't* have fought with me in the den Saturday morning?"

Henry nodded. "It has. I don't know whom you fought with Saturday morning. But I do know who was wearing those white flannels Friday night. That affair in your den is a minor problem. Mrs. Lundy, her relation to Andrew, and the name 'Joe Lundy' on the face of this building, is another. Time will explain them. Neither of them, in my opinion, affects the main issue."

"We are getting nowhere," I grunted irritably, standing up. "What do you want to do first? Go over the resort, see the mine, or interview Furie?"

"The building, I suppose, as we are in it. Lord! this heat!"

We soon finished with the resort. As we started down the gallery stairs it occurred to me to glance at the west end of the north wall where, the night before, I thought my providential door was located. I saw no door, of course.

On the way over to the Two Brothers Deacon said that he thought he would see Furie alone. This suited me for I wasn't keen on climbing the trail to the shanty where I had told Henry he was likely to find the old fellow.

"Very well," I agreed. "I'll drop you at the canyon and come back for you in half an hour. I'll put in the time poking around the mine buildings. We'll go into the mine together."

Henry stopped the car at the gash in the flank of the Skeletons and I took him into the canyon and showed him the shanty.

"Look out he doesn't put a bullet in you."

Henry scoffed at the idea, but I noticed he had his automatic handy, and I watched him anxiously until he passed through the door of the shanty. Evidently Furie was at home for he did not reappear. Going back to the sedan I drove on to the mine buildings. In view of the blistering heat, I concluded it would be as well to put the machine in the stable alongside of the police car Lucy had commandeered. I could easily walk back to canyon and as Deacon would want to see the buildings after we had gone through the mine I would have to return with him, anyhow. When I had spent the prescribed half hour nosing around the plant I trudged back to the canyon. Deacon was coming down the trail, wiping his forehead. He looked wilted.

"God! what a hole!" he breathed. "I'd sooner live in a boiler pit. No wonder the old devil's crazy."

"You found him, eh?"

"Yes. He was mixing a mess of flapjacks and he didn't see me. At first I thought he wasn't alone for he seemed to be talking to a couple of men he called 'Bull' and 'Nap.'

But there was no one around and I saw that he was only talking to himself."

"'Bull' and 'Nap,'" I echoed. "What did he say to them?"

Henry grinned. "I didn't get much of it, but I've an idea he was talking about you. ''Tis a dom shame a ol' he goat like me can't have his bit o' peace without them city sharps a-nosin' in, ain't it, Bull? Whut's that, Nap? Ye reckons he got the daylights skeared outen him? Uh-huh, it'll hold him fer a bit. He-he-he!' He saw me, then."

I chuckled. "Probably he meant me. 'Bull' and 'Nap' are figments of his imagination, of course. Did you get anything out of him?"

"Just about what you told me."

I thought for a moment. "Does this conversation with 'Bull' and 'Nap' strengthen your opinion that it was Furie who tackled me in the resort last night?"

Henry looked troubled. "It should, I suppose. But after talking to him, I don't know. I don't know what think. By the way, here's a souvenir for you." Grinning sourly, he handed me Furie's eight-sided eyepiece. "It seemed to be necessary to him, although I don't believe it helps his eyesight as much as he imagines it does, and I thought relieving him of it was one way of disarming him."

This was Henry's first expression of uncertainty and it delighted me much more than his 'souvenir' did, but I examined the lens curiously. He had snapped the wire close to the glass.

"Wonder where he got it," I mused. "The lens is extraordinarily heavy, even for a pair of old-fashioned spectacles."

"I don't know and I don't care," Deacon growled, wiping his face. "Let's get out of this infernal heat."

We made our way to the cavern-like gash in the opposite wall of the canyon and, preceded by the white beam of Deacon's torch, plunged into its forbidding blackness.

Inside, the air was cooler and we breathed our relief. The gash was some ten feet wide at the bottom. How far up it extended our light beam failed to show us.

"Furie's 'earthquark' must have been powerful medicine," Deacon growled.

The passage was as crooked as a manzanita stick; its walls were of slaty formation, very rugged, and beetling in places. Bowlders, rubble, and earth littered the floor and the dangerous nature of our exploration was made vividly clear to us when a ton or so of debris, loosed apparently by the echo of our footsteps, crashed down a yard or so behind us.

Before its roar had ceased to hammer upon our eardrums thunderous echoes sprang up around us, behind us, above us, in front of us, poured out of other artificial or natural caverns ahead of us, until we were submerged in a flood of sound that hissed and cannoned and boomed about our bodies like water loosed by a broken dam. Never had I heard so frightful a medley of sound. We stood until it had subsided.

Presently, we found ourselves on the threshold of tunnel, the roof and sides of which were timbered. The slash had cut across this timbered tunnel like one slash across another in a cheese, and continued into the bowels of the mountain on the other side of the tunnel. Deacon splashed the light beam into the tunnel. Some of the timbering was smashed. Smaller tunnels radiated from it in different directions and I concluded this one was the main bore of the mine. Bringing the light beam back into the slash, Deacon swept it over the wall above our heads. A vein of quartz some three feet wide on a level with my head caught the light in a way that arrested our attention. Excited, I seized a knob-like projection of the vein. It was loose, it came away in my hand, and Deacon bent the light beam upon it.

"Gold!" I whispered. "Furie's ledge!"

"Rotten with it," Henry whispered reverently.

17
"Jerry"—And Another

I don't think the discovery of any form of wealth is comparable with that of virgin gold in its effect upon the human
emotions. We looked at each other with a fine dew breaking out over our faces. My brain seemed to have become
a well of flame. A strange intoxication gave wings to my
feet. I wanted to dance, to shout, to embrace my companion. And Deacon, who is seldom demonstrative, was
similarly affected.

"Looks like that stuff we found in Ogden's desk," he
muttered.

"The same," I said unsteadily.

"I had it assayed," he went on. "It ran twenty thousand
to the ton."

I whistled. "If there's any depth or breadth to the vein, or
if the hanging wall is good, it may run into millions. . . .
Hello! what's this?"

We saw it at the same moment. A small, square, shining
object, it stood in a niche just below the vein. My hand
beat Deacon's to it and I presented it to him triumphantly.

"A silver snuff-box," he grunted. "It hasn't been here
long by the look of it."

"It comes from one of the French Louis periods," I observed. "Notice the chasing."

"Well, whose is it? You look as if you know something."

"It belongs to Nathan Hyde, Henry," I announced significantly.

He didn't say much, but I could see that he was deeply moved.

"Hyde, Hyde," he muttered in perplexity, turning the thing over and over in his hand. "It isn't like him to put a valuable down and forget it."

I chuckled. "He must have been deeply stirred. Taking snuff from his Louis snuff-box is a sort of a ceremony with Hyde. He indulges in it only when in his opinion an event is also an Occasion."

Henry nodded reluctantly, pocketing the snuff-box.

"Coming upon the vein was enough of an Occasion to make him forget it, eh? Well, we had already concluded he knew something about the mine."

His tone implied that there was nothing more to it than that, but I knew the snuff-box had given him something to think about, and I laughed to myself as we went on into the timbered passage. A little of the timbering had collapsed and some debris had fallen in, but apart from the gash made by the earthquake not much damage had been done. Rusted track rails, sprung and twisted, here and there ran along the tunnel and radiated into those tributary to it. We had gone some distance in the direction of the original entrance, passing an ore cart and several miners' drills when I stopped abruptly, clutching Deacon by the arm.

"Look!"

I went a little sick for I have no stomach for the grewsome. The beam made a great pool of yellow light and I had almost tripped over the thing which lay within it. Deacon mopped his face and I heard him draw a deep breath. The skeleton was that of a tall man. It lay face up, arms folded. A few rags clung to the bones, high-laced boots in fair condition covered the feet and ankles, a stout leather belt encircled the waist. Undoubtedly the skeleton had lain there many years, but from the uneven distribution of dust on it I judged it had been disturbed recently.

Deacon looked at me grayly. "Who is it, John?"

I knew very well who it was and so did he. Dropping to our knees, he held the torch while I gently ran my hands through the accumulations of dust and gravel around and under the skeleton. I brought to light two bone buttons, four metal ones, a bit of candle, a two-inch wire nail, and a stub of indelible pencil. That was all.

"Somebody else has been at him," Deacon muttered.

"Furie."

"Probably. The scavenger! How long has it been here, do you think?"

"Thirty years," I said.

Deacon gave me a look. "You don't *know*."

"See this!" I ejaculated.

The fifth right rib of the skeleton was nicked and split in the region of the heart.

"Bullet, by the look of it," Deacon commented. "Must have finished him."

"Here's something else!" I cried suddenly.

My fingers rummaging below the surface dust beneath the skull had encountered a crackly substance that felt like paper. I drew it forth. Paper it was. A small newspaper, in fact, yellow and brittle with age. In spite of my care it split in two as I opened it and spread it on the floor of the tunnel. The newspaper was about half the size of a modern daily, of old-fashioned make-up, and it had but four pages. At the head of the front sheet was the legend:

TORRIDITY FIREBRAND

A WEEKLY NEWSPAPER

Torridity, Skull Valley, Calif., Monday, July 6th, 1896.

Items of local interest occupied the front page. Some of the headlines were characteristic: Gun Fight Along Main. Another Hold-up at Lundy's! New Boss for Lucky Three. Bad Medicine Closes Down. And so on. A good deal of the text had become illegible. I turned the page.

Part of the top margin of the third page had been torn off. With it had gone the date line. We stared at the torn margin in silence, our hearts pounding in our ears. The curtain had lifted. Dust and bone had become living tissue. The scent of drama was in our nostrils. But only for a moment. A page torn out of the book of many lives . . . and the book lost. Well, we would find it.

"This is where Furie got your pistol, John," Henry said at length, and I hardly knew his voice.

"Yes." My own sounded strange in my ears. "This is the pencil he used." I stared down at the remains below me. "'Jerry'—what were you to Andrew?" I whispered. "Brother, cousin, friend—*what?*" I looked up at Deacon, but my eyes were swimming and I could hardly see him. "Well?" was all I could manage.

"I suppose—*this* was Andrew's reason for keeping the mine closed," he said huskily. "It's a good thing you found the note in that cartridge, John."

"You mean you'd have assumed Andrew had killed man himself, thirty years ago?"

He nodded. "We should have had to. Andrew steadfastly refused to open the mine. Why? Because of what we have just found: the skeleton of a man who has been murdered. The inference would have been inescapable."

"Demonstrating again the unreliability of circumstantial evidence," I remarked dryly. "Here is my theory: Dillon killed 'Jerry' thirty years ago and he killed Andrew three days ago. He killed Andrew because Andrew had just found out that he, Dillon, had killed 'Jerry.'"

"Perhaps you are right," Henry admitted wearily. "I don't know. I'm not sure of anything. But if you are right, why did Andrew leave this body here, instead of giving it proper burial?"

"When we know that we shall know what turned Alex Peterson into Andrew Ogden," I replied sententiously. "Depend on it, he had some good reason. Andrew never did anything without reason."

"I wish MacNair was here," Deacon muttered, getting up. "He's got a solid head on his shoulders. This thing is too much for me." Henry is humble-minded, for all his tenacity of will. "You'd better take care of that newspaper. We'll need it. That bit of pencil, too."

The blocked door of the mine was just beyond the body, and we were returning silently to the slash through which we had entered the tunnel, when I heard quite distinctly a small sound. It might have been caused by rubble falling in the slash, but somehow I felt that it was of human origin. So did Deacon, for he snapped out the light and dropped his hand onto my arm.

"What's that?" I whispered.

"Ssh!"

He guided me into one of the tributary passages ana we waited, scarcely breathing, for what was to happen. The darkness clung to us like pitch. And yet it was alive and tingling, as darkness sometimes is. Intangible softnesses seemed to run through my hair and caress my eyes and cheeks and throat.

Another sound. Louder, this time. And then a ray of light pierced the blackness of the slash. Deacon's hand gripped my arm and we shrank back against the wall of the tunnel. I could hear the breath whistling in his nostrils; my heart seemed to be pounding in my throat. The ray of light expanded, dimly illuminating the slash, which we could see from where we stood, and spilling into the tunnel. We drew back again, plastering ourselves against the wall.

The light came from an electric flash and we saw vaguely the figure of a man in the darkness behind it. But his face was invisible and his body was so distorted by the leaping shadows that I could not tell whether he was large or small. Nearer came the light and we backed still further into the tunnel. The man turned the beam on the auriferous wall, but instead of focusing it on the gold vein he ran it up and down the wall and over the floor beneath it, as if he were looking for something. When he had done this for several minutes he stepped through the break into the main tunnel and flashed the beam ahead of him over the walls and floor. The darkness behind the torch still concealed his face.

He proceeded down the tunnel and the darkness thickened again.

"Who is it?" Henry whispered

"I don't know. I've an idea he's after that snuff-box."

Henry nodded. "Get a look at his face. It may be Hyde. Don't show yourself."

We waited, steeped in silence. The darkness began to as the man returned. Brighter grew the light. He passed the small tunnel which concealed us, playing the beam before him. Coming to the slash, he stepped into it and again swept the auriferous wall with the beam. Deacon's hand tightened cruelly on my arm. I could feel him straining forward like a hound on leash. The man played the beam up and down, to and fro, but still without revealing his face.

Was it Hyde? Somehow, I thought not. We must see his face. But could we manage it without disclosing our presence?

Deacon was on the point of rushing out upon him when the man suddenly turned the light straight up and full upon his own face. If Deacon's fingers hadn't been biting my arm like diamond drills I should have cried out in amazement.

The man was Roy Hammond, the San Felipe lawyer!

18

The Ace of Spades

Deacon's breath blew gustily on my cheek and I knew he was as hard put to it to keep from rushing out on the man as I was myself. I had never cared for Hammond overmuch and as I stared at his meaty face he was less attractive to me than ever. He looked perplexed and dismayed, but as we continued to watch him his head inclined towards the gold vein and avarice also became a part of his expression. For a moment longer this play of feeling was visible to us; then Hammond swung the torch downward and his face was again lost in shadow.

Flashing the beam to and fro, up and down, he turned and made his way back along the slash. The light was completely gone before we permitted ourselves to speak or move.

"Roy Hammond!" Deacon muttered in bewilderment.

"Jerry, Furie, Mrs. Lundy, Dillon, Hyde and—Hammond," I couldn't help murmuring ironically. "Your field of investigation is widening, Henry. Shall you let him go?"

He did not answer for a moment. "Yes, I think so, he said wearily. "Where did you leave the car?"

"In one of the sheds at the mine. He won't see it unless he goes up there. What do *you* think his game is?"

"I don't know. Probably he was after the snuff-box. That couples him with Hyde. Neither of them would want it found here. The thing's got me buffaloed, John."

This delighted me. "An excellent state of mind," I said. "As soon as a man admits his fallibility he begins to get somewhere. What next?"

"San Felipe. I am going to work on Hyde, Hammond, and Mrs. Lundy."

"You haven't found her, yet?"

"No. Queer, isn't it? A woman in that get-up. She must have changed it or be lying low. We'll find her, of course. Are you coming with me?"

"Yes," I said. "I've had enough of Skull Valley for a while. I'll send a mechanic for my car. What about Furie?"

"He'll be here when we want him. I doubt if he would survive anywhere but in the desert."

As we made our way along the slash I dwelt silently on my own reasons for wanting to return home. My desire to see the children and to hear Jerry account for his extraordinary flight to Skull Valley was not the least of them, you may be sure. And I don't think I ever longed for anything quite so much as I did for the sound of their voices and the sight of their eager faces. It didn't occur to me that they mightn't be at home waiting for me, wondering about my absence, perhaps setting out to look for me. And then, also, I wanted to relate my experiences to MacNair. How would his brutally logical mind interpret them to me? Yes, I had a good deal to look forward to.

Neither Furie nor Hammond was in sight when we emerged into the canyon, but as we came out into the open desert I caught the flash of a windshield on the trail which led across the valley. Deacon had seen it, too.

"That'll be Hammond," he said.

I nodded. "He's not going by Pitchfork. I'll bet he didn't come by it, either."

Wheel tracks were visible in the gravel at our feet and it was evident that Hammond hadn't gone up to the mine.

"Probably he doesn't know we are here," Deacon grunted.

The sun was lustier than ever and by the time we reached the mine buildings Deacon was mumbling profanely and mopping his face with a sopping handkerchief. He found nothing in the abandoned plant that interested him, and when we had each eaten a couple of sandwiches and refreshed ourselves of the warm water in the canteen, we set off. As Jerry's flannels were in the back seat there was no need to stop at Torridity and I was mighty glad to see the last of its huddle of buildings vanish over my shoulder, for the town had come nearer than I liked to burying my old bones.

A crackling in my pocket reminded me of the newspaper we had found in the mine tunnel and I carefully spread it out before me. One of the headlines I had noticed in the mine again caught my eye and I read the paragraph beneath it.

ANOTHER HOLD-UP AT LUNDY'S!
WHERE IS THE LAW?

Ten thousand in gold and cash were stolen from Mr. Joe Lundy's safe early this morning. This is the fourth of a series of thefts and hold-ups in Lundy's Place in the past three months and it is by far the largest amount yet taken. The town is in a fine state when a man cannot conduct a respectable business venture without being subject to outrages of this sort, and the *Firebrand* calls on Deputy Sheriff Billings do his duty. The *Firebrand* has it on good authority that Mr. Lundy has brought an expert from San Francisco to see what's what; and he has ordered his men to shoot to kill! Citizens of Torridity look to your gold! *And your guns!* (We know of half a dozen good ropes itching to stretch the hombre's neck, Joe. Ye Ed.)

The item was interesting and amusing and something of a sidelight on conditions of that day, but nothing more, apparently, and why it should occur to me that there might be a connection between Mr. Lundy's misfortune and Andrew's death I couldn't for the life of me tell. But the notion had got into my head and there it stuck.

"Listen to this, Henry." I read the item to him.

"Pity the poor devil if they found him," he muttered grimly. "Torridity was one wild town from what I hear."

"At least they had respect for Mr. Lundy's property," I chuckled. "And you must admit the swift efficiency of the period. Probably they got their man."

Of my feeling that the item might have bearing upon the matters which occupied our minds I said nothing. Henry is intolerant of feelings.

On the fourth page I found a sizable advertisement.

JOE LUNDY'S PLACE
Poker
Black Jack
Faro   Roulette   Drinks
THE COOLEST PLACE IN THE TOUGHEST
TOWN IN THE HOTTEST SPOT
IN THE WEST
JOE LUNDY'S PLACE
COME ONE   COME ALL

"Quite a respectable business venture," I reflected aloud. "Advertising must have influenced newspaper policies then as now."

Henry grunted disgustedly. It was too hot to talk.

Pitchfork Canyon, to which we presently came, had lost none of its grim terror, but we managed the ascent without disaster in something under two hours. From the top I looked back over the desert. Opalescent hues played upon its breast like color in a pastel sunset. It beckoned to me as it had the day before, but I turned away from it with a shudder. I had lifted its veil of beauty, felt its savage fury, found death hidden in its vitals. . . .

It was three o'clock when we reached San Felipe. Deacon dropped me at a downtown corner, muttering something about seeing me later. He had been in a gloomy mood ever since we left Torridity and I had attributed it to his bewildered state of mind. Henry had been so sure of certain things, regretfully sure, it is true, but sure, nevertheless, and our discoveries had shaken his conclusions more than he had admitted. Needless to say, his perplexity had delighted me and I had let him alone.

Hailing a taxi, I settled into it, keenly anticipating the joyful reunion before me. I had expected Deacon to insist on driving me home and I was relieved when he didn't, for I wanted the children to myself. My longing for a sight of Lucy's face had become almost a physical ache and when the taxi got into a traffic jam I could hardly sit still on my seat. Lucy had come to me as a little thing, but I had never dreamed that she would ever fill my heart as completely as she did. I suppose I am a sentimental old ass who ought to have had half a dozen of his own. One of these days I would lose her. The realization twisted my heart, but I knew I could reconcile myself to it if I might have her a little while longer. Jerry was a fine lad, too.

If only Andrew had lived to see the flowering of these young lives! But he hadn't and we had still to clap a rope around the neck of the devil who had killed him. Well, in a little while now, surely. . . .

I began to think of what we'd have to say to one another, Jerry and Lucy and I. What with Jerry's mad flight to Torridity, Lucy's daring pursuit of him, my own experiences in the town, and the discoveries Deacon and I had made in the mine, we'd have enough to keep our tongues

wagging until midnight. There'd be a fire crackling in my
den, Polyandria purring in front of it, Lucy perched on
the arm of my chair, and Jerry sprawled on the rug. And
Mrs. Moffit would bring in a pitcher of chocolate and a
deep apple pie. Yes, we'd have a real domestic night of it!

Mrs. Moffit met me at the door. So overcome was she at
sight of me that I thought she would embrace me.

"Where is Lucy?" I demanded, pushing into the house.

Mrs. Moffit had been weeping a good deal and now she
began to weep again.

"I don't know, Mr. Peebles. I haven't heard a word of
her since I went to Circle Sunday morning. Nor you, neither. Nor Mr. Jerry. And what with the house being broke
into and your lovely door ruined—simply *ruined*—and the
police doing nothing about it—"

"Not here! Not here!" I shouted. "Nonsense, woman!
Of course they are here!"

"Indeed they are not!" she wept hysterically. "And I
haven't seen Miss Lucy since Sunday morning. And what
with you going off and the house being broke into and
your lovely door—

Thrusting her aside, I rushed into my den and took up
the telephone. Deacon was in his office.

"What have you done with Lucy and Jerry?" I bawled
at him.

"They are not here, John," he said in a troubled voice.

"Where are they, then?"

"I don't know."

"You don't know!" I sputtered. "Of course you know!
Or your men do! Where are they?"

"I don't know where they are, John. They are not here.
The boy hasn't given himself up. We haven't seen either of
them."

I hung the receiver up, an empty feeling about my heart.
If I hadn't put the instrument down I should have dropped

it. My legs began to tremble and I collapsed into a chair. They hadn't been seen! They hadn't come back! What did it mean? Where were they? What had happened? Yesterday afternoon—they had had plenty of time! Where were they? That sandstorm? Good God! And then I pulled myself together. This would never do. Because they hadn't come home it didn't follow that they were stranded in the middle of Skull Valley. Certainly not! Jerry had too sound a head on his shoulders. But sometimes sound heads— Nonsense! They were safe—somewhere! Must be! But where? Why hadn't they telephoned?

Mrs. Moffit was in the room. Staring at me piteously. She began to weep. She was going to collapse or become hysterical. I have a horror of weeping women.

"Mr. Peebles!—there's something the matter—Miss Lucy—they haven't turned up—" she was beginning.

I stopped her sharply. "There's nothing wrong! The children will be home to-morrow. What have you got for supper?"

She must have belicved me for after a sniffle or two she dried her eyes and gave me her melancholy smile.

"A beefsteak pie—"

"Good!"

"And a caramel pudding."

"Excellent. Early, please," I went on briskly. "I haven't had a square meal since Sunday morning. I'll bathe and change first."

Brushing her out of the den, I went to my bedroom and began to prepare for my bath. But my mind was still in a ferment of apprehension; at moments, actual dread possessed me. Should I start out to look for them at once? Should I raise a general alarm? Should I organize a search party? Or should I leave it entirely to Deacon? When I found myself standing in the bath tub with my shoes on I decided it was time I made up my mind. And make it up

I did forthwith. I would give them until noon to-morrow. If they hadn't turned up then I'd start back for Torridity in a hired car.

This decision arrived at, I grew calmer.

Cleansed of the grit of Skull Valley, I got into clean linen and a fresh suit. I was fumbling for my billfold in the right-hand hip pocket of the trousers I had taken off when my blood suddenly turned cold in my veins. My billfold was there right enough, but there was something else with it, the sinister smoothness of which seared my hand as if it were a hot iron that I held—instead of a playing card of the ace of spades.

It hadn't been a nightmare—and Furie had lied!

19

Marked Cards

The possibility that my experience behind the bolted door might be reality of a grim and terrible kind hadn't occurred to me since a few minutes after my return to consciousness this morning and I had put completely out of my mind the thought that it was anything else but nightmare. What else could I have done? There was nothing sane or reasonable about the experience; it didn't respond to any principle of logic. In what other category could I have placed it? And yet here I was with proof of its reality in my hand! Drained of the power to think, I groped for a chair.

Every detail of the experience stood out in my memory as sharp as a beacon on a dark night. The fearful quietness after the storm . . . the shapes at the table . . . the striking of the faulty match . . . the two men playing poker in the dark . . . the card I had automatically stuffed into my pocket and forgotten about. And then . . . my hand going over that cold face. Ugh!

"But they couldn't have been dead!" I groaned. "Sitting there like that. Poker hands before them. In the dark! And they couldn't have been alive! It isn't reasonable. It *must* have been a nightmare!" And then I looked at the ace of spades again and knew that it wasn't.

I tried another tack. Why had Furie lied to me? Were he and Dillon in the thing together? If not, what object could he have had in deceiving me? For he certainly hadn't found me in that room in which I had come to my senses. I was sure of this now. As I had supposed at first, the room into which I had fallen was in the north wall of the building. I hadn't seen a door, but there must be one. Furie, then, had gone to the trouble of climbing through the window of the north room, unbolting the door, and carrying me into the room off the west side of the gallery. If he weren't Dillon's accomplice he must have guessed something of the conditions under which I had fallen into the north room; and in either event he had smashed in the door of the west room to create in my mind the impression that it was this room into which I had fallen. A shrewd old rascal, if he were crazy!

But why?

Evidently because there was something in the north room that he wanted to conceal. *What?* The poker players? Probably. And who, or what, were the poker players? Were they dead men? Had Furie killed them and left them there mocking themselves? That would be the act of a maniac. Was Furie—had Furie—? The thought staggered me.

There was another thing, too. The recurrence of this "poker" motif. It seemed to run through the tragic affair like a scarlet thread in a tapestry. Andrew had detested the game, yet we had found the implements of it in his safe; the phrase the "poker game that cracked the town," and some nonsense about playing poker for a human life were a part of the Peterson legend—if it were legend; and then I had come upon that ghastly game in the north room. What did these recurrences mean? Had some game for a human life once been played by Alex Peterson, Torridity gambler, later on Andrew Ogden, staid San Felipe business man? I could not dismiss the question as "nonsense." It required a definite answer. An answer I was unable to give. My brain reeled. For a moment I thought my reason was going.

And then I took fresh hold of myself. This would never do. I would let the matter rest until after supper when I would see Henry—hard-headed Henry—or MacNair—brutally logical MacNair—and give one or the other a chance to express an opinion about my experience.

On my way out of the dining-room I stopped by my old English door and gazed at it sadly. Thompson certainly had done his utmost. As Deacon had said, I might use it for kindling.

When I had disposed of sizable helpings of Mrs. Moffit's beefsteak pie and caramel pudding I went into my den. Polyandria gave me an affectionate greeting. After I had rubbed her ears I went to my desk, took out my little red notebook, and began to pencil in it. I had a good many notes to make and I was still writing when Mrs. Moffit ushered in Luther MacNair. He had telephoned while I was at supper.

"Hello, there," I greeted him. "When did you get back."

"This morning," he said briefly, as we shook hands. "Ah, the little red notebook."

I nodded. "The little red notebook is bursting with information. Did you have any luck in Los Angeles?

"A little."

"Well, keep it to yourself. I, Watson, will tell you my adventures and you, Holmes, may put two and two together and make five." He seemed in no humor for our little game. "When did I see you last?" I went on. "Only yesterday morning, was it? Seems like a month. I've been through a good deal, MacNair."

Whereupon I told him every detail of my experiences. He listened without comment, grim, unsmiling, as ruthlessly mechanical as a locomotive piston. When I had done, I laid my exhibits before him: the Torridity *Firebrand,* Furie's eyepiece, the ace of spades. Deacon had Jerry's flannels and Nathan Hyde's snuff-box.

"What do you think of my poker players?" I demanded, when he had read the item about the robberies in Lundy's Place.

MacNair looked up with a frown as though I had broken in on a train of thought; then he laughed grimly.

"Your poker players? I should say they were part of the pattern. Everything you have told me about—young Ogden's flannels, Hyde's snuff-box, the skeleton in the mine, even that bit of indelible pencil—is a part of the pattern. But most of the parts are missing and those that we have are at odds with one another and we see nothing but confusion. When the pattern is complete we shall probably have as intricate a bit of mosaic work as you or I ever saw."

I nodded. "You think there's something to this yarn about poker being played for a human life?"

"Why not? Queerer things happened in the old West."

"That's true. But what about my two men?" I persisted. "Were they dead or—what?"

"You were there, Peebles. I wasn't."

"But Holmes is supposed to be all-seeing," I murmured. "You might hazard a guess."

"I might hazard a dozen guesses. We want the truth. What do you think yourself?"

"They couldn't have been alive," I said.

"Hardly," MacNair grunted. "The point is: were they dead?"

"I don't know whether they were or not," I said thoughtfully.

"Neither do I. When we know, our pattern will be that much nearer completion. But it seems to me that their physical condition when you found them is less important than what they were doing."

"They were playing poker," I drawled.

"Exactly. But why?"

"We don't know that, either. If the children are not here by to-morrow noon I am going back to Torridity.

While I'm there I'll call on my poker players. In fact, I'll go in any event. . . . Hello, what's this?"

I was fiddling with Furie's eyepiece. Chancing to look through it, I saw, to my surprise, the grain of the top of my desk enormously magnified. I had been struck by the thickness of the lens when Deacon gave it to me in the canyon, but I hadn't examined anything through it at close range and I had supposed the lens had belonged to a pair of old-fashioned steel-rimmed spectacles such as my grandmother had worn.

"Look through this," I said, handing the lens to MacNair.

"Excellent for close-up work," he grunted, "But I don't see how Furie managed for distance."

"I doubt if he got much out of it at all," I said. "Its effect upon him seemed to be largely psychological. It seemed to give him confidence in himself, sureness of movement and speech. Deacon thought so, too. Probably he found the lens somewhere, it tickled his fancy, he had it drilled, and now he can't get along without it. A man of his age is entitled to his little oddity."

'True. Some of us go in for pistols, some for tomatoes. But I've got an idea he isn't as blind as he pretends."

"What makes you think that?"

Whipping five playing cards out of his pocket, Mac-Nair tossed them in front of me, faces down. By their backs I recognized them as part of the deck Deacon had found in Ogden's safe. Turning the cards over I saw the ace of spades, king of hearts, queen of diamonds, jack and ten of clubs.

"A straight, in poker," I muttered.

"Never mind the faces. Look at their backs through the lens. I was nosing over them with a lens down at headquarters this morning while you and Deacon were perambulating around Skull Valley."

Taking up the cards, I put the lens to my eye.

"These cards are marked," I shouted, almost dropping the lens.

MacNair nodded. "You wouldn't have seen the marks without the lens. They are practically invisible to the naked eye. Just the high cards are marked. The rest wouldn't matter."

I studied the cards through the lens again. Their backs were covered with a design of red and white lines, circles, and flourishes in intricate filigree. A line on two corners of each card, the one corner being diagonal from the other, was slightly thickened. The two marks on each card were the same, but no two cards were marked alike. On one card two curved lines were thickened; on another, two straight lines; on another, two half circles; and so on. In no instance was the thickening longer than half an inch and it had been done so delicately that it was almost imperceptible to the naked eye.

The chances of the crooked player would be increased enormously," MacNair was saying. "He would see the backs of the cards as they were dealt and remember the markings. The method isn't perfect, of course—a card would escape him now and then, and he would require a trained memory and a quick eye—but in crooked gambling a certain percentage of losses is desirable."

"But he couldn't see the marks," I exploded, "unless he had the eyes of a hawk!"

MacNair took the lens out of my hand and stuck it in his right eye, leaning forward a little.

"I see the marks fairly clearly as you hold the cards," he observed dryly. "Quite clearly, in fact."

I stared at him, dumbfounded. "You think— Good Heavens! you connect that lens with these marked cards! Nonsense! No one in his senses would play a man with a magnifying glass in his eye!"

"Not if the glass were set in one of the eight-sided rims of a pair of old-fashioned spectacles?" MacNair drawled.

I half rose in my seat. "You mean— Good God!" I whispered reverently. "The 'poker game that cracked the town'!"

"Precisely. The 'poker game that cracked the town.' The town of Torridity thirty years ago. How it cracked it we don't know."

"And what—who was the stake?" I breathed.

MacNair gave his cold-blooded laugh. "Ah! the stake. That will be another part in our pattern—when we know."

"And the players? The players, man?" My breath was coming fast. I steadied myself against the desk.

"Ogden would be one of them," MacNair drawled, with maddening deliberation.

"And Dillon was the other!" I shouted.

He seemed to ponder this. "I don't know so much about that. Who is Dillon?"

"You know perfectly well who Dillon is!" I stormed. "Have pity, man. Tell me!"

Again the cold-blooded laugh. His eyes, I saw, held neither pity nor humor.

"One man's bet is as good as another's, Peebles. We've got a fast track. Pick your horse."

He got up.

"The traditional Holmes!" I complained bitterly. "Very well, MacNair."

I followed him out to his car.

"Promise me one thing," I begged.

"Yes?"

"That you'll let me be in at the finish."

MacNair drew a chamois over the instrument board. "Of course. Watson is always in at the finish."

And with this he left me.

I went slowly back to my den. After some thought I took up the telephone and asked for long distance. I was presently talking with an old colleague who lives in Los Angeles.

20

The Woman in Black

Contrary to my expectations I rested well that night. When I awoke the morning was brilliant with sunlight and Mrs. Moffit's head was inside my room.

"Oh, you are awake, sir!" Her relieved tone suggested that she had feared I might not waken again. "Will you have a dish of tea and a bit of toast?"

"Yes," I said briskly, "and a whole grapefruit, a basin of cereal, bacon, two eggs, and two more bits of toast."

She opened her eyes. "Well, now! And you looked so poorly last night. But you have a mite of acid on your stummick, so you mustn't take more than half a grapefruit. I'll bring a tray in to you."

"No, thanks," I said, throwing back the bed covers. "I'll be at the table in twenty minutes. And—a whole grapefruit, Mrs. Moffit." She fled at sight of my pyjamas.

I was there to the minute and I did justice to her efforts, which included a whole grapefruit. A man takes some filling after a day and a half on gritty sandwiches and warm water.

The meal put away, I telephoned Deacon. To my sorrow, he had no word of the children and I strengthened my resolve to start for Skull Valley if they were not back by noon. Until then I would not permit myself to think too much about them. My head was clear and I must keep it so for what might lie before me. I went out into the garden. It was good to have a hoe in my hands and Polyandria drowsing in the speckled sunlight again.

MacNair had not announced his plans to me and as my own actions depended largely on his I presently decided to call him up. As I approached the patio door, voices came to me. One of them was Mrs. Moffit's dismal treble. The other, a woman's voice also, had a masculine edge and a chanting, throaty quality that arrested my attention. I did not recognize the voice but it roused in my breast a curious nervous excitement. They came into view. Dumbfounded, I slipped behind a hydrangea bush.

Mrs. Moffit was showing my lilies to The Woman in Black!

It did not occur to me to doubt that she was Mrs. Lundy. "Tall," "angular," and "all sinew and bone and tight-shut mouth," were the terms in which Hubbard had described her, and as I stared at her porcelain-white, ascetic face I saw that they were fitting. Her long black coat and dress, the latter reaching to her buttoned shoe tops, were unrelieved by the slightest touch of color and I wondered how Deacon's men had missed her.

"The lily is the vessel of purity." Her voice reminded me of a priest of one of the mystic religions chanting in a temple. "Dew falls into it and becomes holy and those who are sprinkled with the dew of purity likewise become holy. The dew of the lily is the baptismal water of our priesthood," she went on. "These are beautiful."

There was silence for a moment.

"Mr. Peebles looks after them as if they was babies," Mrs. Moffit sighed. "He's always hoeing and digging and watering at them."

"Perhaps he, also, has had a vision of the Truth," the strange voice chanted.

"I'm sure he won't mind if you want to pick a few. He's lovely, that way. The kindest man!"

I thought it time to reveal myself and I stepped from behind the hydrangea.

"Have your friend help herself, Mrs. Moffit," I said lavishly.

My housekeeper started. "Oh! I didn't know you was there, Mr. Peebles. Why, why—this is Mrs. Lundy, the demonstrator of our circle. Mr. Peebles, Mrs. Lundy."

Perplexed, I held out my hand. The woman's grip was firm and strong.

"Your lilies are as beautiful as the Truth, Mr. Peebles," she chanted, looking at me steadily with brilliant black eyes.

I bowed. "Thank you. That is gracious praise. Mrs. Moffit said you were—forgive me if I did not understand?"

"Demonstrator of the Forty-ninth Circle in the Fifth Realm, Cosmic Indulgence," she informed me serenely.

Light broke upon me. "Ah! Cosmic Indulgence!"

I gave the woman a long, shrewd look, but her brilliant eyes met my stare serenely and I knew my Los Angeles and its religious extravagances well enough to perceive that she was sincere in her belief, whatever its tenets might be.

"You have heard of our beautiful faith, Mr. Peebles?"

"Hmn!" I said. "Yes. From Mrs. Moffit." The latter cast a doubtful eye at me. "Do you mind coming into my study for a few minutes before you go?"

She did not seem surprised. "Of course not. Shall I come now? I was just leaving. We are always glad to answer questions about our faith."

I smiled dryly. "Come this way, then. Mrs. Moffit can gather you a bouquet of lilies while we are talking."

I took her through the patio door, leaving Mrs. Moffit goggling at our backs.

"Mrs. Lundy," I said briskly, when I had got her perched on the edge of a chair in the den, "my questions have nothing whatever to do with your faith, Cosmic Indulgence."

Her mouth tightened. "What else can you have to question me about?"

There was in her tone that strength I had felt in her grip. Evidently, she was no ordinary woman.

"I don't wish to be impertinent," I said earnestly. "You will see what I am driving at in a moment. Tell me: have you been questioned by the police?"

She opened her eyes. "The police! Goodness, no! What about, man?"

"Have you been in town ever since Friday night?"

"I have."

"Where, may I ask?"

"What right have you to question me, sir?" Her throaty voice had thickened with anger.

"Please!" I begged, raising my hand. "You will understand in a moment."

"Well, I was in my room at the Central Hotel."

"You were not out at all?"

"Not until this morning. I was meditating. Four days of continuous meditation are required of the priestesses of our faith every month."

Knowing my Los Angeles, I credited even this!

"Haven't you read the newspapers?"

"I never read the newspapers."

"Indeed!" I began to understand. "You called on Mr. Andrew Ogden last week, didn't you?"

"I did."

"He gave you a check for a thousand dollars?"

"What has that got to do with you?"

"Evidently," I said, watching her closely, "you do not know that Andrew Ogden was murdered in his library last Friday night."

She looked at me, gaping. "Murdered!"

I explained the circumstances under which I had found Andrew's body and added a word or two about the check stub. Color flooded her porcelain-white face.

"Do you mean the police want to see me about that check?"

"They want to ask you about it, naturally. Do you mind telling me why Mr. Ogden gave you a check for such a sum?"

"It was a contribution to our cause."

I stared at her, astonished. "Do you mean to say Ogden gave you a thousand dollars for this—this—" Her eyes were hardening and I remembered myself. "—for your faith?"

"Certainly."

I fell silent. Andrew had hated humbug of every description. Humbug in art and music, humbug in literature and politics and religion. Sometimes I thought he went too far, for I regard myself as a bit of a liberal. (Lucy insists this is the essence of humbug!) Andrew *couldn't* have fallen for any such nonsense as Cosmic Indulgence, whether the woman believed he had or not.

"Mrs. Lundy," I said placatingly, "you must forgive me for going into personal matters, but Andrew Ogden was my friend and I am determined to get to the bottom of this affair. Are you, or were you, the wife of Joe Lundy, who kept a resort in Torridity thirty years ago?"

She seemed to freeze before my eyes. "What if I refuse to answer you?"

"But you won't," I begged, leaning forward. "Let me explain. My niece Lucy is engaged to Ogden's son, Jerry. Jerry is suspected of killing his father. I believe he is innocent and I want you to help me prove he is. Won't you do so by answering my questions? It means a good deal to me." Lucy says I am sentimental enough to wring tears from a money lenders' convention.

"All right," the woman yielded suddenly. "But you are touching on a phase of my life I have tried to forget. Not that I am ever likely to forget it!" she added bitterly. "Yes. I am Joe Lundy's wife. What else?"

"Thank you, Mrs. Lundy," I said gratefully. "Were you married to him then?"

"Yes. But I did not live with him in Torridity. I spent a week there once. That was enough." The thin lips tightened. "I didn't approve of Lundy's Place. The town was abandoned when the mines were closed down. My husband was shot about that time."

"Shot!" I exclaimed. "Killed, you mean? Is he dead?"

"He might as well be. He was shot in the head and he has been feeble-minded ever since. The bullet creased the scalp. He remembers nothing about the town—or the shooting. Joe has been a great trial to me, but lately . . . the Truth . . . has sustained me." A rapt look came over her face.

"Forgive me for causing you pain," I murmured.

"It doesn't matter. Some women are born to suffer. Go on, Mr. Peebles."

The tragedy of her life clouded my spirit and it came upon me overwhelmingly that even Cosmic Indulgence might meet a definite human need.

"Since you were at Torridity for a week or so you will know something of the town at that time," I suggested diffidently.

"It was a place of evil!" she replied scathingly. "Wide-open vice prevailed. My husband's resort was the most notorious there."

"Did you hear of a man named Peterson while you were down there?" I asked. "Alex Peterson?"

"Alex Peterson!" the woman cried in so tense a voice that I was startled. "Alex Peterson shot my husband!"

"Good God!" I shouted, springing to my feet. "Alex Peterson—shot your husband! Nonsense! He was the best friend I ever had!"

"He shot my husband, I tell you!"

The bitter emphasis of these words struck me in the face like the blow of a fist and I fell back into my chair. Some influence powerful enough to re-mold Andrew's personality, to lengthen his moral stature, perhaps, had come into his life. What right, then, had I, who knew nothing of him as he was at that time, to deny the word of one whose tragic life witnessed to its truth?

"Do you know why Alex Peterson shot your husband, Mrs. Lundy?"

"I don't," she replied, in the same bitter tone. "It doesn't matter much—now. Only—if Joe deserved it, *I* didn't. Alex Peterson left him for dead. Joe responded to medical treatment and he was brought back to me several weeks later. I have had him—ever since. Thirty years. . . . If it hadn't been for the Truth . . ."

The tragedy in her face wrung my heart.

Did you see Alex Peterson when you were down there?" I asked gently.

"Yes, I saw him. Several times."

"Can you tell me anything about him as he was then?" I went on persuasively. "In fact, tell me what you remember of Torridity and the people you met there."

She nodded slowly. "Yes, I remember him. He wasn't a man one forgot easily. There was a sort of quality about him. A quality no one else in that sink of iniquity had. He was fairly tall, supple as wire, and flat hipped. His face had something of the eagle in it—that lean, reckless, fighting look, you know. Women notice those things. He always wore an expensive Stetson trimmed with a silver buckle, a white silk shirt, fine riding boots with silver spurs, and two revolvers mounted with gold. The revolvers were loaded with gold bullets, and he had a row of gold bullets in an embossed cartridge belt around his waist. I suppose those decorations would have been ridiculous on any one else; but somehow they weren't on Peterson. They seemed to fit him. His type was quite new to me and for that reason I remember him so well. I didn't know, then, the misery he was to cause me."

Mrs. Lundy fell silent and I respected her mood. What an extraordinarily vivid personality Andrew's must then have been to have made so distinct an impression on this woman's mind! He hadn't been typical of the West, but one would have found him nowhere else but in that period of its development which ended with the birth of the twentieth century. What tragic event—for it must have been tragic—had transformed him into the Andrew Ogden I had known?"

"Do you happen to know how he came to be called 'Ten-to-One'?"

Mrs. Lundy nodded. "Yes. I heard a good deal about him while I was down there. He made his fortune gambling in mining properties. He was an inveterate gambler no chance was too great—and he'd risk every dollar he possessed. When he came to Torridity—in 1892, I think it was—he hadn't ten dollars in money to his name, but he was dressed just as I have described him. Stetson hat with its silver buckle, white silk shirt, those fantastic gold-mounted revolvers, and that cartridge belt stuffed with gold bullets. . . . And not ten dollars to his name. Can you see the man, Mr. Peebles?"

"Yes, yes," I muttered tensely, for my interest was at fever heat. "You have made him amazingly vivid. Go on, Mrs. Lundy."

"His young brother, Jerry, came with him—"

"Jerry!" I cried. "His *brother!* Yes, go on." So it was his brother! My old heart was hammering like a riveting machine.

"He swaggered into my husband's resort. Men were drinking at the bar and watching two scorpions fighting in a coffee can. Scorpions, Mr. Peebles! And they were betting on the result! A dozen grown men with nothing else to do but bet on a scorpion fight!" The thin lips hardened and I repressed a smile. "Peterson treated the audience of this elevating spectacle to my husband's vile liquor; then he bet on the result of the fight. Bet his last dollar, Mr. Peebles—at ten to one. He bet on the smaller scorpion and it won. After that he was never known as anything else but Ten-to-One Peterson."

"He must have made money rapidly," I put in suggestively, for she had fallen into silence again. It was hard to curb my patience, with the truth pulsing beneath my fingertips.

Mrs. Lundy gave me her strange eyes again. "Prosperity comes in floods sometimes—I am told." The bitter droop to her mouth touched me. "Peterson staked out several claims and sold one of them well. After that, he plunged recklessly again and again—and he nearly always won. His fortune and his reputation pyramided together. He became famous—or infamous—from one end of Skull Valley to the other. But the Two Brothers mine—he gave it that name himself—was his most recklessly extravagant venture. He put everything he had into it. Everything, Mr. Peebles! The town had begun to bet on his gambles and it waited breathlessly for Peterson to vindicate his judgment. It needn't have. He won. Nothing could stop him. The Two Brothers paid handsomely. It paid after the other big mines had closed down. It paid until the town was abandoned two years later.

"Peterson became one of the two wealthiest men in Torridity. The other was my husband, Joe Lundy. Joe was a gambler, also, but he gambled in human frailty. How I despised him! It is dreadful to have to care for a man you despise, Mr. Peebles! But I have got over that now."

Her eyes closed as if she were trying to shut something out. There was nothing I could say.

"I must tell you about my husband," Mrs. Lundy went on, a little wearily. "In his way he was as striking then as Peterson—I shall not speak of him as he is now—though you couldn't have imagined a more dissimilar pair. Joe was large and bulky, and taller than Peterson, but he was so stoop shouldered that he actually seemed shorter. His head was always thrust forward like a lantern hung on a beam; his face was long and irregular and wax-colored. I once heard a man say Joe's head looked as if it had been worked out of clay by an unskilled hand. He had bristling black eyebrows that gave him a Satanic expression he was very proud of. His eyes were deep sunken and near-sighted, and he wore a pair of old-fashioned glasses with steel frames and eight-sided lenses—"

"Eight-sided lenses!" I ejaculated, and my hand went fumbling to the lens in my pocket.

Mrs. Lundy nodded, but there was a distant look in her strange eyes and I don't think she had noticed my astonishment.

"His soul was as shapeless as his face," she went on in an empty voice. "But he is different now. Only the shell is left."

Mrs. Lundy fell silent again. Her eyes seemed to look straight through me. I was glad of the pause for it gave me time to digest the morsel of information she had unconsciously given me. The thought that Furie's "eyepiece" might have some connection with Andrew's death came into my mind from I know not where. That eight-

sided lens had belonged to Lundy—those marked cards—
Andrew had shot Lundy. There must be some connection.
I couldn't get rid of the thought.

"Joe and Peterson ruled Torridity," Mrs. Lundy went
on, "much as political bosses rule our cities. Joe hated
Peterson because of his success and his good looks. Probably Peterson returned the feeling to some extent, but I
am not sure. I do know that Joe wanted to ruin Peterson
and I suppose that shooting came out of his hatred. The
town was too small for both of them, and Joe would be a
dangerous enemy. . . . Is there anything else, Mr. Peebles?"

Her question disconcerted me. It implied that she had
little more to tell. After whipping my interest up to fever
heat she calmly asked me if there was anything else! That
was like a woman. I was bitterly disappointed, for actually
she had told me nothing that illuminated the problem of
Andrew's death.

"I was only there a week," she went on, reading my
thoughts, "and thankful to get away. I always recall that
week with loathing. After my return to Los Angeles I heard
nothing from my husband."

"But when he was brought back you surely heard what
had happened?" I exploded. "About the shooting, I mean.
It's dreadfully important, Mrs. Lundy."

She shook her head sorrowfully. "Joe came to me on a
stretcher. I have had him ever since. All I know is that he
was shot—by Alex Peterson."

"Who brought him to you?"

"Torridity was abandoned about that time and Joe was
taken to Peskella by his men. One of the men telegraphed
me from Peskella that Joe was there—that he had been shot
by Peterson, and that a doctor who had been working as
a miner had attended him. I had Joe brought to my home
and I have since heard nothing from any one who lived
in Torridity at that time. And I don't want to!" She spoke

with such bitterness that I knew she was telling the truth. "I supposed I would hear the details of the shooting, but they didn't come and I didn't care. I had a broken man to nurse. That was enough. (The details—didn't matter."

I meditated for a moment. "You mentioned Alex Peterson's brother, Jerry," I said hopefully. "Can you tell me anything about him?"

"Very little. I only saw him once. He had his brother's lean face and arrogant eyes, but I heard that he was wild and undisciplined. Peterson shouldn't have brought him to such a place. Vice and gold were the town's twin gods. I shouldn't be surprised if the boy came to a bad end."

I could not answer for I was thinking of what Deacon and I had stumbled over in the Two Brothers mine.

"Didn't the size of that check Ogden gave you surprise you?" I asked at length.

"Yes, it did," she said frankly. "I had been soliciting subscriptions along the avenue and I met Mr. Ogden at the gate. He didn't seem interested until I happened to mention my name. Then he looked at me sharply and asked me if my husband's name had been 'Joe.' I said it *was*—that he was still alive. He looked at me hard, then he invited me into the library. His first question was the one you asked me. Was I the wife of Joe Lundy who kept a resort in Torridity thirty years ago? The question angered me, but he promised me a hundred dollars for the cause if I would answer it. So I told him what he wanted to know."

"How did he take it?"

"He seemed dumbfounded. And when I told him that my husband had not died in Torridity and that he was still alive, his face crimsoned and he began to pace up and down the room, muttering to himself. Then he sat down and wrote me that check. It was for a thousand dollars. You may imagine my surprise. He asked me for my address and showed me out."

"Where is your husband now?" I went on.

"At our home in Los Angeles."

"Is he able to get about?"

"Yes."

After pondering for a moment, I leaned forward. "Mrs. Lundy, have you ever heard of a poker game played for a man's life?"

She frowned. "That is a strange question, but I have. Yes, I have. My husband has talked about such a game in delirium several times."

"Do you know anything about that game?" I pressed.

"Nothing. And I don't want to. It sounded like rubbish to me. I don't approve of poker."

"Has it ever occurred to you that the shooting of your husband and that poker game he talked of in delirium were connected?"

Her strange eyes held mine, but she did not change expression.

"Yes," she admitted. "It has occurred to me. But I don't know. And I don't care—now."

I nodded understanding, but I wasn't finished yet. "Mrs. Lundy, I am going to surprise you."

"Nothing surprises me," she replied wearily.

"You did not recognize Andrew Ogden?"

"Recognize him! Why should I? I never saw him before."

"You are sure?"

Her face became thoughtful. "No, I am not sure, now you speak of it. There was something familiar about him. His face, his voice, his manner—I don't know which."

"You haven't guessed why he gave you that check?"

"No."

Her nostrils quivered a little, but her face was calm and her eyes were steady.

"He gave it to you," I said slowly, gripping tensely the edge of my desk, "because—thirty years ago—he was Alex Peterson."

She stared at me, becoming ashen of face. Her Adam's apple jerked up and down the bony ladder of her throat and she clenched her strong hands until they gleamed like lumps of chalk.

"So that was it!" she cried, scorching anger sweeping the desert of her face. "A thousand dollars to pay for thirty years of misery! The best of my life given to looking after a broken hulk while Alex Peterson grew rich! Well, I am glad he is dead! I wish my hand had driven that dagger into his neck!"

But as I stared at the woman, shocked by her venomous words which, in the intensity of their bitterness, I had never heard equaled on human lips, her face was slowly transformed. Transfigured, I should say. The bitterness faded out and the harsh lines softened; the clear porcelain white returned and her eyes became divinely tender.

"No," she said, in a rapt voice, lifting up her spiritualized face. "I didn't mean that. I should thank him, for through him I came to the Truth."

And as I marveled at the transforming power of these mystic beliefs she dropped her eyes to mine.

"You self-complacent people with your traditional creeds think our faith absurd. You call us neurotics. You say that we are afraid of reality, that we are trying to escape from life. We are. And can you blame us, when reality has made life unbearable? My faith has anchored me to sanity. If I had not found it I should have killed myself. Remember that the next time you sneer at your housekeeper." She stood up. "Is there anything else?"

"Only this," I muttered, subdued of spirit. "Go down to police headquarters and tell them what you have told me. If you don't, the first policeman you meet will take you up."

I let her out through the front door and gave her the lilies Mrs. Moffit had left on the porch. As she went down the walk, the blooms on her arm, I saw in her gait a grace, a dignity, a measured stateliness, which I knew was the gift of her strange faith, and I became a little more tolerant of human bewilderment.

When she had gone I stood in the hot sunlight thinking over what she had told me. Andrew, in his Alex Peterson days, had shot the resort-keeper, Joe Lundy. Was this why Dillon had blackmailed him? If it were—and purely it was—no wonder Andrew had given the woman a check for a thousand dollars! The irony of being blackmailed for twenty-five years for a crime one hadn't committed staggered me. A crime, indeed, that hadn't been committed at all! Poor Andrew! Had he, become blind with fury and reverting to his former reckless character, attacked Dillon and been killed by the man? Perhaps. But why had he shot Lundy? And what about the man, 'Jerry'? I shook my head wearily and turned into the house. A gleam of light, but a night of darkness still. When would the dawn come? There would be a long reckoning with Dillon when it did.

On the threshold of my den I stopped with a shout of joy.

Jerry—dressed in khaki—and Lucy were standing at the French window, hand in hand! And Deacon was behind them.

21

Prodigals

I leaned against the door jamb, my legs as weak as a new-born calf's, and I saw that I would be making an ass of myself, if I didn't look out. But there I stuck like a fool, blinded by tears, and mumbling at them as if I had swallowed my teeth. They didn't come towards me, either, and I wondered why. Wiping my eyes, I saw that Jerry's thin face, dark and handsome and a trifle arrogant, was drawn with grief. This was natural. But as I gazed at him a queer sort of fear that contrasted oddly with the arrogant and the grieved look crept into his dark eyes. When I found it in Lucy's, also, I was disturbed. The look was quickly gone from the eyes of both of them, however, and Lucy drew Jerry's arm around her waist in a defiant, protective way that hurt me.

"Lucy!" I mumbled. "Come here. You, too, Jerry. Both of you!"

I managed to stumble forward and they swept towards me, simultaneous "Uncle Johns" on their lips, and took me into their arms. It was good to feel their young bodies against my own, I can tell you. Jerry smelling of dust and Turkish cigarettes, and Lucy her own sweet self and, I fear, smelling of Turkish cigarettes, too. None of us spoke— none of us seemed able to—until I suddenly remembered

Deacon. He was regarding us from the window with a melancholy expression. Disentangling myself, I blew my nose.

"Where did you find them, Henry?" I demanded gruffly.

"I didn't find them, John. They dropped in at headquarters and persuaded me to drive up here with them."

"Captain Deacon didn't know whether to come with us or lock us up," Lucy said, with a sad little smile. "We came through the garden to surprise you, Uncle John."

"I don't blame Deacon, either," I growled, blowing my nose again. "Where have you children been?"

Neither of them spoke; neither of them looked at me. Haggard of face, Jerry whipped out a cigarette, made a boggle of lighting it, and flung it into the grate. At that moment he reminded me of the Andrew Ogden, the reckless Alex Peterson, I had imagined, but had never known. So vivid was my impression that if I had still doubted Ogden and Peterson were the same man my doubts would then have vanished. But the defiant look was back in Lucy's eyes. It worried me. Deacon was watching, waiting. It was decent of Henry to have come up, instead of holding them at the station.

"Mrs. Lundy was here," I said, to help things along.

"That so!" Henry exclaimed. "Where is she now?"

"On her way down to headquarters. You just missed her. She has a good deal to tell you."

I don't think Jerry had heard what I said to Deacon for before Henry could respond the boy broke in suddenly, addressing the fireplace:

"I feel like a skunk!" And then, miserably: "You are entitled to take the hide off me, Uncle John."

At this Lucy ran to his side and slid her arm around his waist, challenging Deacon and me with defiant eyes.

"It's my fault, Uncle John!" she exclaimed emphatically. "You mustn't blame Jerry. I made him do it."

"Made him do what?" I inquired, alarmed.

Jerry raised his eyes to mine. Shamed and wretched of expression, they seemed to beg my forgiveness. What on earth had he and Lucy been doing? He was about to speak when Lucy's face lighted up as if she were inspired. Putting her fingers on his lips, she whispered to him. Then she looked at me.

"We'll tell you afterwards, Uncle John." Her voice was tremulous, but her eyes were steady. "There are other things that should come first. Jerry was with his father Friday night before—before it happened." She paused, her eyes humid with grief and pity and tenderness. "Uncle Andrew told him everything . . . nearly everything, that is. Jerry must tell those things first."

"I agree with the young lady," Deacon observed dryly. "The young man certainly should tell those things first. I came to hear them."

This was reasonable enough and I must be forgiven for not perceiving the subtlety of Lucy's finesse until afterwards.

"But you might as well tell us what Mrs. Lundy had to say for herself, John," Deacon said dryly.

I did so, putting it briefly. They listened attentively. Jerry nodded his head now and then, as if what I were saying coincided with his own knowledge. Just as I finished, the telephone rang. My old colleague in Los Angeles was calling and I talked with him for a few minutes.

"Go ahead, Jerry," I grunted, when I had hung up.

"Mrs. Lundy told you the truth," he said earnestly. "But she didn't touch the meat of the story. It's the queerest tale you or Captain Deacon ever heard. It's a long tale, too."

"Get at it, then. Mrs. Moffit shall bring us in some lunch while you are talking."

22
The Gambling Fool

"Mrs. Lundy has told you how Dad came to Torridity," Jerry began, his dark eyes fixed on me, as if I and not Deacon were the one he had to convince. "You know what he looked like and how he dressed, then: his white silk shirt, his silver spurs, his gold-mounted guns and gold bullets, and all that. You know about him bringing Jerry—Uncle Jerry, I suppose I'll have to call him—to Torridity. You know how he got the name, Ten-to-One, and how he made a fortune by gambling in mining properties. And Mrs. Lundy seems to have given you a pretty good idea of what Torridity was like in those days."

"You don't need to go into that, my boy," I said. "Tell us what happened to your father—how Alex Peterson turned into Andrew Ogden. I know it happened, but I can't get it down." My eyes clouded. "How about you, Henry?"

"Let him get on with his story," Deacon grunted.

Jerry threw him a defiant look that again reminded me of the Alex Peterson Mrs. Lundy had pictured for me.

"It'll come fast enough for you, Deacon, when I get started," Jerry growled. He turned to me again, a burning earnestness in his eyes. "I know how you feel about Dad, Uncle John. It must come pretty hard. But when I tell you about his last night in Torridity you'll understand. It took thirty-five years to make Dad what he was that night. It took six hours to turn him into the man you knew. Funny, how you can cram a lifetime into an hour or two. It would have broken a weaker man, that poker game—"

"Poker game!"

I flung the words back at him and I felt, rather than saw, Deacon stiffen. "There *was* a poker game, then?" I said huskily.

"The game that cracked the town, Uncle John."

His somber eyes held me rigid in my chair. "You mean—they played poker—for a man's life?"

"Yes, Uncle John."

"Who was the stake?" Deacon rapped out.

Jerry ignored the question and Deacon's face darkened; but Henry made no response. I suppose he realized that the boy couldn't be expected to feel any too amiably disposed towards him.

"Dad had a remarkable memory for details," Jerry went on, "and he made those ghastly six hours so vivid that I felt as if I were down there myself. He remembered the minutest details, the conversations that took place and the very tones in which they were uttered. He lived the whole thing over before my eyes. You won't wonder at this when I'm done. I can't make you see it as he made me see it, but I'll do my best.

"Dad's six hours began just before sunset on Monday, July 6th, 1896. He was in his cabin on the Two Brothers property. His men had gone into Torridity, half a mile away—Deacon told me you were down there, Uncle John. Dad had been doing some book work, but he was about ready to go into town himself when the door flew open and Uncle Jerry tumbled into the cabin and slammed the door shut behind him. His eyes were wild and Dad asked him what was wrong. It took him a minute to get it out.

"'They're after me, Alex!' he gasped.

"'Who are after you?'

"'Lundy—the bunch. They're going to string me up—'

"'They're—*what!*' Dad shouted.

"Uncle Jerry got his wind, then, and he started to pour his yarn out on Dad. It seemed they'd taken him down to Lundy's and given him a miners' trial. Lundy had been judge. He'd made a break for it—got away—they were after him. He shouldn't have headed that way, but he didn't know what he was doing. He'd been a fool—crazy. Alex had treated him white when he ought to have taken a rawhide to him. Now he was roping Alex into it, low-down hog that he was. Alex must hand him over to Lundy.

"'It isn't your funeral, Alex. I'm going back. I'll take it without squealing.' He said this with his head up and the crazy look gone out of his eyes.

"'What have you done now?' Dad roared at him. Uncle Jerry had been up to every kind of deviltry imaginable since they'd come to Torridity.

"Jerry had started in to tell him when they heard shouting off towards the town. Dad sprang to the window. The sun was setting and the desert looked like a painted plain— you know how the beauty of it at sunset takes you by the throat, Uncle John? Half the town was racing towards the Two Brothers—crazy mad, by the way they were coming. Most of 'em were shouting and waving their arms, some of 'em had guns, a few carried ropes. It looked bad and Dad knew it. He'd seen mining-town lynching gangs on the rampage before and he knew what they were capable of doing.

"'Come on, son! Pronto!' he shouted.

"But Uncle Jerry shook his head. 'I shouldn't have come here, Alex,' he said. 'I'm going back. It isn't right to rope you in on it. You've always treated me a darn' sight better'n I deserved. So long.'

"He dragged open the door he had burst through a moment before and was for making off across the desert

when Dad jumped on him from behind and swung him
towards the flank of the Skeletons behind the mine buildings.

"'Move, I tell you!' Dad roared. 'Get into the mine—'

"'See here, Alex,' Uncle Jerry began.

"'No back talk! Move, you fool!'

"'It's not your funeral, Alex—'

"Dad must have been pretty husky in those days. He
grabbed Uncle Jerry by the shoulders and hustled him towards the mine tunnel, Uncle Jerry fighting him as hard as
he could. An ore cart stood on a pair of steel rails which
ran into the bore and Dad neatly upended Uncle Jerry and
dumped him into it.

"'Keep your head out of sight and shut up!' he growled,
running the cart into the mine. 'Those hombres mean
business, by the sound of 'em?

"They did, I guess. A bullet flattened against the overhang of rock above the tunnel entrance and the crowd let
out a frightful yell as they saw what Dad was doing. It
gave him a pretty clear idea of what he was up against.
A heavy redwood door hung at the tunnel entrance. Dad
shut the door and padlocked it; then he set his back to the
door, dropped his hands to his gun belt, and waited.

"In those days a huge overhang of rock stuck out of
the mountainside above the door like a hump on a camel's
back. Old-timers had prophesied that it'd come down
some day and block the mine, but Dad hadn't much faith
in prophets. I don't mean that he was careless of the lives
of his men, however reckless he might have been with his
own, but a hard-headed realism seems to have tempered
that imaginative turn of mind of his which ran to white
silk shirts and gold bullets, and he had a great respect for
facts. He had satisfied himself that nothing short of an
earthquake or the deliberate dynamiting of the overhang
would bring it down and that was enough for Dad.

"The crowd swooped onto the mine property, making a fearful racket, but when they saw Dad standing in the shadow of the overhang, thumbing his gun belt, they stopped and piled up in a semi-circle, hemming him in. Not too close, though. One or two of 'em were fingering their guns, but they kept 'em where they belonged. Dad wasn't a gunman, but he had that *quality* Mrs. Lundy spoke of, that picturesque arrogance, if you like, which had made him one of the two top dogs in Torridity. His famous forty-fives were the most feared weapons—and the least used—in the Skull. So they stood there, watching him, figuring that a gold bullet would be as uncomfortable as a lead one, I guess. . . . I'm trying to put it over to you as I got it from Dad. Not so much what Dad said, either, as the impression he gave me? Do you get the picture, Uncle John?"

How could I have failed to get it? Jerry's boyish eloquence, the fine ardor of his dark eyes, the flashing movements of his slender, strong hands had carried me back to Torridity—the Torridity of yesterday. The man I had known as Andrew Ogden was before me. I saw the evening sun glint on the gold bullets at his waist and on the filigree work on the butts of his guns. I heard the shouting of the human wolves semi-circled about him drop to a throaty growl, then to a silence as taut as a wound-up spring. I heard the creak of a cooling engine, the gusty breathing of the mob, the rattle of a falling stone. The sun was dropping behind the Skeletons, the purple shadows were mysteriously lengthening, the cindered earth seemed to heave on its couch in relief. Yes, I got the picture! And so did Deacon. Wasn't he sitting there with his hands clenched, his frosty blue eyes wide open, his lips parted a little?

"Get on with it, son," I whispered.

"Dad knew he couldn't hold them like that much longer," Jerry resumed. "They weren't carrying ropes for nothing. He must make some definite play or they'd swarm over him."

"'What'll you have, Lundy?' he drawled.

"Lundy shuffled forward. His wife has told you about him, Uncle John. He stopped half a dozen feet away from Dad, his heavy loosely jointed body in a slouching attitude, his hung-on head thrust forward.

"'What'll you have, Lundy?' Dad drawled again.

"Lundy blinked through his eight-sided glasses. You'll hear more about those glasses presently.

"'That brother uh yourn, Ten-to-One,' he said.

"'So?' Dad commented.

"'Yeah. We need him right bad.'

"'What for?' Dad demanded.

"'Crackin' my safe this mornin'—steady thar!'

"I can see Dad lunging at him, gun in hand, eyes bleak with fury. Lundy's nerve was superb. Youve got to hand it to him for that. He just stood there, casually blinking at Dad, saying nothing.

"'Take that lie back, Lundy,' Dad muttered at him.

"'I reckon not,' Lundy grinned. 'It ain't no lie.'

"'You've got two minutes to prove it!'

"'Aplenty.'

"'Get at it, then,' Dad barked.

"Lundy began. It seemed that fifty ounces of gold had been taken out of his office three months before. Two weeks later three hundred dollars had been lifted from his bar while the crowd was out watching an adjoining resort burn down. Still a month later some one had shot up Lundy's faro game and pulled in five hundred dollars. Dad knew of these affairs. Everybody in Torridity did. About the time the faro game was shot up Lundy heard that a Pinkerton detective was in San Francisco and he had written to him to come down to Torridity. The detective had come and he had insisted on Lundy keeping his presence in Torridity secret. Lundy had agreed, but the news had leaked out somehow. The town weekly newssheet had it.

"The previous Saturday being the Fourth of July and pay night a good deal of dust and currency had come into Lundy's by Sunday night. Around ten thousand, Lundy said—three thousand in raw gold. Lundy's safe was an old-fashioned contraption that a clever devil could crack with a can-opener and the Pinkerton man thought the thief was likely to try his hand again early Monday morning. Lundy's office was upstairs, there was a storeroom off it, and the Pinkerton man said he'd hide in the storeroom and if the thief showed up, step out on him. Lundy could stay down in the hall. It had sounded reasonable and Lundy had agreed.

"At this point in his story Lundy broke into coldblooded laughter. He packed one of those inhuman cackles that a decent man wouldn't own, Dad said. Yes, he'd gone up to his office at sunrise. And the Pinkerton man? Lying on his back with his hands lashed to his legs and a gag in his mouth! The window was broken in and so was Lundy's tin-can safe and Lundy was out a matter of ten thousand dollars.

"'Mad?' said Lundy. 'Yeah, but I ain't nothin' to what that Pinkerton sharp was when I tooked the rag outen his mouth. I tho't he'd burn the hall down, he talked that hot. He'd gone to the windy for a breath uh air and the blankety-blank hombre had clouted a gun over his head. Mad? Yeah, I was mad, but not as mad as yuh'd think. Them detectin' sharps is all right fer the cities, but they ain't w'uth tobaccy spit out here. An' because I hired the Pinkerton sharp ain't no reason fer keepin' me own eyes shet.'

"According to Lundy, the description of the man who shot up the faro game resembled Uncle Jerry.

"'I sez nothin' to the Pinkerton sharp—' Lundy went on, 'I let him fiddle his own tune—but I sez to myself, I sez, "keep yore eye on that Jerry lad, Joe."'

"Well, before Lundy looked up the receipts Sunday morning he mixed a handful of salt with the gold dust. That afternoon he and Burke and Webb, a couple of prospectors, and Fitch, a gambler, had gone up to Uncle Jerry's room in the Red Gold Hotel. Uncle Jerry wasn't home, but they found a couple of bags of dust—and there was salt in them, Uncle John!"

"A frame-up!" I whispered.

But I seemed to know instinctively that it wasn't. My mind flew back to the item in the old newspaper Deacon and I had found in the mine and I thought of MacNair's "intricate bit of mosaic work" and his "parts of a pattern." Gradually, the pattern was emerging from the shadows of thirty years ago. . . . I had a sense of inevitability as inescapable as the climax of a Greek tragedy.

Jerry shook his head sorrowfully. "It wasn't a frame-up, Uncle John.

"'That's the damnedest lie your tongue ever let loose, Lundy,' Dad flashed at him. 'I'll give you ten seconds to swallow it!'

"Lundy slouched where he was, a thumb hung in his gun belt, and pretended he was grieved.

"'It ain't no lie, Ten-to-One,' he said. 'I wisht it was. We took the lad down to hall, gived him his trial fair and square, an'—well, three hundred citizens uh Torridity heard him admit he done it! That right, boys?' Lundy blared at the crowd.

"Dad went sick at the roar the mob put up. You see, Uncle John, it hadn't occurred to him that Lundy's accusation was anything more than a cleverly concocted lie built on another of Uncle Jerry's fool breaks. But he couldn't dispute the testimony of three hundred witnesses—some of them his own men. What deviltry had got into the lad? Dad asked himself. Uncle Jerry was as wild as an unbroken colt, impatient of restraint, useless maybe but he'd never been vicious. There must be something else Lundy hadn't told, Dad reasoned. There must be. He kept his gun up.

"'Where's that Pinkerton man?' Dad demanded of Lundy.

"But Lundy wasn't telling. 'He's around somewheres. Yuh wouldn't be expectin' him to show his face after what the kid done to him?'

"'Just that,' Dad shouted. 'Tote him out.'

"Lundy stuck his lantern head forward, goggling at Dad through his eight-sided glasses. 'Now, looky here, Ten-to-One,' he argued. 'The fella's feelin' purty bad, uh course, but *this* is the p'int. There's a wad uh money missin' an' we got an idee Jerry had a pardner. If he had, and the sharp keeps his face shet an' hangs around a couple uh weeks more, he may be able to rope the pardner in, too. Nacherally, he wants to stage a comeback. An' I wants my money. So I guess yuh'll have to fergit him. The boy's admitted he done it. Ain't that enough?'

"'A pardner!' Dad had jumped at that. It might account for Uncle Jerry's fool play. Partly, anyhow. He looked over the faces in front of him. Some of them he didn't know. Floating labor constantly drifted in and out of the town. Most of 'em looked tough enough for any kind of deviltry.

"'God help you if you are lying, Lundy!' Dad threatened. Then he addressed the mob. 'Listen, men. I am going into the mine to talk to my brother. The door'll be open—you can rush us if you feel like it—but there'll be twelve of you shaking hands with the devil before you get him. How about it?'

"'We don't mind yuh talkin' to the lad, Ten-to-One,' Lundy grinned. 'Get at it.'

"Dad unlocked the mine door and swung it open. Jerry was waiting for him on the other side of the door. Dad grabbed him by the shoulders.

"'You heard what Lundy said?'

"'It's true, Alex,' Uncle Jerry groaned. 'You'd better hand me over to 'em. It'll save trouble.'

"Dad blew up, then. 'You damned fool!' he stormed. 'If you'd wanted more money why didn't you come to me?' He flung Uncle Jerry against the tunnel wall. 'I couldn't bear the sight of him,' he said.

"Dad stood at the door of the tunnel, staring off across the desert. I can see him there now, Uncle John. The sun gone and the shadows covering the desert's burned-out nakedness. Lundy and his gang quiet and waiting. A sort of graveyard stillness in the hot, dead air. You know how it is down there at night. You feel as if you were the last man God had let live. And Dad was thinking: Jerry was Jerry . . . his kid brother. He had no one else. The boy was weak. In a way, it was his, Alex's, fault. He shouldn't have brought the boy to this sink-hole. Yes, it was his fault.

"'Scared, son?" he asked gently, facing Uncle Jerry again.

"The boy's head flew up. He thought the world of Dad. 'Uh-huh,' he replied. 'Might as well admit it. What's coming on, Alex?'

"Dad passed up the question. 'Let's hear about it, son,' he said.

"It appeared that before the first robbery ten weeks back Uncle Jerry had lost a couple of thousand dollars playing black jack at Lundy's. The game was crooked, he said. Uncle Jerry was sure of this and Dad, knowing Lundy's, thought it likely enough. Anyhow, Uncle Jerry had lifted the gold in Lundy's office and the money in Lundy's bar, and he'd held up the faro game. Those jobs gave him back the money he'd lost, but instead of profiting by his experience, he'd sat in at a poker game with Nat Richey and Tex MacCoy—two of the cleverest card sharps in the Skull. They cleaned him, of course. That was on Saturday afternoon—the Fourth of July.

"Uncle Jerry seemed as if he couldn't get the rest of it out, but Dad kept prodding him and it soon came. Richey and MacCoy had taken six thousand from him. Two thousand was his—or Lundy's—the rest . . . was Dad's. There had been a couple of hundred ounces of gold in Dad's safe. He was to have shipped it on Tuesday. Uncle Jerry had intended to put it back that night.

"You can imagine what Dad felt. I think he'd sooner have had Uncle Jerry stick a knife in his back. He said he had to take his eyes off the boy and turn towards the desert again. It was getting dark now. The shadows helped him to get himself in hand. Lundy and his gang hadn't moved; they weren't making any noise. Probably they sensed what Dad was going through.

"Uncle Jerry went on with his yarn. He'd been going with a man who had drifted into the camp recently. He wasn't telling the man's name. Nothing would get that out of him. He wasn't yellow—that way. This man had suggested pulling off something big—Lundy's holiday receipts, say. Uncle Jerry didn't want to go in that deep, but he had to put Dad's gold back before Tuesday morning and, well, they'd done it. And he reckoned that was all.

"Dad didn't speak. And he couldn't bear to look at Uncle Jerry. A couple of minutes passed with Dad still staring off into the dusk and saying nothing. Uncle Jerry couldn't stand it any longer.

"'For God's sake speak to me, Alex!' he begged. 'Let 'em string me up—it's coming to me—but don't look like that!'

"Dad softened—he couldn't help it, I guess—and turned round. 'It hits me pretty hard, son—your doing this,' he said. 'I can't blame the boys much. Who was in with you?'

"'I'm not telling,' Uncle Jerry said stubbornly.

"Dad nodded. 'All right. I won't hold that against you. Here's one of my guns. Don't use it unless you have to.' He handed Uncle Jerry the gun and dropped an arm over his shoulder. 'Look here, son. I'll do the best I can for you. But if things go wrong—the cards of life are stacked now and then—you'll take your medicine, eh?'

"Uncle Jerry stuck out his jaw. 'You can bank on me, Alex,' he promised.

"'Good boy!' Dad cried. 'I'll get you out somehow. I'm going to lock you up now and talk to the boys. You'll find candles and a water canteen somewhere. So long, son.'

"He gripped Uncle Jerry's hand and went out. The door padlocked, he faced Lundy and the crowd again.

"'Satisfied?' Lundy grinned.

"Dad didn't answer him. You see what he was up against, Uncle John? Uncle Jerry had broken the first law of the mining camps. Down there in those days a man's gold was more sacred than his life, Dad said, and the mob had come to see that Uncle Jerry got what they believed was coming to him. Argument or pleading wouldn't touch them. Many of them were friendly towards Dad, he had staked a few of them from time to time, but gold was the most vital thing in their lives. As Dad said: 'They'd sanctified it with blood and sweat. Nothing else was comparable with it. Jerry had violated the vessel of their faith. I didn't blame them!' A rotten mess, and Dad couldn't see any way out of it.

"And then all at once an idea struck him. Lundy was notoriously fond of money. Could he be bought off? Maybe. But if he could, would the miners, who were sticklers for the rough-and-ready frontier code, consider Lundy entitled to take satisfaction in cash? They might and they mightn't. It wasn't much of an idea, but Dad was desperate. He stepped nearer Lundy.

"'See here,' he began, 'the boy's been led into this. I'll make the money good. Let him go. I'll see he doesn't slip again.'

"Lundy was amused. 'You will, huh!' He broke into that horrible laugh of his. Dad wanted to strike him on the mouth. 'Hear that, boys?' Lundy drawled.

"They had and they buzzed like a hive of bees, Dad said. 'No!' 'Give him the rope!' 'Hang the devil and be done with it!' 'Let the hombre swing!' and the like tossed back and forth.

"Lundy shrugged. 'It ain't no use, Ten-to-One,' he said. 'He's had his trial fair and square. Miners' law. We found him guilty. Gold-thievin' is gold thievin' an' the boy has got to swaller his med'cine. It ain't the first necktie party we've had around here and I don't rec'lect Ten-to-One Peterson doin' any objectin'.'

"This was true, Dad admitted to me. He hadn't. But circumstances alter cases, Uncle John. Dad had never before realized this so clearly. The responsibility was his. He'd brought Uncle Jerry into the toughest town in the West and it was up to him to get him out. He drew still nearer Lundy.

"'You can call 'em off if you want to,' he said, his voice emphatic but low—almost a whisper. 'I'll pay you fifty thousand dollars if he goes free.'

"Lundy gave him a hurt look, Dad said, but his eyes flickered queerly behind his eight-sided glasses. 'Now, if that ain't addin' insult to injury!' he drawled. 'An' me a-tryin' ter pertect the morals uh the town. I'm ashamed uh yuh, Ten-to-One!' But his voice was low, too.

"Dad took a deep breath. 'A hundred thousand, Lundy,' he whispered.

"'Lordy! bribery comes high, don't she?' Lundy replied, but he hadn't raised his voice. 'His eyes were as hard as gun barrels,' Dad said. 'I knew I'd made an impression.'

"'Yore bluffin', uh course, Ten-to-One,' Lundy went on. 'No kid ever borned uh woman is worth a hundred thousand of any man's roll!'

"'I'm not bluffing,' Dad came back at him. 'Do you take me?'

"'Not fer half a million, Ten-to-One.'

"Lundy's words said one thing, the glitter in his eyes another, but Dad understood. Lundy was afraid of the men. His fear was natural—Dad knew something of frontier passions. The gathering darkness had blurred the men's bodies, but Dad felt something of suspicion in their attitudes. They didn't trust Lundy, he decided, and they resented the undertones that had passed between him and Lundy. Lundy's expression seemed to say: 'Look out. They won't stand for any monkey business. It's up to you, Ten-to-One.'

"But Dad was puzzled about Lundy. He felt there was something else in the man's mind beside his natural fear of the mob. What it was he didn't know, but his feeling was this: Lundy was playing with an idea that embraced Dad's proposal—and something else. It was this unknown quantity, this 'something else,' that troubled him. He didn't trust Lundy, any more than the miners did. Lundy would poison his own mother to further his ends. What was he up to? Well, one thing at a time, Dad reflected. The mob, not Lundy, was his immediate problem. He thought for a moment, then he came to a decision.

"'What are you figuring on doing, Lundy?' he demanded loudly.

"'My dooty,' Lundy drawled.

"'Meaning?'

"'The execution uh justice.'

"Dad went into action, then. His gun flew into his hand and he leaped back against the tunnel door. The light was so poor by this that the shadow of the overhang concealed his position.

"'Don't move,' he warned.

"Lundy remained where he was.

"'Listen, boys,' Dad said curtly. 'You don't hang my brother to-night. I've got six reasons why in my hand. The boy has got six more. Start shooting, if you like. You can't see me—Lundy'll go down first. Then five more of you. You'd get me—the boy, too—but we'd check out with plenty of company. Don't move while you are thinking it over. You, too, Lundy, or I'll drop you!' You get the situation, Uncle John?"

"Get it!" I whispered. "Rather!" It was another addition to that gallery of imperishable pictures my memory was never to let go. Jerry went on.

"The crowd began cursing and yelling to one another to do this and that, but they didn't move up. Dad kept his back to the door and his gun steady. The voices of several of his men were raised in his behalf, but he hadn't much hope. At last the racket lessened and Lundy shouted:

"'What's yore proposition, Ten-to-One?'

"'This,' Dad said bluntly. 'Jerry stays in the mine all night. Meanwhile, I'll look at the evidence with you. In the morning I'll talk it over with the boys.' He didn't dare ask for more than a 'stay of execution.' 'If you prefer shooting, I'm ready.'

"The racket started again, but Lundy quietened them.

"'Looky here, boys,' he argued, 'this hangin's got to be done respectable.' Peterson is the lad's brother, an' come to think of it, I reckon he's entitled to look over the evidence—meanin' that gold uh mine—if he wants to. So I moves we postpone the execution uh justice until sun-up. If *I'm* satisfied, the rest uh yuh ought to be.'

"'Yeah, that's right,' a voice roared.

"'Peterson's figurin' on gettin' the boy away!' another yelled.

"Lundy snickered. 'He's due fer a disapp'intment, then. The lad stays in the mine. I set one uh yuh to watch the mine—outside—and three uh yuh to watch Peterson.

Peterson holds the key and does as he pleases—pervided he leaves his brother alone. How's that?'

"It sounded reasonable enough from every point of view, Dad thought, but he didn't trust Lundy. The men mulled it over for a minute or so, then one of them shouted:

"'All right, Lundy. It's your funeral.'

"'That suit yuh, Ten-to-One?' Lundy drawled.

"Dad wasn't sure whether it did or not. He was afraid of Lundy. Still, a delay was something. Anything might happen between now and dawn.

"'Yes, I reckon so,' he answered casually.

"Holstering his gun, Dad took out his keys. Two of them were alike. He slid one of those two off the ring and shoved it well under the mine door.

"'Jerry,' he called.

"Uncle Jerry heard him. 'Yes, Alex?'

"'I've pushed a key under the door. If anybody comes from me to let you out—I don't know what'll turn up— shove it out to him. But make sure he's on the level. I'll do my best, son.'

"Dad then moved out of the shadow of the overhang. 'I'm holding you responsible, Lundy,' he said grimly. If anything happens to the boy before sun-up, God help you!'

"Lundy laughed like the devil he was. 'He's never helped me none, yet, Ten-to-One, so I reckon I'd be in fer a tough time.'

"Turning, he faced the mob. 'Burke, Fitch, Dillon, Webb— you boys there?' he called . . . What's wrong, Uncle John?"

I had jumped out of my chair as Jerry pronounced that potential name, and so had Deacon.

"'Dillon,' you said!" I shouted, almost beside myself. "That's the man—your father's murderer. What did he say Dillon looked like?"

Jerry laughed mirthlessly. "He didn't say, Uncle John."

"Why didn't he?" Deacon rapped out.

Again the boy laughed and once more I was reminded of that Andrew Ogden I had never known. "He had his reasons. We're coming to that. I'll get on with the yarn, if you don't mind."

We settled back into our chairs. But I was trembling with excitement and Deacon was red in the face. The room seemed to be charged with the destructive violence of a thunder storm. Jerry went on.

"The men Lundy had named came forward. It was quite dark now, Dad said—there was no moon—and their faces were indistinct, but he was more or less familiar with all four of them. Burke and Webb were big surly brutes, prospectors both of them, and jealous of Dad's success. They could be depended on to defend the crowd's point of view. Dillon was a tall, rangy fellow whom Lundy had recently taken on as bartender. Dad wouldn't tell me any more about him. Fitch was a gambler and a gunman. The crowd was satisfied.

"'Got yore guns, boys?' Lundy asked. They had.

"'Burke, Fitch, Webb—yuh'll watch Peterson,' Lundy commanded. 'Dillon stays by the mine. Sabe, all uh yuh?' They did and Lundy told the crowd to ramble on home. 'You know where thar's plenty uh good liquor,' he said. 'But keep sober. Big doin's to-morrow.' The men began to disperse. Pretty soon Fitch and Dillon, Webb and Burke, Lundy and Dad, were the only ones left.

"'Any time yuh want to look at that evidence'll suit me,' Lundy snickered.

"He went off towards the town, then, trailing that ghastly laugh of his out behind him. It had the edge of a rawhide. Dad looked around him. Dillon stood to the right, near the mine door. Burke and Webb and Fitch were in front of him, waiting to see what he was going to do. Tough birds, he reflected.

"None of them spoke. Dad rolled a cigarette."

23
Painted Ladies

"It was just nine by Dad's watch. The sun rose at four. He had seven hours' grace and he knew he was in for the biggest night of his life. Fitch and Burke and Webb hadn't moved. Dad looked them over, his hand at his gun belt. No, he decided, shooting wouldn't do. He might get one or two of them, but hardly three or four. Dillon's skill with a gun was unknown to him, but Fitch was a killer, and the other two knew how to handle their forty-fives.

"Dad was ready to spend every dollar he possessed to save Uncle Jerry, but whether it was an honest and un-qualified acceptance of his offer that Lundy had in mind, or not, he couldn't decide. That sense of 'something else' buzzing in Lundy's head wouldn't let go of him. What was the devil after? The only thing to do was go and see.

"'It meant leaving Jerry alone with Dillon and whoever else might turn up,' Dad said. 'But I couldn't help it. He was locked in, he had one of my guns, and I knew he'd give a good account of himself, if he had to.'

"Dad struck off towards the town and Burke and Webb and Fitch fell in a hundred feet or so behind him. He knew their types—they'd hang on to his heels like blood-hounds—and he wondered where it would end. The night was hot, but the air was clear as a crystal ball. It had a sort of a velvet sheen to it, Dad said. The stars seemed so close he could almost have reached up and turned them out. You know what those desert nights are like, Uncle John.

"A terrific din was pouring out of Lundy's Place. Shouting, laughing, women squealing, ragtime on a tinny piano, and all that. Nothing unusual about it, of course. Lundy's enjoyed itself that way. A hush fell as Dad entered. He went up to the bar and bought a drink.

"'Where's Lundy?' he asked.

"The barkeeper seemed nervous. 'Upstairs,' he replied.

"As Dad made his way towards the gallery stair, Fitch, Burke, and Webb came in. The crowd looked anxious, Dad said, but when he paid no attention to the three men everybody brightened up. One or two of the miners whom he knew well expressed their sympathy, but most of 'em were hostile.

"Dad stood at the top of the stair and looked down into the hall. The piano had started again and the crowd was milling around the floor or drinking at the bar. They all seemed animated by the same impulse: to have as good a time as Lundy's Place could offer them, Dad said. As he watched them, it came over him that they were all of a kind, men and women. Not a hair's breadth of difference between one and another. The same speech and thoughts and desires. They might have been members of a single body.

"'Sheep,' Dad muttered to himself. 'Queer, I never thought of 'em like that before. Think alike, act alike. Whether it's lynching a man, buying a woman, or swallowing booze. Wax! Get 'em hot enough and you can shape 'em any way you please.'

"These were his thoughts as he stared down into the hall and I mention them because they bear on what follows. The comparison to wax sent Dad's eyes to a colored poster tacked in the well of the stair. There were a good many like it stuck around the town just then. It went something like this, Dad said:

"'GREATEST SHOW ON EARTH
PROFESSOR DRYDEN POPE'S WAXWORK WONDERS
UNPARALLELED! UNPRECEDENTED! UNEQUALED!
DIRECT FROM TWO YEAR RUN IN NEW YORK
See
Lifelike Representations of
President Cleveland
Madame Du Barry
Sitting Bull
Buffalo Bill
Bluebeard
Napoleon
And Other Famous Personages
LUNDY'S PLACE JUNE 21ST AND 22ND
Eight O'clock
FIFTY CENTS   FOUR BITS   HALF A DOLLAR'

"This probably isn't an accurate description of the poster, Uncle John, but it's near enough. The point is, Professor Dryden Pope had left without paying his bill and Lundy had confiscated the show. You'll get the significance of that presently.

Several of the alcoves and some of the rooms were occupied, but the alcove in the northwest corner of the gallery was empty, and Dad went towards it. This alcove was always empty, for the reason that a door in the north wall, close to the corner, led into Lundy's office, or 'secret' room as Dad said it was sometimes facetiously called. Of course it wasn't a 'secret' room, except in so far that the door when it was closed wasn't visible to the casual observer. Everybody familiar with the resort knew it was there. Many of them had been in it—some of 'em to their loss.

"Lundy had an imaginative turn of mind, Dad said—crooks have as a rule, I guess—and while the building was being erected he got a notion to have a concealed room built into it. The idea wouldn't work, of course—the construction of the building was too simple—so he compromised on that so-called 'secret' room. The door opened at a joint in the solidly-built 'board and batten' partition which ran across the north end of the building, and it extended from the floor to the ceiling. When the door was closed you hardly knew it was there.

"Dad went to the door. It was ajar. He pushed it open and looked in. Lundy and the two gamblers, Richey and MacCoy, were sitting at a round table. Richey was a tall, thin man with a yellow face. MacCoy was much shorter and heavy-set and he had a blue chin and sly fingers. Both of them were well-to-do, but neither of them had much in the way of reputation, as I've told you. Dangerous men, Dad said. Lundy was fiddling with stacks of poker chips."

At this point Jerry stopped and refreshed himself from a glass of milk Mrs. Moffit had brought in a short while before. The pause gave me time to assemble my wits. That feeling of tragedy inevitable had never left me. Indeed, as the boy had swept on through his narrative, and the intricate pattern of MacNair's "mosaic" had gradually revealed itself to me, my feeling had become one of stark horror. And then Jerry had proceeded to describe that poster hung in the well of the stair, his father's thoughts as Andrew lifted his eyes to it, and the partly concealed entrance to Lundy's "secret" room, and humiliation had for the moment superseded my horror. Wax dummies! I had begun to suspect something of the sort. But what an unmitigated ass I had been!

However, that sense of stark horror quickly took precedence again in my mind and, sick at heart, I looked at Deacon. He still sat rigid in his chair, his blue eyes like marbles, his lips parted a little. And Lucy? Her face was the color of parchment. I don't think she had lifted her eyes from Jerry's since he had begun to speak. . . . But Jerry was commencing again.

"Those poker chips Lundy was fiddling with must have given Dad an inkling of what the man had in mind." Jerry paused, in his eyes a haunted look that added to my weight of grief. "I won't pretend that what I have told you is an *exact* description of what was said and thought and done, Uncle John," he went on earnestly. "I insist it is true in spirit, though—you know what I mean. But it's different with what I'm going to tell you now. Dad had what follows as clear as a letter on a dictaphone record and he passed it on to me that way. And I can't forget it any more than he could. There are some things time *can't* rub out. So I'm giving you the letter as well as the spirit, this time.

"'Howdy, Ten-to-One,' Lundy greeted Dad, waving his hand. 'Come in.'

"Dad described the room. A hanging lamp lighted it. There were half a dozen chairs, an old desk, the table, a couple of cuspidors, and an old-fashioned safe with a broken lock. A brewery calendar with a picture of a woman in tights hung on the south wall. Windows faced north and west. The room was oblong, and it ran about a third of the way across the building. A door in the east wall led into a storeroom which occupied the other two-thirds of the end of the building. I have seen the room. It is still as he described it.

"Dad took a chair and rolled a cigarette. Lundy offered him matches, but Dad refused them, having plenty of his own. He said he felt that they had been waiting for him, that with himself there the cast was complete.

"'Sizable crowd below,' Richey commented.

"Lundy rattled the poker chips. 'Yeah,' he agreed. 'Business ain't what she was, though.'

"'The old town's lasted purty well,' MacCoy put in. 'Longer'n I figured. When yuh pullin' up stakes, Joe?'

"Lundy didn't know. The Bad Medicine shutting down would make things worse. But he wasn't kicking. He'd done pretty well there. 'Yuh got to calc'late on these minin' towns blowin' 'emselves out. Two Brothers still goin' strong, Ten-to-One?'

"Dad grunted that it was, and went on smoking. Lundy said something about him always having been 'a lucky hombre,' and rattled the chips again.

"'Me an' Mac an' Rich was thinkin' uh havin' a little poker,' he said smoothly.

"'So?' Dad grunted.

"'Yeah. They plays a purty stiff game,' Lundy went on. 'But yuh ain't no slouch yuhself, Ten-to-One.'

"Dad acknowledged the compliment and Lundy remarked that he was partial to a stiff game himself.

"'I was jest thinkin' you an' me has known each other four years an' I ain't sat in a game with yuh yet. Funny, ain't it?'

"'Is it?' Dad answered dryly.

"Lundy got the inference, all right, but he didn't take it up. 'Mac an' Rich is fair itchin' fer a game,' he went on. 'Ain't yuh, boys?'

"'Itchin' is right,' Richey admitted, and MacCoy supported him.

"Dad drew on his cigarette. The warm smoke steadied him. 'There's plenty of easy money downstairs,' he said.

"Lundy leaned nearer. 'Yuh've got the repitation uh bein' the gamblin'est hombre as ever come into the Skull, Ten-to-One. Yuh think nothin' uh bettin' down to yore shirt, they tell me. Don't it seem as if a couple uh high fliers like you an' me ought to git together?'

"'Sometime, maybe,' Dad said.

"Lundy stuck his ugly head still nearer. 'Now's as good a time as any, ain't it?'

"Dad didn't think so. He'd come to talk about his brother. That evidence against him. Lundy said there wasn't any hurry about that. He could see it after the game.

"'You'll show it me now,' Dad shouted suddenly. 'Where is it?'

"Lundy drew back. 'Scared?' he drawled.

"MacCoy said it looked that way and Richey guessed Dad had never sat in a *real* game. Lundy laughed.

"'Queer, how some hombres gits their repitations, ain't it?'

"At that they all began to grin and chuckle and Dad said he had to sit tight or he'd have lost his head. He knew what that 'something else' in Lundy's mind was now and he could hardly keep himself from wiping the smirk off the man's ugly face. Dad said he'd never heard of anything quite so damnable.

"And then he got the other side of the picture. He knew what Lundy was after. Why not meet him halfway? The proposition was ghastly, but nothing else had presented itself, or seemed likely to. Mad? Maybe. But could he think of anything better? He hadn't been able to, so far. And Jerry was waiting for him, his face yellow in candlelight . . . blackness behind him . . . a rope ahead . . . Jerry, his kid brother! And it was he who had brought him here! It must have been pretty awful for Dad. You—you get the picture, Uncle John?"

Get it! Would it ever pass from my mind? The boy's voice had broken with emotion. His face was haggard. I had forgotten the others.

"Get on with it!" some one croaked. It must have been Deacon.

"They stopped their infernal cackling, Dad said. Lundy's eyes were as hard as rock drills. MacCoy and Richey were staring out of their damned inhuman faces at him.

Dad was asking himself: Would the miners back him up
if he won? They might, if the issue were put to them in a
sporting light. 'A gambling debt was one of their funda-
mentals,' he said, 'like birth and death and a man's gold.'
But he couldn't be sure.

"Lundy's play was said to be crooked. MacCoy's and
Richey's were known to be. Lundy had cleaned Tex Mullins
of sixty thousand, and Pastelli, the Paso del Norte gambler, of a hundred thousand, in that very room. But Dad
had never yet met a crooked player he couldn't trip. They'd
have to be pretty good. What should he do? The dead heat
of the room stifled him. He could scarcely breathe. Suddenly, he made up his mind.

"'This goes for the three of you,' he said threateningly.
'Your play is said to be crooked. Maybe it is maybe it isn't.
But—one crooked play and I'll give you a gold filling.'

"Lundy slapped his holster. 'Lead'll go just as fur as
gold, Ten-to-One. And it's cheaper. Yuh'll play?' His voice
fairly crackled.

"Dad nodded and Lundy's eyes blazed. Then his face
fell into poker lines, as Richey's and MacCoy's had already
done. Lundy asked if there was any limit. Dad said there
wasn't and Lundy's teeth clicked together.

"They looked at each other, Dad and Lundy, with complete understanding in their eyes. Dad knew that he was
in for the biggest hour of his life and I guess Lundy felt
much the same about himself. Richey and MacCoy didn't
count—they were just bits of staging demanded by the
necessities of poker. Dad said he actually had a feeling of
exhilaration.

"Lundy spread half a dozen sealed packs of playing
cards out on the table and stacked more chips alongside
those already there; then he sat down opposite Dad. Mac-
Coy sat on Dad's left, Richey on his right. Just then Fitch
stuck his head into the room, but when he saw what was in

the wind he pulled out. Lundy took off his glasses, saying he didn't suppose Dad'd mind if he changed them for his other pair. These were for distance. He couldn't see the pips with 'em.

"Dad had nothing to say. Everybody knew that Lundy was nearsighted and that he used a second pair of steel-framed glasses for card playing and reading. He took them out of a case which he kept in the breast pocket of his gray drill shirt and put them on. The lenses of this pair also were eight-sided, but they were much thicker and they magnified his eyes. The other pair he put away in the case.

Meanwhile, Dad had picked out a deck at random, glanced at the seal, broken it, and drawn out the cards. He counted and shuffled them and spread them out face down. The backs were covered with an intricate design of red and white lines, circles, and flourishes. Apparently they were all right and he pushed them towards Lundy.

"'Leary, ain't yuh?' Lundy grinned.

"'Cautious, that's all,' Dad replied shortly. 'You'll bank?'

"'Yeah. Chips.'

"Dad always carried a fair-sized roll with him in those days and he peeled off five hundred dollars in fifties and tossed it down in front of Lundy. MacCoy and Richey pushed across similar amounts. They had a great deal of money on them.

"'Chicken-feed!' Lundy grunted, as he gathered in the money.

"They agreed that one another's checks should be honored. Lundy shuffled, Dad watching the flash of his hands and the fall of the cards. He knew Lundy wouldn't miss an opportunity.

"'Cut!' Lundy grunted.

"MacCoy did so. Richey slid forward a blue chip, Lundy dealing meanwhile. Dad followed the deal closely, but the cards appeared to come straight. They picked up

their hands, Dad, MacCoy, and Lundy anteing in turn.
Dad held three nines, an ace, and a jack. He discarded the
odd cards. Lundy picked up the deck and looked from one
to another. Richey asked for three, Dad for two, MacCoy
for one. Lundy dealt and took one himself.

"Dad found a three and a six in his draw, but he felt
fairly safe and when Richey dropped he shoved forward
a stack of reds. MacCoy saw the bet and Lundy flung his
cards down in disgust, exposing a couple of pairs. Dad's
three nines were good over the three fours in MacCoy's
hand, and he drew in the pot.

"'That Ten-to-One's the luckiest hombre as ever come
down the Skull,' Dad heard a voice behind him growl.

"'It ain't lucky to win the first pot,' some one else muttered.

"For a minute or two Dad had been aware of feet moving behind him and as he glanced over his shoulder he saw
that half a dozen men, Fitch and Webb among them, stood
around the door. There were many more behind them and
he could hear others coming up the stair. They must have
sensed something of the significance of the game, he said,
for none of them moved towards the table. Dad wasn't
superstitious, but the last remark bothered him. Were these
men to see the greatest victory of his life—or his ruin? It
took him a moment to shake off the notion. Hadn't he won
the first pot in games he'd cleaned up in more times than
he could remember?

"Richey shuffled, Lundy cut, and Richey dealt. The
men at the door were quiet now. You could feel the tension
quickening, Dad said.

"On Richey's deal Dad got two jacks which he drew to.
MacCoy asked for three cards, Lundy for two. Richey took
three himself. Dad didn't think Lundy or MacCoy were
drawing to theirs. He had caught another jack and on the
strength of it bet a stack of reds. MacCoy raised the stack.

Lundy meditated, narrowed his eyes at Dad for a moment, then saw the raise. Richey dropped and Peterson contented himself with a call. But Dad's jacks had gone back on him—Lundy had filled a straight with his two-card draw.

"'Turn an' turn about, as me old mother uster say,' Lundy snickered as he drew in the pot. 'A couple uh pairs, huh, Mac. An' yores, Rich? Three eights. Tough luck, ol' timers. Yore deal, Ten-to-One.'

"Dad said the pressure outside had forced several of the men into the room, but they all kept around the door. The room began to reek of cut plug and burning kerosene and sweat. There wasn't much talk. A word here and there. Dad won the third hand. The fourth went to MacCoy, the fifth to Richey. On the sixth hand Dad bluffed with a couple of sevens. MacCoy and Richey dropped out early, but Lundy had bet some two thousand dollars before he drew back and Dad reaped the pot. At the end of an hour Lundy had lost around four thousand. Richey was about even, Mac-Coy was a little ahead.

"'Ain't that Ten-to-One luckier'n a b'ar in a bar'el uh honey!' a man behind Dad growled.

"Lundy allowed himself to look disturbed. He leaned forward, drumming on the table.

"'Kid's play, Ten-to-One,' he muttered.

"'So?' Dad answered coolly.

"'We ain't gettin' nowheres,' Lundy went on.

"Dad nodded and they stared at each other in silence. Lundy's eyes were hostile, but the look of complete understanding in them was more evident than ever—probably due to the thick-lensed glasses, Dad said, and he supposed the same expression was in his own. Lundy leaned back.

"'Let's get at it, then.'

"Dad couldn't mistake his meaning. Lundy didn't look at either Richey or MacCoy. In the intentness of his concentration on Dad he seemed to have forgotten they were there. Dad, of course, had long since realized that they were as unrelated to the issues of the game as the wax figures Lundy had confiscated two weeks before. 'Wax!' Dad thought. That was what they were. 'Wax in Lundy's hands.'

"The next four pots didn't alter the standing much.

"'Your deal, Lundy,' Dad said again.

"MacCoy cut and Lundy laid down five cards to each. The room reeked like a tannery now; Dad loosened the neckband of his silk shirt as he scanned his cards. He had three queens, a trey, an ace. Pretty good, Dad thought. He had a feeling that the game was coming to a head. His eyes leaped to Lundy's, then dropped to his cards again. An honest draw to the value of his hand was his play. Richey discarded three, Dad the ace and the trey, MacCoy three. Lundy dealt three cards to Richey, two to Dad, and three to MacCoy; then he laid the deck down.

"'Standin' pat, eh?' MacCoy whispered.

"'I reckon these'll do me.' Lundy's voice shook, Dad said.

"Dad drew the two cards towards him, wondering what was Lundy's pat hand? The chances favored a full house; an ace full, possibly, he said. A straight seemed too small to enter into account. A flush was likely, but not to be feared. A straight flush was mighty rare.

"And then Dad slipped the index corner of his draw carefully into sight and his heart stopped dead for a second. The fourth queen was staring up at him! He had a hand that was within two of being unbeatable! With the aces broken, only four kings and a straight flush could top him. Standing pat wasn't an indication of fours and it wasn't likely Lundy had that rare bird, a straight flush, in a pat hand! If he had, the devil was camped in his pocket. No, Dad argued, Lundy's pat hand was either a tower hand or a bluff. And he'd like to see Lundy bluff four painted ladies! . . . It looked as if the Ten-to-One luck were holding out, Uncle John.

"Lundy sat with his shoulders hunched up and his cards held close to his eyes. He looked like something out of hell, Dad said. His eyes, leaped from his own hand to the back of Dad's; his lips twitched, grinning, and he moistened them with the tip of his tongue. The men behind Dad seemed to have stopped breathing, so dead still was the room, yet Dad said the air quivered like a harp string. Somebody behind him whispered:

"'Bet, yuh fool!'

"It seemed to ease the tension for a moment and Richey slid forward a stack of blues. Dad measured it with a couple more. MacCoy scratched his chin, thinking, then he matched the three blue stacks with another three. It was now Lundy's bet. His hunched-up shoulders almost paralleled the sides of his head and he blinked owlishly at Dad, who was trying to fathom his expression. Dad knew he was clever enough to simulate any expression he wanted and he couldn't make up his mind whether the uncertainty in Lundy's eyes was real or not. Lundy muttered something to himself, then he suddenly raised MacCoy a stack of blues.

"Richey skinned his cards, hesitated, made a rapid calculation, and measured Lundy's four stacks with five. Dad saw the bet and raised it two stacks of blues. MacCoy dropped out.

"Lundy blinked at Dad, peered at his cards, goggled at Dad again, then shoved forward every chip, blue, red, and white he had left. Richey's face was saffron, Dad said, but he was game. He measured Lundy's bet stack for stack, and raised it by another.

"The bet was Dad's again.

"He knew instinctively that this was to be the final hand and for the first time since he had picked up the fourth queen he felt afraid. He wouldn't have minded if only the half million or so he was worth were at stake—he'd bet down to his silk shirt on a sight less than four queens often enough—but this was different. Jerry—his own flesh and blood—waiting with a noose hanging over his head—the living stake—it was ghastly. Like buying and selling a man. But what else could he do? This was the only way and he had taken it. His head was buzzing like a mill saw. The room stank of those desert rats at the door! Why didn't they get back to their holes and give them air! He got himself in hand again. He must have faith in his painted women. Sit tight! That was it.

"Dad then pushed forward all his chips, topping Richey's bet by some four thousand dollars. Somebody behind him whispered: 'This is poker!'

"Lundy's eyes were like points of frozen light, Dad said. He grabbed a writing pad off the desk, scribbled an IOU, and tossed it among the chips. It was for ten thousand dollars. Richey grunted like a stuck pig and reached for the pad. Then he stopped and skinned his cards.

"'No,' he muttered, 'I'm out.'

"Lundy looked at Dad. Richey and MacCoy looked at him. Everybody looked at him. Dad thought he caught a gleam of mockery in Lundy's eyes, but the devil dropped his eyelids and he couldn't be sure. He brushed the sweat from his forehead. He said he'd have given a hundred dollars for a drink of cold water. Lundy was sliding the pad to and fro on the table, blinking at Dad like some beastly prowling thing. All at once, Dad seized the pad, wrote an IOU for twenty thousand, and shoved it on top of the others.

"Lundy grunted, calculated, or pretended to, and wrote again. The IOU was for forty thousand.

"Dad wrote another for sixty thousand.

"You couldn't hear the drawing of a breath now, Dad said. The room was like a death house. And he and Mac-Coy and Richey sat like dead men. Lundy was noiselessly chewing his lips, fingering his pencil, his cards, the pad, opening and shutting his eyes. Then he wrote an IOU for a hundred thousand dollars.

"Dad said he forgot the stinking heat, Richey, MacCoy, the jam at the door. He only saw Lundy's fist, the backs of his five cards, the blinking eyes behind them . . . and beyond, a white-faced boy in a dark tunnel. . . . He was asking himself if the devil or chance had given Lundy the four kings or the rare straight flush. It must have been pretty awful for him, Uncle John. Telling me, put him through it all again. He pulled himself up. Lundy was probably betting on a full house. He'd stick by his queens.

"There was a quarter of a million in the pot. A hundred and fifty thousand or so of it was Lundy's, and ninety thousand Dad's; the remainder had been MacCoy's or Richey's. Dad calculated swiftly. At that time he had available in cash and bonds some three hundred thousand dollars, so he could bet another two hundred and ten thousand. He thought about it for a moment longer, then he put his cards down and wrote a check on his Los Angeles bank for three hundred thousand dollars, payable to Joe Lundy. Tearing up his IOU's, he slid the check under one of the stacks of blues.

"Lundy breathed gustily, took off his glasses, wiped his face with a dirty handkerchief, and picked his teeth with a sharpened match. Putting his glasses on again, he whipped out a checkbook and scribbled a check for three hundred thousand dollars, payable to Dad. Then he struck the sharpened match, burned his IOU's, and scribbled on the pad. Tearing off the sheet, he pushed it, with the check, under one of the stacks of blues, but in such a position that Dad read it easily. Lundy had written:

                    "Jerry Peterson goes free,
                    "Joe Lundy.

"'It'll cost yuh the Two Brothers to call me,' Lundy whispered.

"Dad said he had known it was coming, just as he had known it was Lundy's mad ambition to ruin him that had driven him to propose this crazy game; but his vision turned black as he read that damned writing, felt the essence of it drip onto his brain like corrosive acid. It was just as if a curtain had dropped between his eyes and his hand, the pot, and the other three. He wondered if the thing were real . . . if he weren't going mad. A sort of mirage, perhaps. And then he saw that dark tunnel again and a white-faced kid listening and waiting, and he knew it was real. . . . God—awfully real. The curtain lifted. Had Lundy the four kings or the straight flush? The possibility of him having the one or the other racked Dad horribly for a moment, then he shoved it to the back of his mind and grabbing the pad wrote a transfer of the mine property in Lundy's favor.

"'That'll stick in any court,' he said, tossing it over.

"The room was dead still for a moment, then a gasp of admiration broke from the men at the door and the pressure behind pitched them into the room. Dad said it came to him in a twinkling, then, that the issue had been presented to the crowd in the proper sporting light and that if he'd won they'd probably back him up. But had he? Lundy's voice quietened the room.

'Good enough!' he bawled. 'Stick yer Henry John to it, Mac.'

MacCoy witnessed the transfer in a shaking hand.

Lundy returned it to Dad. Tearing it off the tablet, Dad slid it under his check.

"Lundy began to laugh, then, Dad said. Leaning back in his chair, clasping his cards over his belly, he let it belch out of him in horrible body-heaving bellows. It must have shocked even those tough nuts behind Dad. Lundy kept it going until Dad could stand it no longer—he'd been through enough to drive most men mad.

"'Show your hand!' he roared, jumping to his feet.

"There must have been something in Dad's face that told Lundy he was going too far. He shut off his bellowing and spread his hand—slowly, one card at a time—you know the dodge, Uncle John.

"He had a straight flush—the one, two, three, four, and five of hearts!"

24
"Bull" and "Nap"

Jerry fell silent. I found myself mopping my face with a handkerchief and staring into his tragic eyes.

"Am I getting it over, Uncle John?" His voice seemed as remote as the Torridity of thirty years ago.

"I have been living down there ever since you began," I mumbled huskily. "Poor Andrew! I don't wonder at the change in him!"

"It would have smashed a weaker man—you were right about that, young fellow. Get on with your story."

I had forgotten Deacon and it was with something of a shock that I realized he was there. His clear blue eyes were haunted by that tragic look I saw in Jerry's and Lucy's, and which, I suspect, haunted my own, and I remembered again that Andrew had been Henry's friend, also.

Jerry ran his hand gently over Lucy's dark head and she drew closer to him, pressing her cheek against his knee. He resumed, then, and in a twinkling I was back in Torridity.

"The mind'll take in only so much, Uncle John, and at first Dad didn't get the full import of Lundy's straight flush. He said it was Lundy grinning up at him and beginning to draw in the pot that drove the thing home. It gave him a pretty awful minute or two. Himself bankrupted and Jerry as deep in the mess as ever! It must have taken all the iron in Dad to keep him from drawing gun and going berserk.

"Lundy began to laugh again. Dad said if he'd stayed within sound of it he'd have killed the man. Half the town had forced its way into the building. They packed the gallery, the stair, the hall. Men and women. Human wolves, Dad called 'em. He rammed his way through them—they let him pass when they saw the look in his eyes. A few of them were sympathetic and expressed their sympathy, but they had nothing else to give him.

"Outside, he dropped onto a bench which stood at one end of the veranda that fronted the building. He said he couldn't get away from Uncle Jerry's eyes. The mine tunnel was just in front of him. Uncle Jerry was sitting in it, his lips white and his eyes staring. Twisting his hands—starting desperately to his feet at every sound—sinking back—covering his face—counting the minutes—measuring the hours. And in five hours it would be sun-up. . . . The sweat poured down Dad's face as he told me.

"Fitch and Webb and Burke came out. They saw Dad and nodded to one another. Each of them wore two guns. Burke crossed the street to a bench outside a poolroom, Webb lounged over to the rail at the other end of the veranda, and Fitch sat on the step.

"Dad jumped up with a crazy notion of ending it then and there, but he forced himself down. It wouldn't do. They'd have Jerry strung up inside of ten minutes. Fitch and Webb had started up at the same time, but they, also, settled back. No word was spoken.

"He couldn't go on like this—Jerry's precious five hours dribbling away—but he must *think* his way out, or he'd have the whole town on his back. He said he had a feeling of defect somewhere. 'A false note,' he called it. Something wrong. He began to grope around in his mind, but he couldn't get it. And all the time he was thinking of

Uncle Jerry . . . seeing his eyes staring out of that damned tunnel. There *must* be some way out. But where—what—how?

"Lundy's Place began to come to life again—shouting and singing and laughter. Dad tried to shut his ears against the row, but it grew louder and louder. Some one shouted, 'Drinks on Joe Lundy!' and the building shook with feet treading up to the bar. Glasses clinked, bottles smashed, a couple of good-natured pistol shots were fired. Free drinks meant that Lundy was taking the easiest way of making himself solid with the miners.

"Dad hadn't got rid of that sense of 'something wrong.' There was something wrong. Of this he was positive. Something wrong with that game. Why couldn't he pin it down? He became desperate. He'd make a running fight of it. Get Fitch with his first shot, Webb as he spun round at the step, and Burke as he started across the street. Then, hell-bent for the Two Brothers! He'd deal with Dillon, release Uncle Jerry. They'd saddle Gunpowder and Bluebell and try for Pitchfork or Shinbone. They'd never make either—he'd do well to get to the mine—but it'd be better than seeing Jerry swinging against the skyline at sun-up. And he could think of unpleasanter ways of checking out.

"All this had gone through Dad's mind in a split second or so. His hand fell to his holster, he half started up, and then he dropped back.

"Some one was standing on the ground behind the end rail along which ran the bench he was sitting on. He saw it was old Pat Furie, a prospector. Everybody knew Furie, Dad said. He was a little wisp of a fellow with a shock of gray hair, China-blue eyes, face wrinkled like a walnut—but you know about Furie, Uncle John. He wasn't really old then, except in the sense that the desert makes a man old. Fifty or so. Furie stuck his thumb in Dad's ribs.

"'What do you want?' Dad growled.

"'Lundy cleaned ye, huh?' he chuckled, so low that Dad scarcely heard him.

"Dad told him to take himself off and mind his own affairs. Furie 'he-he-he'd'—you know that crazy cackle of his, Uncle John, and stayed where he was. Fitch looked up but he slumped back again. Furie didn't count in Torridity. He was generally regarded as 'queer but harmless.' Thumbing Dad again, he nodded significantly towards Fitch and Webb. Something in his attitude cautioned Dad.

"'What's wrong with you?' he muttered.

"Furie 'he-he-he'd' again. 'Lundy cleaned ye, Ten-to-One. I knowed he would! He's been a-layin' for ye an' now he's got ye. He-he-he! Old Furie ain't the fool folks thinks he is. No-sirree!'

"Dad held his tongue with difficulty.

"'Lundy's a slick hombre,' Furie rambled on. 'Yes-sir-ree! An' so's old Pat Furie! Only nobody don't know it but hisself. I sure figgered on ye bein' smarter'n to let Joe Lundy make a fool o' ye, Ten-to-One. Yore a ter'ble disapp'intment to me.'

"The racket inside was deafening by this, Dad said, and as Furie had spoken scarcely above a whisper Fitch couldn't possibly have heard him.

"'Out with it, desert rat!' Dad growled, grabbing him by the arm. 'What do you mean he made a fool of me?'

"'He-he-he!' Furie cackled. 'Them cards ye played with—'

"'Yes?'

"'They was marked—'

"'They weren't! I looked.'

"'With the nekked eye, ye did,' Furie whispered. 'Not through Lundy's maggifying glasses—his other pair. I cotched a look through 'em once. Reg'lar maggifyin' glasses. He-he-he! Pat Furie ain't nob'dy's fool! No-sirree!'

"Dad had to grip the rail hard to hold himself down. The backs of the cards so faintly marked that the markings were invisible without the aid of magnifying glasses which Lundy had worn in the guise of glasses! No wonder the four queens had let him down! Dad was crazy mad for a minute—he'd always prided himself on being too shrewd to be taken in by so simple a trick as that!—but he soon cooled down. He'd have to keep his head if he were to profit by what he had learned. Furie had slid back into the shadows. Dad recalled that Furie had been cleaned by Lundy several years before and he supposed this was his revenge.

"Dad thought for a space. Then he got up and moved towards the door, rolling a cigarette. Fitch raised his head.

"'Slow coming?' Dad asked casually.

"'Start a-roarin' any time yuh like, Ten-to-One,' Fitch drawled.

"Dad grinned at him. 'Lundy upstairs still?'

"'I dunno,' the man answered.

"Dad shoved into the resort. The crowd was busy getting drunk as fast as it knew how. They stood against the bar six deep, crowded the alcoves, slithered around the floor. Drinks on Joe Lundy didn't come often, Dad said. A drunken miner climbed onto a table and emptied his six-shooter at the roof. Dad's appearance checked the hilarity for a moment, but he nodded amiably here and there and they went at it harder than ever.

"Pushing up to the bar, he took a drink and asked if Lundy was still upstairs. The barkeeper said he hadn't seen him come down and he shoved Dad's money back to him. 'All drinks is on the house,' he explained.

"Dad mounted the stair, forming his plan. He would call Lundy's crooked play and force him to submit the magnifying glasses and the marked cards to a committee

of miners. On the strength of Lundy's fraud, he'd then
demand Uncle Jerry's release and the return of the check
and the mining transfer. Pretty daring, you'll admit, Uncle
John. It might work. And it mightn't.

"From the top of the stair Dad looked down over the
hall. Fitch and Webb had come in. They saw him and took
up positions near the two doors of the building. Burke,
Dad supposed, was outside. He leaned on the newel post
for a moment, smoking his cigarette, then he ambled
over to Lundy's 'secret' room. The door was open and he
entered.

"Lundy was sitting at his desk with his ordinary glasses
on, working over some figures. He grinned when he saw
who it was, but his eyes narrowed and his hand slipped
down to his gun belt. The cards and the poker chips were
still on the table, but the money, the check, and the transfer were gone.

"'Hello, Ten-to-One,' he drawled. 'What'll yuh have?'

"Dad glanced over his shoulder. Nobody had come after
him. The row downstairs was deafening. He shut the door.

"'Those cards and that other pair of glasses,' he said
coldly.

"'Huh!' Lundy grunted.

"'Yuh heard me!' Dad shot back at him.

"'What's eatin' ytih!' Lundy bawled. He got up, his
thumb hooked in his belt.

"Dad had intended to stay cool, but he was at the end
of his endurance and at Lundy's insolence his good intentions blew up.

"'You damned sharp!' he roared. 'Those cards are
marked. That pair of glasses you wore—'

"He didn't finish. Their forty-fives seemed to flash at
the same instant, Dad said, but his must have cracked
half a second sooner, for Lundy's slug plowed through the
brewery calendar and the pine boards behind it. Lundy

reeled sidewise against the table, dropping his gun; then he pitched to the floor and lay on his side. Blood began to trickle down his right temple.

"Dad was pretty badly shaken, I guess, but he couldn't pretend to regrets he didn't feel. Lundy was a rascal and he'd brought it on himself. Dad slid over to the door, expecting this would be the end. Well, he'd done his best. Uncle Jerry would take it like a man, he knew.

"When he opened the door he saw that the rush he had expected hadn't begun. It didn't look as if it were going to, either. The row was worse than ever and the crowd was guzzling Lundy's hospitality as if nothing had happened. Another tipsy miner had climbed onto a table and was emptying his gun at the roof. Several men were trying to take the weapon away from him. It didn't take Dad long to realize that the shooting upstairs had been identified with that downstairs and that it was supposed to be part of the general jollification.

"But just then he saw Fitch break away from a group of men near the front door and come slowly down the hall to the stair. Dad quickly shut the door. Fitch's casual gait didn't indicate that he suspected something was wrong— probably he was just coming up to satisfy himself that Dad was still with Lundy. And Lundy was dead on the floor!

"Dad had intended to submit the cards and Lundy's other pair of glasses to the miners, but with Lundy dead and the miners full of his cheap whisky, he doubted if this were wise. He was pretty sure it wasn't, in fact. They'd be more than likely to fall in with Fitch and Webb and Burke, lynch him and Uncle Jerry, and inquire into the merits of the case afterwards. He thought of the north window. No, there wouldn't be time. He must do better than that. An opportunity had been given to him—he must work it to the utmost.

"Could he trick Fitch into entering the room, then knock him over the head? Maybe. But there was something else in the back of his brain. 'Fermenting,' Dad said. He'd have it in a minute. Maybe he'd better tackle Fitch, though. But if Fitch were too quick for him, he'd have the mob pouring up like a young tornado, and with Lundy dead on the floor, they'd be wax in his hands.

"Wax!

"That was it, Uncle John.

"I suppose if Dad had had time to think it over he wouldn't have done it, but the idea took him unawares and he acted on the impulse. You know how it is. When you think a thing over at a sane moment you wonder how you got by with it. But you did get by.

"He slid over to the door and opened it an inch or so. Fitch was loitering on the stair, talking to one of the girls of the place. Good enough! Shutting the door, he hurried into that storeroom I mentioned a while back and struck a match. Professor Dryden Pope's wax figures stood in two rows near the door. They were a sad-looking crew, but not unlike the originals. The figures were half size—waist up.

"Dad grabbed Napoleon Bonaparte—the figure had lost his famous hat—and after pulling the table out of the immediate range of the light above, planked him down sidewise on the chair Lundy had occupied during the game. The gallery door was still shut. Dad rolled Lundy into the shadows behind the table, stripped him of his gray shirt, and drew it over Napoleon's head and shoulders. Then he crowned Napoleon with Lundy's Stetson, set Lundy's glasses on his nose, and lowered the light.

"Some one knocked on the door.

"Dad dropped into the chair, faced Napoleon, and casually lighted a cigarette. The illusion wasn't bad, he said. If Fitch contented himself with looking into the room it might work. But if he entered or spoke to Lundy, that was the end of it. Dad let his hand slide round his gun belt, at the same time blowing a cloud of cigarette smoke between himself and Napoleon.

"The door opened.

"Dad glanced over his shoulder. Fitch was looking in. Nodding casually to him, Dad exhaled more smoke into Napoleon's face. Sweat started out on his forehead and trickled down his cheeks, his heart seemed to be climbing into his windpipe. He said he wondered if there were any limit to what a man could endure. But he forced himself to address Napoleon.

"'I want to talk with you about that evidence, Lundy,' he said calmly.

"Fitch drew back and shut the door. Dad wiped the sweat out of his eyes, but he didn't move for at least a minute. Then he crept over to the door and peered out again. Fitch was leaning over the gallery rail, smoking a cigarette. Downstairs the hullabaloo was worse than ever. Everybody seemed crazy drunk. Celebrating his downfall, Dad reflected. Well, he'd show them a thing or two now. Good job he'd got over that notion of appealing to their sense of honor.

"He bent over Lundy and went through his pockets, but he found neither the mining transfer nor the check, although he recovered the original stake he had lost to Lundy on the final hand. What he had won between the start and the finish of the game he didn't touch. The check and the transfer weren't in the safe, Lundy's desk, or the pocket of Napoleon's shirt. He could think of nowhere else to look, so he went over the ground again. Without result.

"Dad didn't dare wait any longer. He'd stop payment of the check when he got out of the valley. Lundy's heirs would probably find the transfer and his loss would be the Two Brothers. A fair-sized loss, of course, but not as great as would be generally supposed, Dad said; for contrary to the local impression the greater part of the known richness of the mine had been exploited—although it was still a valuable property.

"But Dad stopped to look at the dummy and that second impulse took him. 'Why not make it two of a kind?' he said to himself. 'They might hold him if he only looked in.'

"If he'd thought about it first for, say, two solid minutes, he wouldn't have done it, for he hadn't one chance in ten of putting it over. But it was just another of those gambles he had been taking all his life and he didn't stop to think. That was Dad in those days, Uncle John.

"He glanced through the door again. Fitch still hung over the gallery rail, smoking. Shutting the door, Dad peeled off his shirt and hustled into the storeroom. Sitting Bull looked the likeliest candidate and he tore off the dummy's headdress, drew the silk shirt over its head and shoulders, and set it down on the chair opposite Napoleon. Then he put his own Stetson on Sitting Bull's head, well over the eyes, placed a chair so that the absence of legs wouldn't be easily noticed from the door, gave Napoleon's Stetson a cocky tilt, and considered the effect.

"'Not bad,' was his thought. And it wasn't bad in that light, Uncle John. I've seen those dummies.

"There was a handle on the outside of the door of Lundy's 'secret' room, then—it's gone now. When the door was unlocked, or unbolted—a bolt was inside—you turned the latch and pushed it open. Just then, the latch clicked.

"Dad dropped behind Napoleon's chair, puffing out cigarette smoke. The door opened an inch or so and Fitch's face appeared in the crack. Dad had to press his hands to his naked body to quieten the pounding of his heart. The door opened wider. Fitch must be coming in. Dad's hand slid around to his forty-five. But he found words on his lips instead.

"'What yuh want?' he snarled, in a fair imitation of Lundy's high-pitched voice.

"Fitch stopped. 'Nothin', Joe. I was jest takin' a look-see.'

"'Git out, then!' Dad shouted in the same voice. 'I'll call yuh when yore wanted!'

"Fitch slammed the door shut.

"Dad stood up, breathing hard. Pretty close, you'll admit, Uncle John. Of course, Fitch had no reason to believe the two figures he saw were not Dad's and Lundy's, and that was the long chance Dad had played, but I don't think one man in a hundred could have carried it off.

"It wasn't likely that Fitch would look in again for a while. Dad crammed the marked cards into a pocket and raised the sash of the north window to the top. He knew if any one were out below he'd be seen against the lighted window, but he'd have to risk that. Burke was probably watching the front and side windows. Climbing through, he dropped to the roof of the lean-to beneath it, then to the ground below. He listened. Nothing happened. He hadn't been seen, evidently. Dad felt pretty good at this, you may be sure, but he knew he'd have to be careful. The trick wouldn't be turned until he and Uncle Jerry were at the top of Pitchfork. He remembered, then, that he'd forgotten to bring Lundy's magnifying glasses. Well, he wasn't going back for them.

"The night shone like an ebony stick and as Dad plunged into it he had a queer sense of the desert's being alive and sentient. 'Sentient'—that's how he put it, Uncle John. I knew what he meant, too. Down there at night you feel as if you were in the grip of something you don't understand, but which understands you. Something elemental. Dad couldn't shake it off.

"He came to the mine property with his gun in his hand. There was no time to be lost and he called Dillon by name.

"But Dillon didn't answer. Dad called again. Still he didn't answer.

"Dad peered into the shadows of the overhang. He said its dark stillness seemed to flow out upon him like a deep river and lose itself in the shadowy sea of the open desert. Had Dillon laid some sort of a trap for him? he wondered. The quickest way to find out was to move towards the mine door, and this he proceeded to do. But Dillon wasn't in the shadow of the overhang. There was no sign of him anywhere. 'The desert looked empty of all life but my own,' Dad said.

"'Jerry!' he shouted.

"There was no answer and Dad's heart turned cold.

"'Jerry!' he roared. 'Jerry! Jerry! What's wrong with you? This is Alex!' And he hammered on the door with the butt of his forty-five.

"Uncle Jerry didn't answer and Dad took out his keys. The padlock and hasp were just as he had left them. Nothing could have happened, then. But his hands shook so that he could hardly fit the key into the lock and turn it. And when he had swung the door open the blackness of the tunnel seemed to catch him by the throat in a throttling grip. Ghastly, Dad said.

"He went into the tunnel, calling to Uncle Jerry. There was no reply. He found a match, but before he could strike it his feet collided with something soft and heavy. Uncle Jerry's name rose to his lips, but he couldn't articulate it. A minute passed before he was able to strike the match.

"It was Uncle Jerry he had stumbled over. He lay on his back dead with a bullet wound in his chest."

25
The Final Gesture

That sense of Greek tragedy to which I have referred, together with my previous knowledge, had prepared me for some such climax as this; and as Jerry's voice faded out again we found ourselves looking at one another with melancholy eyes. Jerry hadn't merely told us the story: he had made us live every minute of it. His boyish earnestness escapes me when I try to set it down on paper. I could think of nothing to say; and neither, apparently, could Henry. Presently he began again.

"The match went out. Dad found a bit of candle in one of his pockets. He struck another match, lighted the candle, and dropped the burning match. As the match touched the ground fire spurted up, sizzled for a moment, and burned out. Dad said he supposed a little powder had been spilled by one of the mine hands. Grief drove the incident out of his mind and I don't believe he remembered it for thirty years, Uncle John. There was no reason why he should have.

"Holding the candle, Dad knelt by the body. Uncle Jerry's face had a fierce, intent look on it, he said. His hands were clenched. The wound was around the heart. There was a good deal of blood. Dad's other gold-mounted pistol lay beside the body. Near it was a copy of the Torridity

weekly newspaper—the *Firebrand*. A story about the robbery at Lundy's was on the front page.

"Dad turned the cylinder of the forty-five. One cartridge had been discharged. He put the gun down and went
to the door with the light. The key he had pushed under
the door was where he had left it—between the truck rails.

"I can see now the look on his face as he went back to
the body, Uncle John. . . . He was quite sure what had happened. Uncle Jerry had concluded that Dad wouldn't be
able to do anything for him, he had become despondent,
and he had killed himself. His despondency had been natural, but it hadn't occurred to Dad that he'd take his own
life. And then Dad wondered if Uncle Jerry hadn't reasoned that he'd caused enough trouble and that this was
the better way out. He hoped it was that. In the days that
followed he made himself believe it was.

"Uncle Jerry was nearer to him than any one else—he
hadn't any one else, then. Those few minutes by Uncle
Jerry in that God-awful tunnel must have about torn the
bowels out of him. They became the keystone of his life—
the life he'd yet to live, I mean. He talked to the body as
if . . . as if Uncle Jerry were listening. The sweat stood out
on his face as he told me. He told me what he said . . . the
very words. I can hear them on his lips now. . . .

"'Why did you do it, son? . . . Didn't I tell you I'd get
you out? We'd have been heading for Pitchfork by this . . .
God, why didn't you make him wait?' Dad blamed himself
for taking Uncle Jerry to Torridity. 'It wasn't any place for
a colt of a kid like you. And you've left me. I don't blame
you, son! I failed you all along. I thought too much of
making money and being the big toad in this burned-out
puddle hole of a valley. . . . I'm through, son. You hear
me? . . . I'm pulling out tonight as I ought to have done
long ago. I've had enough raw meat to last me till I cash
in. . . . Maybe some day I'll feel you've forgiven me.'

"He began to think about giving Uncle Jerry decent burial. But where should he put him? Another of those impulses which had governed Dad's life struck him, then. Dad said it hit him like a bolt of lightning, but I believe he'd have done it, even if he'd had time to think it over. . . . He could never bring himself to work the mine again and as Uncle Jerry had chosen to die in it why not make it his tomb?

"'It was the only thing I could do for him,' he said, 'and it was the sort of extravagant gesture that appealed to me in those days. "A hundred thousand dollar tomb for Jerry," harmonized with that crazy pattern I had woven of my life—like "Ten-to-One" and "gold bullets" and "silver spurs."'

"The mine wasn't his, now, but if Lundy's heirs found the transfer, as they probably would, he'd negotiate for the property. Ninety or a hundred thousand should buy it back.

"Dad was still holding the candle and he had started to get up when the light flashed on the small blade of a clasp knife. It was Uncle Jerry's knife and there was a stub of indelible pencil beside it. The pencil hadn't been sharpened recently and Dad couldn't figure out what Uncle Jerry had used the knife for. But the pencil suggested a note and he picked up the newspaper. There wasn't any writing on it, but he noticed that part of the top margin, including the date line, of the back sheet, had been torn off, and Dad went through Uncle Jerry's pockets, fully expecting to find the missing scrap of paper with some word for him on it.

"A little money, some matches and cigarettes, and other odds and ends were all he found. There was no scrap of writing either on the body or near it, and he supposed that the margin had been torn before Uncle Jerry had come into the mine. Bitterly disappointed, he placed the knife, the pencil, and the other trifles on the newspaper.

"Dad got up, thinking of Dillon. Queer, his going off like that, he reflected. Perhaps he had decided that Jerry was safe enough and that he was wasting his time guarding the mine. That must be it. There was another queer thing, too, Dad thought. That wound in Jerry's chest. Suicides usually fired at their heads. Well, he couldn't get around the locked mine door, the key under the door where he had left it, and the exploded cartridge in the gun at Jerry's side. Jerry had killed himself right enough. He wished he could have got his hands on Jerry's pardner. Probably it was some one he didn't know. Pity the poor devil if Torridity got a rope around his neck!

"Dismissing these thoughts, Dad hurried outside. To do what he had in mind would take some little time and he hadn't a moment to spare. To tell the truth, Uncle John, I don't know how he could have expected Sitting Bull and Napoleon to carry off that deception long enough to give him time to make his preparations. Probably he didn't think about it until afterwards. But that was Dad—*then*. 'Ten-to-One' hadn't been tacked on to him for nothing.

"The town was still quiet. Dad looked up at the overhang. It clung to the mountainside, he said, as a slice of cheese which the cleaver hasn't completely severed clings to a half drum. He'd examined the overhang many times. He'd even had the base of it drilled to test its solidity. It was some two hundred feet high, Dad said, a hundred wide, and thirty thick at the bottom. The fissure between the overhang and the parent body varied in width from five to ten feet. The bottom of the fissure was some thirty feet above the top of the mine door and was fairly accessible by a rough trail.

"Dad went into the powder house and lighted a carbide lamp. There was plenty of dynamite. Getting a wheelbarrow, he began to trundle the stuff to the foot of the fissure trail, working desperately, reckless as ever of consequences. When he had got out as much of the dynamite as he thought he would need, he carried it into the fissure, a case at a time. There was still nothing doing off towards the town.

"The last case carried into the fissure, Dad rushed back to the powder house and gathered up a broken box of electric fuses, three great coils of copper wire, a battery box, a screw-driver, a hammer, and a pair of wire cutters. He left the battery box at the foot of the trail; the other articles and the carbide lamp he took up into the fissure.

"Dad forced the cases open, stuck fuses into two cartridges in each case, and attached two short lengths of copper wire to the other end of each fuse. He then shoved the dynamite, some of it loose, but most of it boxed, into old drillings, holes, and crevices at strategic points and packed it down with earth and rubble. The lengths of copper wire which stuck out of each pocket of dynamite he connected to his main lines.

"With the carbide lamp slung on his arm, he hurried down the trail, paying out the wires. Picking up the battery box, and still paying out the wires, he raced to a point about a hundred and fifty yards north of the overhang. The coils ran out there, and he connected them to the battery box. His gesture was about complete, Uncle John.

"He cut back to the building and looked in at the bunkhouse. None of his men were in—thanks to Lundy's free whisky—and he made for the stable. Gunpowder, the gray, whinnied to him but he saw nothing of Bluebell, the mare. Fredericks, his foreman, was fond of riding at night, and he supposed Fredericks had taken her, as he often did. So much the better. Dad watered and saddled the gray and led it outside.

"'We'll need everything you've got, old timer,' he whispered.

"He then drove the six mules out and switched them across their rumps. They ambled off a little way and stopped. It was the best he could do for them. Diving into his cabin, he wiped the sweat off his body, got into a clean shirt, clapped on an old Stetson, and picked up a half-filled water canteen. A last look around the cabin and he hurried outside, hung the canteen over the pommel of his saddle, and plunged into the mine, carrying the lamp. He said he couldn't go without another look at Uncle Jerry.

"Dad had just got to the mine door when he heard shouting off towards Torridity. Turning, he saw lights. The lights grew brighter, the shouting louder. He wondered what they'd done to Bull and Nap. Then he went in to Uncle Jerry. It took him a minute to steady his voice.

"'I'm here to tell you good-by, son,' he said. I can hear him saying it now, Uncle John. 'I'm giving you one grand funeral. It's all I can do. I reckon they'll not bother you. You can lie here forever. . . . Can you hear me, son?'

"He dropped to his knees and tried to recall the burial service, but it wouldn't come; so he repeated the Lord's prayer. Slowly, clearly, calmly, Dad said. His telling of it made me think of a cathedral service.

"The shouting began to boom in the tunnel. Dad picked up Jerry's knife, cigarettes, and money. The pencil had rolled off somewhere. He slipped the newspaper under the head, folded the arms, and took up the gold-mounted gun. But as he slid the gun into his holster a thought struck him and he drew it out again and placed it beside the body. It was just another of Dad's impulses, Uncle John. A good soldier—he was always going to think of Uncle Jerry, as that—had a right to be buried with his weapons. . . . Besides, as Dad put it, 'I'd done with gold-mounted guns and gold bullets and silver spurs and all that frippery.' He said it had come upon him with crushing force that his life had been nothing but one extravagant gesture after another. Uncle Jerry's funeral was to be his last gesture.

"'Good-by, son,' he whispered.

"A last look and he was racing for Gunpowder. In the saddle he sent the gray charging at the battery box, drew up, picked up the box, and with the plunger raised peered off towards Torridity. He could just see a fan-shaped shadow sweeping across the burned-out plain. They were after blood, by the row they were making.

"Dad knew that he hadn't a second to lose, yet he hesitated to drive the plunger down. He made his thoughts during that moment particularly clear to me, Uncle John. The simple act of driving the plunger down would seal Uncle Jerry up in the mountain, it would end his own activity in the Skull, it might even bring about the abandonment of the town. And in a strictly personal sense, it would mark the ending of one phase of his life and the beginning of another. He was through with posing and fool nicknames and crazy gambles for the rest of his life.

"The shadow swept on towards the mine. Dad shut his eyes for an instant; then he shoved the plunger down and flung the battery box away. Gunpowder shot forward.

"Dad said nothing happened for a split second or so, and he had a horrible fear that his connections were faulty. Hell broke loose, then. He thought his eardrums would burst beneath the roar of the explosion. The ebony night smoked and rocked. Gunpowder screamed like a witch and went on like a rocket. Dad thought he saw the fan-shaped shadow crumple back on itself. A fearful grinding, crunching, crashing sound followed the roar and it seemed to Dad that the entire eastern flank of the Skeletons was sliding down into the Skull. Gravel and pebbles showered upon him and as they pelted Gunpowder's haunches the gray screamed again and went on like a cannon ball. . . .

"It was just dawn when Dad got to the top of Pitchfork. As he looked down over the Skull he felt as if he were tearing its fingers from his throat. He swung the gray around and faced the west. It was then that the name he had been looking for came to him. 'Andrew Ogden.' It was a good name. . . .

"That's the Torridity story, Uncle John."

26
The Lead Bullet

The throb and beat of Jerry's voice ceased on that final word and we sat in silence again. Lucy was weeping softly, I had to dab furtively at my eyes, and Henry blew his nose more vigorously than usual. Our reactions to the Torridity story were precisely the same, I suspect. We had lived through an emotional experience of great intensity. Horror and grief and terror, pervaded always by a sense of relentless tragedy, had followed one another in swiftly changing sequences. And then the end of the drama had plunged us, emotionally exhausted, into the depths. It would take us a minute or two to get over our sickness of spirit.

Jerry's dark eyes had glowed and hardened and his lean face had flushed and whitened beneath the dramatic sweep of his tale and I had been reminded of that other Jerry whom Andrew had left in the Two Brothers mine. Poor Andrew! Life had thrust a knife into his heart and kept it there.

The precision with which the fragmentary evidence MacNair and Deacon and I had discovered fitted into the various parts of Jerry's story was amazing. Our evidence had suggested much, but it actually had revealed little, and this exquisite dovetailing of cause and effect fascinated me. Even my experience in the "secret" room had become clear. Wax figures, indeed! But the less said about *that* the better!

I had not missed the pathos of Furie's devotion to his Bull and Nap. For thirty years he had guarded and cherished them! No wonder his terror that they might be destroyed or taken from him had driven him to deceive me about the room into which I had fallen! They were a shabby substitute for human society, but the desert does strange things to a man, and I thought I knew what they had come to mean to his longing, lonely spirit. Poor Furie! I gave Bull and Nap credit for saving what sanity was left to him.

Our case was far from complete, however. Jerry, I believed, had more to tell us.

"And so," Henry muttered, breaking the silence, "that was the 'poker game that cracked the town.'"

Jerry nodded, his eyes brooding. "Torridity was abandoned shortly afterwards. . . . I wish I could have put it in the way Dad did. Made you understand what it did to him, I mean."

"You have," I told him gently. "Many things are clear to me now."

"I never felt as if I really knew him," the boy went on. "We were always good pals, of course, but sometimes he seemed like two men."

"Perhaps you thought of him as wearing a mask."

"That's it!" he exclaimed. "I never felt as if I were looking right at him. There seemed to be something in between us. A mask, yes. But sometimes the mask slipped. It's a queer thing to say about one's father."

I nodded understandingly, but Lucy shook her head.

"It was the real Uncle Andrew shining through the mask," she said, with deeper insight than ours. "That awful game, and finding Uncle Jerry dead, and that last gesture—they must have done dreadful things to him. Poor Uncle Andrew!"

"It meant changing his speech, his mode of living, his outlook on life," Henry observed thoughtfully. "But fundamentally he remained the same. A man can't change his nature—much."

"Only sometimes the mask wore thin," I added sadly.

Jerry shut his eyes, his face haggard again. "When I think of the way I harried him about opening that mine!" he groaned.

It was hard to really find one's father and lose him in the space of an hour or two and I started up, intending to drop my arm over his shoulder, but Lucy was before me. Sliding onto the wing of his chair, she gently drew his head to her breast and ran her fingers softly through his dark hair. Collecting pistols is all very well so far as it goes, but it came upon me then that I had missed much of what life has to offer.

"You had better tell us the rest of it, Jerry," I said quietly, as the boy looked up, himself again.

He nodded. "Dad had no trouble about the mine. It was never claimed and he concluded that the transfer hadn't been found. He waited a few years, then he had it transferred to his new name. Queer, what happened to the transfer and the check, isn't it? If Lundy didn't leave the room between the end of the game and when Dad shot him, neither did the transfer and the check—unless Lundy passed them on to some one else, which doesn't seem likely."

"His mind is a blank about what happened to him that night," I said. "He won't know what he did with the papers—or that there were any such papers, for that matter. He must have hidden them so well that nobody has been able to find them. I don't know why he should have."

"The transfer may have been found," Deacon suggested, "and nothing been done with it."

"Hmn," I said thoughtfully, for certain things were becoming clearer to me. "In my opinion the transfer and the check are still where Lundy put them. I've an idea several people have been looking for them. But go on, Jerry."

"Dad stopped payment of the check he had given Lundy, so his bank account was intact. He came up here and put everything he had into land-and-water development. You know what happened. He made the San Felipe valley fertile and he founded the town of San Felipe. Everything he touched prospered. He had wanted to erase as much of the past as he could and he had changed his name and his mode of life. But he knew that somebody was bound to recognize him as time went on and beyond taking another name he hadn't tried to conceal his former identity. Of course he didn't figure on blackmail. But this devil, Dillon, whom Lundy set to guard the mine that night, had, and about five years after Dad came into the San Felipe, he turned up and demanded five thousand a year to keep his mouth shut about the killing of Lundy.

"Dad paid him. I think his decision to do so was a pretty good indication of the change that had come over him since his Torridity days. It wasn't cowardice, of course. As a matter of fact, he always doubted Dillon's ability to make the charge stick. But Dad had married, I was born, and mother was in delicate health. If Dad had kicked Dillon out he would have involved himself a nasty mess and the shock would probably have finished her. So he paid. Mother's health remained about the same until she died ten years ago, and Dad continued to pay. I doubt if in his Torridity days anything under heaven would have made him submit to blackmail. After mother's death he shrank from opening up the case on my account, and he went on paying. A man can get used to anything, I suppose.

"'I don't think Dillon could have made it stick,' Dad said the other afternoon, 'but it would have opened up the ghastly affair and the papers would have screamed from one end of the country to the other. It wouldn't have been good for you. A youngster doesn't easily live down that sort of thing and I didn't feel like taking any chances with your career—especially after the mess your Uncle Jerry had made of his life.' It was conservative Andrew Ogden who said that, not Ten-to-One Peterson, Uncle John," Jerry commented grimly. "Of course, he overestimated the effect the scandal would have had on me, but he couldn't forget Uncle Jerry.

"Dad had made a barrel of money and the five thousand a year meant nothing to him. Dillon sent him a poker chip every year to remind him that the money was due. I suppose this condition of affairs would have gone on indefinitely if it hadn't been for Dillon himself, Mrs. Lundy, and that old desert rat, Furie, who, it turned out, never left Torridity.

"A month ago Dillon overplayed his hand. He demanded a hundred thousand dollars. If Dad came through he'd cancel the yearly payment for ever. If he didn't, he'd make the Lundy affair public. Dad had got into the way of paying the five thousand without protest and this jolt was just what he needed. He blew up and told Dillon he'd never get another cent. Dillon gave him a month to change his mind.

"This was the situation when Dad tumbled into Mrs. Lundy last week. She was soliciting subscriptions for some fool religion. Dad was struck by her name and he took her into the house. It turned out that she was the wife of Joe Lundy, the Torridity resort-keeper. You can imagine Dad's state of mind when she told him Lundy hadn't died. Dillon had been blackmailing him for twenty-five years for killing a man who wasn't dead!"

"Do you know who this man Dillon is?" Deacon demanded sharply.

"I don't. Dad did, of course, but he wouldn't tell me. He said he was going to handle him in his own way. I suppose that's why he sent for this detective, Luther Mac-Nair." A grim look crept into Jerry's face. "He was afraid I might go after Dillon myself."

The boy's tone made me think of Ten-to-One Peterson.

"Furie was next. Queer, isn't it, how life breaks in bunches? Dad had crammed enough to fill a lifetime into those last few hours in Torridity. Thirty years of comparative quiet, then the thing comes to a head, as it were. You can't get away from life. We had a bit of an earthquake two months ago, you remember. It came from Skull Valley way, where it seems to have been pretty violent. It shook open another entrance to the Two Brothers mine and uncovered a rich vein of gold in a hanging wall of quartz. This new vein is a good deal richer than the one Dad worked thirty years ago. I should say there are a couple of millions in it, Uncle John. Furie got into the mine through the split and found the new vein. He'd been gold crazy for fifty years or more, so you can imagine what it did to him."

"Deacon and I have met Furie," I said dryly. "We know about the vein."

"A queer old bird, isn't he? Did you notice his eyeglass? That came out of Lundy's magnifying glasses. But the mine. You know how I nagged Dad to let me open it. I'd give a good deal not to have said some of the things I did." The boy fell silent, his eyes brooding; then he went on again. "Furie came to see Dad Friday afternoon. He didn't recognize him. His sight is bad and a good deal of his memory is gone. The transfer of the mine from Alex Peterson to Andrew Ogden for a nominal sum was a matter of record and Furie came to Dad believing him to be a new owner of the mine. He hasn't the remotest idea who Dad is—was.

"Furie brought a specimen from the new vein and he said he figured he was entitled to a fifty-fifty share in the profits. He has some claim, of course, but when Dad realized that Furie had violated Uncle Jerry's tomb he went crazy. What else had Furie done or found in the mine? Well, Furie had found a gold-mounted forty-five and 'a passel o' bones.' One of the back rib bones had a 'bullet stickin' in it.' Oh, and 'thar wuz a water canteen, a bit o' candle, some buttons, a belt, a pa'r o' boots with plenty o' w'ar in 'em still, an' the like.' Dad must have gone mad for the moment. Furie had dared to violate Uncle Jerry's remains! After he had sealed them up! Closed the mine forever! Where was the gun? Furie had sold it that morning. Dad seized him by the throat. It's a wonder he didn't kill the old rascal. To whom had he sold it? That suave old stick, Nathan Hyde, it seemed. Dad sprang to the telephone, but Hyde had already sold the forty-five to you. And you, it happened, were out."

"I'd give my right arm to have been in!" I whispered. "Go on, boy."

"Furie was whimpering and snarling on the floor where Dad had dropped him. But he was scared and he must have got it into his head that Dad was raving because of the value of the pistol. Anyhow, he pulled out the contents of one of his trousers pockets and planked them down on the desk. 'That's the price o' the six gun. I'll split ye fifty-fifty, Andry Ogden.' Among the trash mixed up with the money was a bit of metal. Furie pounced on it. 'An' that's the bullet that wuz stuck in his rib!' he shouted. Dad got the shock of his life, then. You see, Uncle John, it had never occurred to him in all these years that Jerry hadn't committed suicide. Now, if Jerry had killed himself, the bullet would be gold.

"It was lead!"

I sat bolt upright in my chair and Deacon all but leaped out of his.

"Dad was stunned. His insane rage became the cold rage of Ten-to-One Peterson. He put Furie out and started to think the thing through. It meant upsetting the assumptions of a lifetime, but he soon got it straight. Do you see it, Uncle John?"

"See it?" I shouted. "Of course I see it! And so does Deacon. Lundy hired Dillon, the ex-Pinkerton man to trap Jerry. Dillon got him and double-crossed Lundy by persuading or forcing Jerry to go in with him on something bigger. Jerry agreed and he was caught. Lundy naturally set Dillon on guard outside the mine. As soon as the crowd, and your father, and the men watching him, had gone, Dillon spoke to Jerry, told him to push out the key your father had thrust under the door. Jerry, thinking he was to be freed, obeyed. Dillon opened the door and shot him.

"Why? Because he reasoned that when Jerry felt a rope around his neck, as he probably would, he'd try to save his own life by exposing the plot and naming his accomplice. Dillon himself would have done that very thing. He saw no danger in shooting Jerry. In fact, he thought it safer than freeing the boy and getting away with him. He would report that he had heard a shot in the mine. The miners and your father would investigate. They would find the door locked, the key under it, and Jerry dead with his brother's pistol at his side, one chamber exploded. Being a stranger, he probably knew nothing of Peterson's gold bullets and he reasoned that his alibi was perfect.

"But before Dillon could get hold of Jerry's gold-mounted pistol and discharge it to account for the bullet hole in Jerry's body and thereby insure a verdict of suicide, Jerry, who was mortally wounded, managed to put a bullet in him. The impact knocked Dillon down. Jerry was dying, but in one of those bursts of strength that sometimes come to a man in the last moments of life he penciled those few words we found, stowed them away in the cartridge case, and reloaded the gun. Obviously, he wanted his brother to see the note first and he thought this was the safest way of getting it to him. I expect he reasoned like this: If he stuffed the note into the muzzle of the gun his brother wouldn't see it and it would be destroyed the first time the weapon was discharged; if he rammed it into the empty shell Peterson would probably throw it away; but if he concealed it in an *unexploded* cartridge Peterson, who was a two-gun man and therefore certain to look to the condition of his weapon *at once,* was bound to see that the cartridge had been tampered with, as soon as he broke the gun to replace the empty shell. It never occurred to him that Peterson would leave 'the soldier his weapon.' Jerry died a minute or so later.

"Dillon now came to himself. Seeing that Jerry was dead, he crawled out of the mine, locked the door, thrust the key under it, and—this is surmise, but I'd bet on it—fought his way to the stable, *saddled the mare, Bluebell, and took himself off.* Later on, if he found out that Peterson's bullets were gold, he realized that his alibi was not perfect. It held, however. It held for thirty years—but only because Peterson contented himself with revolving the cylinder of the forty-five and 'left the soldier his weapon.' Trifles are significant sometimes. . . . Are these the conclusions your father came to, Jerry?"

"Just about, Uncle John. Of course he didn't know of that note Lucy told me you found in the gun."

"And you, Henry?"

"I'd like to hear about the young man's departure from his home the night Andrew was killed," Deacon responded dryly.

"I was coming to that," Jerry went on. "You can guess Dad's state of mind. Thirty years of repression had taught him a thing or two, but he was wild to bring Dillon to justice. First, he'd have to take me into his confidence, though, and he called me in and told me everything. It took him quite a while to get it all out and when he had finished it was after eight o'clock. Talking continuously for so long cooled him down and cleared his head, but getting the whole tragic story in a couple of hours like that threw me off my balance. I wanted to kill Dillon with my bare hands and make it as long and painful as I could. Dad refused to tell me who he was. He smoothed me down and we quietly talked the thing out.

"Uncle Jerry must have proper burial. The mine was open. Other people would be getting into it. If Furie talked, as he probably would, we'd have a rush on our hands and a city population camped around the mine a week after the news got about. Naturally, we didn't want Uncle Jerry's tomb turned into a stamping ground for the gold diggers and mining camp riffraff in the West. Dad wasn't particularly interested in the new vein itself, but with Uncle Jerry buried in the family plot in Felipe, where Dad had come to the conclusion he ought to be, his objection to reopening the mine would be gone, and he wanted me to make the most of Furie's discovery. Incidentally, not forgetting Furie.

"Meanwhile, the mine was still Uncle Jerry's tomb and intruders must be kept out of it until we could get an undertaker down there. The thought of people stumbling over him, as Furie evidently had . . . was horrible. Some one must go down there. I was the logical one and Dad said I'd better leave in the morning. But morning wasn't quick enough for me. I was going that night—at once. There was a moon at midnight and I'd been down Pitchfork half a dozen times. Dad finally agreed and I asked him what he was going to do about Dillon.

"'Hang him if it takes every dollar I've got!' he said grimly. The look on his face made me think of Ten-to-One Peterson. 'You'd better be off, if you are going tonight, son,' he went on. 'I'll follow you in a day or two. Stay there until I come. Don't forget food and water. And you'd better carry a gun.'

"'You'll explain to Lucy, Dad?' I asked. 'She's singing at the Chesters'.'

"He promised that he would and he said he'd see you, Uncle John, and tell you everything. Either you or he would bring Lucy home. Those were about his last words to me."

Jerry paused, that brooding look in his eyes again, and we respected his silence.

"It was around nine, now," he resumed. "Driving into town, I stocked up with water, food, and gasoline, and set off. It was midnight when I reached the top of Pitchfork. The moon had come up, just past the full, and the trail was bright as a new dollar, but I had a tough time getting down. It was nearly dawn when I got to Torridity. There was no one there. I drove out to the mine at once."

"Uncle Jerry was there, just as Furie had said. I sat down and looked at him for a while . . . wondering about things. Of course, I was glad he hadn't killed himself. Dad was, too. Queer how a bit of lead fired thirty years ago was still changing the course of human lives—Dad's, Dillon's, mine. I put in most of the day looking over the new vein and the old workings.

"In the afternoon I drove back to the village and went into Lundy's Place. It was like going into a cemetery. All the things Dad had told me flooded my mind. You'd think the place had been abandoned yesterday. But you were there yourself, Uncle John. I went up to the 'secret' room. It—it was like going onto sacred ground. And there were the dummies, pretty nearly as Dad had left them thirty years ago! And Furie was with 'em—he'd just got back— he'd come up to see if they were all right. And—you've got to believe me, Uncle John—he was talking to them and pretending to play poker with 'em. He often does, it turned out. There were chips on the table. It was a show-down. Sitting Bull had three aces! I thought Furie was going to shoot me when I walked in on him, but I calmed him down and he talked a little. The room was a sort of 'holy place' to him, too. He didn't want anybody there. Bull and Nap were all the company he'd had for thirty years and he'd got so he didn't want anybody else. It was pitiable.

"The next day a car drove into the village, but it didn't come up to the mine. And a couple of hours later—Lucy came. We didn't see you, Uncle John."

"I know something about Furie and Bull and Nap, and their poker game," I said feelingly. "Lucy came, you say?"

There was more to follow, I suspected, for with the finish of his story Jerry's voice had dropped oddly and that queer defiant expression had come into Lucy's eyes. Deacon looked at me grimly and afterwards I wondered if he had guessed.

"What then?" I asked encouragingly.

Lucy slowly drew out of her breast a slender pink rib-bon which hung around her neck. "We were married in San Miguel yesterday afternoon, Uncle John," she said.

27
"Who is Dillon?"

I stared unbelievingly at the circlet of gold on the end of the ribbon. And then the full force of the announcement broke upon me. Married! I had lost her! It pinned me, sick and old, into my chair until an uprush of anger at Jerry gave me release. He must have felt the wind of its coming, for he took the words out of my mouth.

"I know what you are going to say, Uncle John!" he poured forth in grief-stricken tones. "I'm a cad to have done such a thing! I don't blame you. Dad dead and not buried—this murder charge hanging over my head—and letting Lucy tie herself up with me! It was a beastly thing to do! Get it out of your system. It's coming to me, God knows!"

"Oh, Jerry!" Lucy cried distressfully. "How can you say that!" And then, so gently that my anger was softened: "It isn't coming to you! You are giving Uncle John a wrong impression. Please keep quiet while I tell him about it, dear."

Her dark eyes, tender, earnest, yet unafraid, held mine.

"Jerry is trying to shield me. It was entirely my fault. He didn't know about his father until this morning. We started back as soon as I told him."

"You didn't tell him until *this morning!*" I exclaimed incredulously.

"If I had told him when I found him he wouldn't have—married me."

"Hardly!" Jerry mumbled.

"But why—what— You young idiots!" I roared, recovering myself. "Couldn't you have waited until this thing was cleared up?"

"Don't you see?" Lucy said patiently. "If a man doesn't need a wife when he's in trouble, when does he need one?"

"Oh!" I gasped, and my anger suddenly left me. "Oh, that's it!" I felt as if I hadn't known Lucy until this moment.

Jerry yearned over her, but she pushed him aside and came to me, her lips trembling.

"You always said I was a funny little thing, Uncle John, but you've been such a dear!" She kissed me and I began to melt like butter. "Jerry was in serious trouble—you and I didn't doubt him for a single minute, but—things looked bad for a while. If—if he should be arrested I wanted my right to stand by him to be a legal one. Don't you see? And there was only one way I could do it. You've always taught me to think things out for myself and what I did seemed right. It nearly broke my heart to deceive him. And I couldn't, I simply *couldn't,* tell him last night—our wedding night. It was dreadful—telling him—this morning. You—you won't scold us, will you, Uncle John?"

Scold them! How could I? Keen as was my sense of loss, my grief was nothing in comparison with the tragedy of Andrew's life. Clever Lucy! She had known what she was doing when she had made Jerry tell his story first. It was a splendid thing she had done, marrying a man with a murder charge over his head, even though she believed him innocent; but it was the sort of romantic, audacious, illogical thing Lucy would do. To me her mind was still an unexplored country. It was ever opening up before me new and enchanting vistas, but this was, I think, the loveliest vista of them all.

"It was fine of you, dear," I told her gently, pressing her tightly to me. "Jerry, if you ever fail this girl of yours I'll take you apart with a jackknife.

"I hope you will, Uncle John," he mumbled earnestly. "Lucy is too fine for me. And she's trying to make it easy for me, bless her, but—well, I can't help feeling that I failed Dad. He told me to stay there until he came. I had gone on my own insistence as much as his—and—I quit my job. When Lucy told me about him—this morning—on top of what I'd done—it pretty nearly finished me."

The boy suddenly dropped his head into his hands. Lucy, with a little cry, ran over to him and, falling on to her knees, put her arms around him. They were quiet for a moment.

"He didn't want to come away," Lucy said tenderly, "but I told him I'd stay there until he did—and that he didn't love me—and that if he didn't want me then he needn't have me ever—"

"Didn't want you!" Jerry burst forth, lifting his head and seizing her shoulders. "I've been crazy for you ever since I left college! And—well, I've got you!" And with this he kissed her very competently indeed. "When she said she'd stay down there until I changed my mind and wanting her the way I did— Oh, damn it, Uncle John! what could I do? I gave Furie twenty dollars to keep his eye on the mine—and what was in it. I hoped we'd be back the next day, but the sandstorm held us up most of the night. That's all."

"Furie earned his twenty dollars," I said grimly. "Don't feel too badly, son. I imagine most of us would have done the same under the circumstances. Eh, what, Henry?" and I turned to Deacon who had been decent enough to hold his tongue.

"Young fools!" he growled. "I suppose it's the sort of thing that's done nowadays."

I chuckled reminiscently. "So I'm told. But if I remember rightly, the young lady who became Mrs. Deacon wouldn't have you unless you eloped with her in the romantic manner. I believe you had to hoist a ladder to her window—"

Henry raised a hand, grinning. "All right, John. They are forgiven." I suppose he was thinking of his imprisonment behind my poor door. "Let's get back to Dillon."

"Dillon, yes!" Jerry exploded. "Dillon's our man. Do you know who he is?"

"Quietly, my boy," I protested. "We are getting there as fast as we can. Tell me: you were wearing white flannels Friday night?"

"Yes. But I changed into these khaki duds before I left."

"Where?"

"In that little room off the library."

"And you left your flannels in that room."

"Yes."

"Were your keys in one of the pockets?"

"They were."

"What time did you leave your father?"

"At fifteen after nine. I looked at my watch."

"I suppose you went out by the hall door?"

"Yes."

"And you went straight to the garage?"

"I did."

"You saw no one?"

"No one, Uncle John."

I rounded again upon Deacon. "Satisfied?"

"Some time ago," he cried heartily. When Henry is convinced he is wrong he always admits it manfully. "You were right, John. Dillon is our man. He killed Andrew, dressed in the boy's flannels, and later planted them behind Lundy's bar. But I haven't any idea who he is. Has MacNair? Where is MacNair, by the way?"

I didn't know.

Deacon was thoughtful for a moment. Then he said: "Did Mrs. Lundy say if her husband is able to get about?"

I nodded. "He is. Why?"

"Nothing. I was just wondering. If his memory is gone I don't suppose he could recognize Dillon. You were right about the motive, too. Andrew was killed because he had found out that his brother Jerry did not commit suicide. Yes, Dillon is our man."

"But who is Dillon?" Jerry shouted tempestuously.

Just then the telephone rang. I took off the receiver.

28
The Last Illusion

When I hung the receiver up two minutes later Deacon, Lucy, and Jerry were looking at me with varying degrees of interest. I had kept my expression casual, but it would hardly have been possible for them not to have sensed something of the emotion released in my breast.

"You'll have to excuse me, Deacon," I said carelessly. "A man has just called me about a matter I must attend to at once. I'm sorry. Your car is at the door, isn't it, Jerry? Do you mind if I use it?"

"Help yourself, Uncle John. The sand storm made a mess of the enamel. Shall I drive you?"

"No, you'd better stay with Lucy."

He didn't repeat the offer and I smiled understandingly. Lucy gave me a quizzical look and Henry a surprised one, but I met them blandly and the expression receded in Lucy's eyes and died away in Deacon's. Meanwhile, I had got my little red notebook out, carelessly fingered the pages, and stowed it away in my vest pocket. In the same careless fashion I now opened the right-hand bottom drawer of my desk, took out my thirty-eight automatic and slipped it into my coat pocket. From where they were none of the three could have seen the pistol.

"I'll get back as soon as I can, Henry," I said, standing up.

He nodded. "I was going, anyhow. I wish MacNair was here. He has a way of getting behind facts."

"You never can tell about MacNair," I commented. "He's apt to turn up when you least expect him."

"Whom are you going to see, Uncle John?" Lucy wanted to know.

"A man," I said irritably. "Don't bother me, girl."

But as Deacon and I went out together I felt that she wasn't satisfied. Henry drove off. Most of the enamel had been scoured off Jerry's roadster, but the windshield was intact. I started the engine.

"Uncle John!"

Lucy had come running after me and I looked into her serious face as she put her foot on the running board.

"Well?"

"Why did you take your pistol?" she demanded breathlessly. "Was it Mr. MacNair who telephoned? Does he know something about Dillon?"

It wasn't a bad guess and I was tempted to tell her it was Dillon who had called me. Discretion came to me in time and I said instead:

"Little girls should be seen and not heard. Go back to your husband, Lucy."

The roadster slid forward and, as I accelerated, leaped into the avenue. A glance over my shoulder showed me Lucy still standing at the curb, bewildered and troubled of expression and distractingly pretty in the warm glow of the late afternoon sun. No wonder Jerry had let her persuade him into that fantastic elopement! What man with salt in his blood could have resisted her! The roadster rounded a bend in the avenue and she was gone.

How long would her suspicions allow her to remain inactive, I wondered.

It was just four now. Night would catch me halfway down Pitchfork. Well, it couldn't be helped. At the first oil station I tanked up with gas and water. I also filled the canteens I had found in the roadster and got a supply of food at a lunch counter. Turning south, then east, I got beyond the city limits. The open country was before me and I sent the roadster on at a terrific rate, praying that I might not encounter a traffic officer.

I love speed. Under any other circumstances I should have thrilled to the quiver of the wheel beneath my hands, but my mind was on Dillon's challenge. He had flung it at me over the wire with a dramatic suddenness, a colossal impudence, that had torn unqualified acceptance of his terms from me before I knew what I was saying. Life or death: which was to be my portion, and which his? Well, I was going through with the thing. It wasn't the first time I had carried my life in my hand. Old dogs might as well break their teeth as lose them.

It was nearly sunset when I got to the top of the Skeletons. As I looked down into the vaporous beauty of the Skull my mind dropped through the well of the years and I saw Alex Peterson flying on the wings of the morning from the scene of his terrific last gesture. A full minute I lingered there, then I moved the car forward into the descent. The last third of the way was covered in darkness and I drove drenched in sweat and with death perched on my shoulder; but luck or the devil must have been with me for I reached the bottom without mishap. A draught of water refreshed me, and I swung onto the Torridity trail.

There was no moon, but the top of the night shone like a jeweler's window.

As the car throbbed over the cindered trail that subterranean life Peterson had sensed seemed to pulse beneath my hands. It throbbed up my arms, it invaded my being. It roused in me something of dread, a bubbling expectancy, a suffocating suspense. The hot wind on my cheeks fanned these strange emotions and I sought relief by taking in the aspect of the desert night. Sand. Cacti. An outcropping of rock sharp as a tiger's tooth. And overhead the brilliant bowl of the night. Ugh! Tenuous fingers encircled my throat. I rode in a splendid tomb, but a tomb. Was it to be mine? I had been a fool to come! Nonsense, I hadn't!

I made out a huddle of buildings in the ebony gloom ahead. But as I peered over the spreading flare of my lights at the buildings, it seemed to me that the town crouched rather than huddled and again I had that feeling of inorganic matter curiously alive. Instead of driving up to Lundy's, I stopped at the head of the crooked street, shut off the engine, and got out. The brooding quietness of the place must have bewitched me for I neglected to switch off my lights. This error nearly cost me my life.

Crack!

As the bullet whined past a matter of six or eight inches above my head, I dropped against the side of the car. The shock of this abrupt rending of the silence held me rigid for a moment; then I reached into the car and switched off the lights. Here was something definite, something I might get my hands on. A feeling of exultation overcame me. I pondered. The flash of the rifle had come from one of the upper side windows of Lundy's Place. So long as I remained in shadow I was fairly safe. Was it Dillon who had fired at me? Everything pointed towards such a conclusion, and yet, for some unaccountable reason, I wasn't sure that it was Dillon.

Pistol in hand, I slid around the back of the car and dived into the shadow of the first building at that end of the street. And then into the shadow of the next and the next until I had come into the shapeless shadow of Lundy's Place. I saw no one, heard nothing; but my previous experience in the resort was still vivid in my mind and it took every ounce of courage I possessed to get myself to the door.

Noiselessly entering the place, I stood with my back to the wall, expecting another shot. It did not come. A tomb couldn't have been quieter. I drew breath. But the stillness did not deceive me. There was at least one person in that building who sought my life. And I was as certain as I was of my own existence that the events which had begun in Torridity thirty years before were to run out their course this night. Oddly enough, I felt as if I were the tool of forces outside of myself; and although I am a timid man I did not permit the reflection that a broken tool does not mar the beauty of the finished marble to turn me back.

I quietly took off my shoes and padded over to the stair. There I paused and listened again. Still no sign of human presence, but I was not deceived. My senses knew. I started softly up the stair. Halfway to the top a sprung board creaked beneath my stockinged feet. It was the board that had betrayed me to Dillon on Sunday night. Reaching the top, I stood with my hand on the newel post.

I saw a light!

A thin line of yellow light, it lay along the floor of the gallery at the bottom of the west end of the north wall and I knew it came from under the door of Lundy's room—the room I had fallen into. I moved towards the door and pushed upon it. It was unlatched. Pistol leveled, I entered. There was no one in the room. The door swung to behind me.

The room was just as I had expected.

A dirty coal oil lamp hung crookedly from the ceiling and shed a feeble glow upon a flat-topped desk, several chairs, a cot with a broken leg, an old-fashioned safe, the door of which was open, and a round table with a deck of cards and stacks of poker chips on it. The north window was broken. Dust and sand furred everything which had escaped constant human contact. Otherwise, the room

looked as it must have done thirty years ago and I, like
Jerry, felt as if I were treading on holy ground.

The wax figures faced each other across the table. Time
and heat and dirt had blurred their resemblance to the
famous warriors they counterfeited, but at first glance
they looked fairly human and not untypical of the country. Stetson hats, one of them with a silver buckle, hung
over their brows; their shirts had faded from the original
white and gray to the dun hue of sand. I could not resist a
sheepish grin at myself for being such an ass Sunday night.

A large brewery calendar ornamented by the face and
form of a voluptuous lady hung on the south wall. Its
year was 1896 and the July sheet, yellow and flyblown,
was uppermost. Sundry scribbling and initials defaced
the mount. The calendar sheets were quite large and they
had evidently shown a disposition to curl for three thumb
tacks held them down at the lower corners and center. The
calendar was a curio in more ways than one and I determined to have it before I left.

"Drop yer gun an' reach!"

The shrill command smote me like the blow of a fist. I
did not move. The automatic hung slackly from my hand
and I knew better than to raise it. Furious at myself and
my mania for collecting, I waited.

"Drop it, ye two-legged varmint!" the voice screamed
passionately. "Drop it or I'll slop yer innards over the
floor!"

I dropped the pistol.

"Face round whur I kin see ye!"

I swung slowly on my heel. Before me was the storeroom Jerry had mentioned and which I, like a fool, had
forgotten. It must have been shut when I came in or I
would have noticed it; now it was open. At first, I saw not
Furie, for he stood within the shadows of the room, but
the long barrel of an old-fashioned Colt, then the ancient

hand that held it, and finally, as he emerged from the obscurity of the storeroom into the yellow lamplight, the old desert-rat himself.

His appearance at that moment was the picture I was to retain of him until the end of my days. His hat registered itself on my memory first. Deep yellow and coarse-strawed, it was of a style in vogue several years ago. A red band encircled the crown through a break in which stuck a bristle of white hair. His shirt was equally astonishing. A combination of green and purple devices, it looked like the discarded regalia of a stillborn American fraternal order. Evidently his recent trip to civilization had been effective in more ways than one. The wild rage of his face transfixed me. His lips were twitching and froth-flecked and curled back over the toothless gums. The deep sunken, malevolent eyes were shot with red from the inflamed lids and it came upon me overwhelmingly that the man was murderously insane and that I was nearer death than I had ever been.

"Well, I cotched ye!" he shrilled, shaking the ancient Colt at me.

"Was it you who fired on me?" I inquired mildly, keeping a watchful eye on him. He seemed to have accustomed himself to the loss of his eight-sided lens.

"'Twar!" he shouted, hopping from one foot to the other. "Pity I didn't plug ye! I'd o' been saved the trouble o' doin' it now. Whur'll ye have it—in the belly or the head, ye hippoty hoppin' horned toad, ye? Fer a couple o' squirts o' tobaccy juice I'd stake ye out in the Skull and let the sun b'il the p'ison outen ye!"

"But what have I done to you?" I demanded casually.

"Whut have ye done?" he screamed. "Whut have ye done? Whut—whut—whut—"

Speech left him. His eyes contracted to points of red. He shook his fist at me, waved the pistol in my face, stamped

and capered until I almost expected him to dismember
and vanish in smoke. His rage, indeed, finally pitched him
over the summit of his emotions and for perhaps three
seconds, his strength spent, he stood and simply quivered
and glared at me.

In that moment of silence I heard the creak of a board.

I had trod on that loose board myself. I had trod on
it several times. Some one was coming up the stair. I had
been groping about in my mind for the explanation of
Furie's insane rage and suddenly I found it; and I also saw
as clearly as if a ray of light had pierced my brain what
had been prepared for me. It was diabolically clever, as
any scheme of Dillon's would be—and the creak of a board
had betrayed it to me. Trifles are often strangely illumina-
tive. Fear gripped, my soul, but I shook it off. My clever-
ness must exceed his.

Furie got his wind again. "Whut—whut—I'll telt ye,
then. An' if ye opens yer trap while I'm talkin' I'll give
it a fillin' o' lead! Yer one o' them p'lice cops! I knowed
it yesterday mornin'. Yer one o' them slicker big bellies
with a stick an' a whistle! Yer after the hombre as killed
that thievin' Andry Ogden and yer got it in yer fool head
I'm the lad as done it! An' yer fixin' to bring me into one
o' them crookit co'rts whur a slick lawyer kin make a old
cuss like me say he killed his mother! Yer fixin' to stretch
me neck and give me six feet o' Californy dirt to stake me
a claim in! Waal, sir, thar ain't nothin' but hide an' hair
o' me left, but I aim to die whur I lives an' do me own
claim-stakin'—"

I raised my hand.

"Shet up, or I'll stake ye out for the buzzards!" he
screamed, prancing on his drumstick legs again. "Don't
I know? Hain't I been told if ye ain't six foot under the
Skull by sun-up they'll be makin' me swear I killed Andry
Ogden when I didn't, an' crackin' me neck fer it? Ol' Hide

and Hair ain't the fool he looks. Whur'll ye have it? The head o' the belly?"

Obviously Dillon had been talking to him. Anything I might say, then, would be of no avail. He was in a frenzy again, frothing at the mouth, shaking his fist, stamping his feet. He'd finish me in a minute or so. Desperately I sought for some means of overcoming him, and I had about made up my mind to rush him when a thought struck me. Dillon was outside, listening, waiting, and it offered the barest chance of success, but I'd try it. I'd try anything.

Furie was into the tale of his tribulations again. "Hain't I tramped Skull and Skeletons nigh on fifty years? Hain't I cotched snakebite and drinked water as stinked!" He was twitching and writhing and foaming like a man in a fit. "Hain't I seen me eyesight go and me teeth drop out? Hain't I weared meself to a passel o' hide and a rattle o' bones? But I've found it!" he screamed and shook the Colt in my face. "Quartz rotten with gold! I'll be rich as Rockyfeller—"

"Furie," I said casually, "here is your eyepiece. Don't you want it?" I held the lens forth in the palm of my left hand.

It took him unawares and his torrent of words suddenly ceased. His eyes became almost sane in their expression; his pistol hand dropped to his side, and he reached for the lens.

"I ain't been jest right since I lost it," he mumbled.

It was then that I caught him neatly under the point of the chin. In my day I was a bit of a boxer and I gave him everything I had. He doubled up at the knees and the pistol dropped unexploded from his nerveless hand; as he toppled forward I caught him and laid him out on the floor.

Scooping up my automatic, I spun around, expecting Dillon to come pouring into the room, preceded by a fusillade of shots. But he didn't, although I knew he was standing out there, waiting, listening. I had gone quietly about the business of knocking Furie out and he evidently didn't know what had happened. Well, I knew what Dillon was waiting for! How was I to turn the situation to advantage? I had saved my life, but I wanted Dillon to force the issue. I wanted him to commit the overt act. I wanted him *to attack me*.

My eyes fell on the dummies and I seemed to see Alex Peterson bending them to his own ends thirty years before. The human mind is keenly receptive to inspiration during periods of violent emotion and all at once I knew what I was going to do. The audacity of the idea caught my breath. Had I been in a normal state mind I shouldn't have given it a moment's consideration. But I wasn't. I was in a state of mind similar to that Alex Peterson had been in thirty years before. Imitating Furie's high-pitched voice, I shrilled:

"Yer head or yer belly—whur'll ye have it?"

I was peeling off Furie's incredible shirt. A button hit the ceiling.

"No, no! For God's sake, no!" I cried, in an agonized voice. "Don't shoot! Don't!"

The shirt was off. I was slipping it over Napoleon's head. Fortunately, it was several sizes too large for Furie.

"Git yer prayers offen yer chest, ye snifflin' polecat!" I screamed.

"Furie!" I pleaded. "They'll get you. They'll crack your neck!"

The shirt was on. So was the astonishing hat. I toppled Sitting Bull into the shadows against the north wall, lowered the light, scooped up the pistol.

"Crack me neck!" I shrilled. "They ain't cotched me yet! An' they won't! An' here's whur I turns ye into buzzard beef, ye rat-eyed lizard!"

"Furie!" I screamed. "Don't shoot! Dillon lied to you!"

I fired once, twice at the ceiling.

"Furie—he's— Ahhh!"

As I staggered back and sank in a heap against the south wall, the door flew open and Dillon rushed in, pistol in hand, as I had prayed he would. A glance at my limp body, and he fired, once, twice, thrice, at the wax figure in the absurd straw hat. Then a long, throaty cry that began on a note of surprise and ended on a note of rage broke from his lips and he lunged towards the straw-hatted figure with the three neat round holes in its head.

I had risen silently.

"Hands up, Dillon," I said gently.

He was whirling on his heel, his still smoking pistol leaping up at me, as I had expected he would. I shot him once, twice, through the heart and his own weapon blew a hole in the floor. My last shot had spun him around so that he faced the door through which he had burst to enact his pretense of avenging my supposed death. I shall never forget the almost comic look of bewilderment frozen on his swarthy face. Then the released tension of his body sent him staggering forward, he crumpled at the knees, and pitched into the blackness of the gallery.

My legs gave way beneath me and I dropped on to the chair Sitting Bull had occupied; the pistol slid from my hand and my head fell forward. I could not have moved or uttered a word to save my life. Decidedly, I was getting on for this sort of thing. How long I sat there I don't know. Furie began to groan, but I took no notice of him. I wished I was back in my den . . . my newspaper . . . my carpet slippers . . . Polyandria purring . . . even Mrs. Moffit with a hot lemonade.

The blare of motor horns and the sound of human voices broke the desert stillness. There was some shouting and my name was called, but I took no notice. Feet pounded on the floor below . . . on the stair . . . on the gallery floor. Lights flashed, exclamations of horror arose, and a body of people poured in upon me. Deacon and Lucy and Jerry, Nathan Hyde and Roy Hammond, and Thompson, the police detective. What the devil were Hyde and Hammond doing here? Lucy began to weep over me and Jerry patted my back. Silly ass! I wasn't sick. Henry wrung my hand and fiddled with his Elk charm, and wrung my hand again. What idiots people are!

"Uncle John, Uncle John, Uncle John!" Lucy sobbed. She had drawn my head to her breast and was bathing my bald spot with her tears.

"That—that man out there!" Deacon shouted unsteadily.

"Dillon," I mumbled.

"Dillon!" he roared, as if he were beside himself. "I tell you it's Luther MacNair!"

"And who is Dillon but Luther MacNair?" I asked wearily.

All of them suddenly fell silent.

Lucy's tears are wonderfully resuscitative. I began to fumble for my little red notebook.

29
"A Simple Act of Justice"

Jerry gave me something to drink and I felt still better. The stuff tasted divinely, but I made a wry face as I swallowed it so that he wouldn't have the satisfaction of knowing I had enjoyed it. Lucy says I am too rigid in my prejudices.

"Quite a family party," I remarked acidly. "Can't a man keep an appointment without half a dozen people chasing after him? It's a wonder you didn't break your necks coming down Pitchfork at this time of night."

"He might have killed you, Uncle John!" Lucy wailed, pressing me to her again.

"Hmn," I said grimly. "I suppose it was you who got Deacon to come. Give Furie a drink of that abominable stuff, Jerry. I had to tap him under the chin."

"How did you know it was MacNair, John?" Henry asked humbly.

I saw that they all were properly dumbfounded and I chuckled. "You'd have known it was MacNair, too, if you hadn't had your eyes elsewhere."

Henry flushed. I felt sorry for him and I turned my attention to Nathan Hyde, who had been eyeing me with an ironic grin. Hyde must have left on short notice for he still wore his morning coat and his pearl-gray spats. Spats in Skull Valley! In that environment he was as astonishing a figure as Furie had been before I had stripped him to the waist.

"Still looking for that mine transfer, Hyde?" I demanded shrewdly.

That ruffled his smoothness a bit, but he replied suavely enough. "No, we were looking for you, Peebles," and he chuckled. "The truth is, Deacon here came to see what Hammond and I had done with you—or to you."

"I don't blame him," I said pointedly.

The old rascal chuckled again. You cannot offend him. But Hammond was inclined to take umbrage.

"It was a deliberate insult!" he blustered. "A man in my position—the recipient of high fraternal honors—a prospective member of the council—"

"See here, Uncle John!" Jerry cut in unceremoniously. "You were supposed to be Watson and you turn out to be Holmes. And the supposed Holmes is the villain. How about it? Get on with your deductions."

I detest explanations, but Deacon was coming out of his bewilderment and I knew he'd be training his guns on me before I was many minutes older.

"Thanks for the comparison, Jerry," I said modestly. "I don't deserve it. I was merely—fortunate. Our affair didn't have a Watson—if I may borrow your figure. Holmes took upon himself the role of Watson as a matter of expediency."

"You mean you knew all along that MacNair killed Andrew!" Henry exclaimed.

"Well, since the day after it happened," I admitted. "But my evidence was incomplete. I didn't believe it would stand up under the attacks of the battery of criminal lawyers MacNair—Dillon—would summon to his defense. So I waited. I waited for him to show his hand—to force the issue. I knew he would. And he did—to-night. I'll give you the evidence item for item. I ruffled the pages of my little red notebook.

"Item One," I began.

"To-day is Tuesday. Jerry left his father at fifteen minutes past nine Friday evening. At exactly half past nine I was called on the telephone, presumably by Andrew Ogden. The speaker asked me to come over at once. His voice was strained and unnatural, but I had no reason then to believe that it wasn't Andrew's. On the way over I saw a man in Jerry's white flannels flying down the drive. I found Andrew dead in the library with his left hand closed around the telephone receiver. The inference at first glance was that Jerry had killed his father as Andrew telephoned me, then run for his life. But—and this is my point— while most people hold the receiver of a telephone to the left ear with the left hand, Andrew was deaf in the left ear and he always held it to his right ear with his right hand. Yet I found him holding it *in his left*.

"I contend, therefore, that it was not Andrew who telephoned me, but the man who killed him; that his murderer was not Jerry, because Jerry would have known which hand to place upon the receiver; and that the murderer telephoned me to come over so that I would see him escaping in Jerry's clothes and conclude that Jerry had killed Andrew. Do you follow me, Henry?" He nodded. "Go ahead, John."

I had my audience and I resumed.

"Item Two.

"After Furie left the Ogden house and before he called Jerry into the library, Andrew wrote a card to MacNair and dispatched it with Stimson. Presumably he intended to summon MacNair to account. I contend that MacNair returned to his house shortly after the card was left there, and not several hours later, as he pretended; that he left for the Ogden house at once; that he saw a light in the Ogden library and that caution or a sense of danger sent him there instead of to the front door; that he overheard

Andrew telling Jerry the story of his Torridity days, without, however, disclosing to him Dillon's present identity; and that he realized if he would preserve his own life and liberty he must make away with Andrew as soon as Jerry had gone. There was no moon and as the shrubbery outside the library window is quite thick he easily stood on the little railed-in balcony without being seen.

"My evidence of this is flimsy. MacNair was having a stucco sunroom built onto his stucco bungalow on Magnolia Avenue. I found traces of plasterers' cement on his shoes and a deposit of it on the balcony.

"Item Three.

"My den was entered before dawn the next morning. I am not sure why MacNair wanted the pistol I had bought from Hyde and which he had overheard Jerry and Andrew talking about. The fact that one of its gold bullets had been fired constituted dangerous evidence against him, and as he believed the pistol might be obtained easily, he perhaps concluded he had better get it out of the way. Or again, since Andrew found no last word on the body in the mine it is not unlikely that the pencil, the torn newssheet, and the flare-up of powder on the floor of the mine tunnel—MacNair had overheard Andrew detail these to Jerry, remember—suggested to his keen mind the possibility that a message of some sort was concealed in one of the cartridges in the revolver. (In fact, I shouldn't be surprised if this had suddenly occurred to Andrew, also.)

"As it happened, I went in and caught MacNair. We struggled. Lucy and Mrs. Moffit came running in just as I was about done for. MacNair took himself off, pretended to collide with some one outside, fired a couple of shots through his hat, and returned. And then MacNair made another mistake. He said he was in the Ogden grounds and that he had heard me call out.

"Now my mind is quite clear on this point. *I did not call out.* MacNair and I fought in silence.

"Item Four.

"Polyandria followed me into the den. Somehow, she got tangled up between us. I heard her yowl and I was sure she lashed out with a paw. After the struggle I found a tiny drop of blood congealing on one of her claws. She hadn't scratched me, so she must have drawn the blood of my opponent. And it must have come from an uncovered part of his person, or the claw would have been cleaned, or nearly so, as Polyandria drew it back through the garment.

"There was no scratch on MacNair's face, neck, or hands, but there was one on his right wrist. Now he couldn't have concealed this scratch without its concealment being noticed, so he at once pulled up his sleeve and showed it to me—obviously to disarm suspicion. The scratch he attributed to my briar rose and we amiably discussed the limitations of circumstantial evidence. It was very touching. The scratch is still visible."

"Good stuff, John," Henry muttered. "Good stuff."

"Item Five.

"MacNair examined the cartridges in the gold-mounted pistol before I did. A few minutes later, when I called his attention to the nicks and scratches Jerry Peterson's knife had made on the one that contained the note, he pretended he had not seen them. That was nonsense. The shell was so defaced that he couldn't have helped seeing them.

"Item Six."

I held up the little red notebook. "Some of my conclusions are written here. When MacNair and I were in my den Saturday night I pretended to him that I was playing the role of Watson and that Watson had as much right to keep his conclusions to himself until the end of a case as Holmes had. We made a joke of it. Well, I had reasons for wanting MacNair to know I believed him guilty, so I put the notebook down on my desk and left the room for a minute or two. When I returned I found the book had been disturbed—as I had expected.

"Item Seven.

"Sunday morning—we shall always remember, Sunday, eh, Henry?—MacNair stopped his car at my house and told me he was going to Los Angeles. As a matter of fact he did not go to Los Angeles. I purposely glanced at his speedometer." Here I referred to the little red notebook. "It registered 6,825 miles. When I looked at it last night, after the car was supposed to have covered a distance of 250 miles, it registered 7,010 miles—an increase of only 185 miles. MacNair went to Torridity to plant Jerry's flannels, for he knew that the trail inevitably would lead us there. I got to Torridity before he left, although I did not know at the time of my arrival that he was in the town. He could have garaged his car in any one of half a dozen buildings. I'll come back to his activities in Torridity presently.

"Items Eight and Nine.

"Last night I telephoned an old colleague of mine in Los Angeles and asked him to make certain inquiries for me. He was able to get the information I wanted at once and he called me back this morning. He told me, first:

"That MacNair was involved in the Phalean oil swindle and that he had to return one hundred thousand dollars before the end of this week or face a criminal court action. A hundred thousand was the amount he demanded of Andrew.

"Second:

"That MacNair was discharged by the Pinkerton Detective Agency thirty years ago for accepting a bribe of ten thousand dollars."

I put away my little red notebook.

"Those," I said, "are the nine links in my chain of evidence against MacNair. In bulk, the chain is impressive; unlink it and you will find that most of the links are weak."

"I don't know about that," Deacon objected. "I thought you had a pretty strong case."

I shook my head. "It might have got a conviction in an English court—over there murderers are hanged—but I doubt if it would have in an American. Do you know what percentage of convictions is obtained in American courts, Henry?"

"It must be pretty low," he admitted.

"It is, and I have always thought if more care were used in the accumulation and preparation of evidence for the prosecution the situation would be improved. That is why I did not turn my evidence over to you before. Consider it by points. Number One favors Jerry, but it does not implicate MacNair; Two is flimsy; Five is doubtful; Six and Seven depend on my unsupported word; Eight and Nine are good contributory evidence, but they don't prove anything; Three is fair and Four—the scratch—is excellent, but in view of the quality of most of the other evidence a clever criminal lawyer would riddle it in ten minutes. A cat scratch, indeed! As if any one of a dozen cats mightn't have scratched MacNair! Several recent murder trials have gone that way. MacNair had been too clever to leave any tangible clew behind him. Moreover, he hadn't been sending men to the death penalty for thirty years without learning a thing or two about evidence and he knew just as well as I did that I hadn't enough to be sure of convicting him.

"So that you may understand what happened to-night I shall try to give you a sort of moving picture of MacNair's mental processes from just before he left for Torridity Sunday morning up to the end. I got this picture by

asking myself what I would do if I were MacNair—not a
bad dodge, Henry!—and I arrived at certain conclusions
which have been verified by what has happened.

"MacNair knew I believed him to be Andrew's murderer
and he began to realize that his attempt to implicate Jerry
wasn't apt to succeed; so he looked around for a likelier
candidate. He fixed on the cunning, half-witted old desert
rat, Furie. Naturally, he would. Furie had neither friends
nor money, and his violent quarrel with Andrew and
Andrew's refusal to recognize his claim on the Two Brothers, had provided him with motive for the crime. Moreover, Furie was just cunning enough to recognize the value
of escaping in somebody else's clothes. The telephone call
to me could be finessed easily.

"But first he must plant Jerry's flannels in Torridity, as
the trail inevitably would lead there. And this on Sunday
morning MacNair proceeded to do. Not to further involve
Jerry, remember, but to support the charge of murdering
Andrew and getting away in Jerry's flannels that he purposed bringing against Furie.

"I, also, went to Torridity Sunday morning. Neither of
us had expected the other to be there—yet. MacNair now
saw that while I might not have enough

evidence to convict him he could not fasten the guilt
on Furie while I lived. And—I was an increasing source
of danger to him. I might turn up something else. It was
then that he concocted his beautiful scheme for disposing
of Furie and me and insuring his own safety at one blow.

"The subtlety of the man's mind was amazing. I am not
surprised at his long record of successes.

"His scheme was absurdly simple. He would shoot both
of us here in Torridity and bring our bodies together. Then
he would report to you, Deacon, that Furie had killed
Andrew, that I had charged Furie with the crime, that Furie

had shot me, and that he, MacNair, had come running up and dispatched Furie just a moment too late to save my life. He had warned me, and so on. Dear, dear! Another pitifully tragic example of an outsider's meddling in police affairs. And—another triumph for Luther MacNair. Later, he would get possession of the little red notebook on my desk. . . . What do you think of it, Henry?"

"Clever," Deacon growled. "Damned clever! We'd have *had* to assume Furie killed Andrew and took Jerry's flannels to Torridity to implicate the boy; for I suppose by this MacNair knew you'd keep your evidence from us until you'd got your case complete."

"Probably I am a trifle close-mouthed," I admitted. "One doesn't easily shake off the habits of a lifetime. MacNair waited until night, but night brought the sandstorm with it and upset his plans. I think the sandstorm saved my life." Here I described that dreadful Sunday night. "That door bolted, he could not get at me. I don't know why he went off. Perhaps he had used all his ammunition. Perhaps Furie appeared with his rifle. Perhaps it was near dawn and he feared he might not be able to consummate his plan before somebody else turned up. You, Henry, probably. He knew you would come. Anyway, off he went.

"And now we come to my reason for letting MacNair know I believed him guilty. *I wanted him to do precisely what he did.* Only Sunday night I wasn't ready for him. He took me unawares."

"You wanted him— I don't get that!" Henry ejaculated.

I chuckled. "I mean that I wanted MacNair to regard me as an increasing source of danger. Such a condition of affairs would be intolerable to him. Don't you see? It would make him force the issue, *commit that overt act which would complete my chain of evidence against him.*"

"You mean you deliberately invited him to murder you?" Henry shouted.

"Something of the sort," I confessed. "Of course, I intended to evade his stratagem, whatever it might be, catch him on the rebound, and convict him by virtue of his unsuccessful attempt to murder me, as you so disagreeably put it."

Lucy was staring at me with fascinated, horrified eyes. She seemed beyond speech. Jerry's mouth hung open. Hyde had forgotten his sardonic grin. Furie, whom Jerry's flask had brought to himself looked saner than I had ever seen him.

"You were always a nervy devil," whispered Henry. "Get on with it, man!"

"It was to be a duel of wits, you see, and I was pretty sure Skull Valley would be the field of honor. Obviously, MacNair would again act quickly. And he did. He telephoned me this afternoon that he was going down to Skull Valley to arrest Furie for the murder of Andrew. Did I want to be in at the finish? If so, I was to come alone. I knew what he meant—and he knew that I did. A sort of unspoken agreement had come to exist between us. Mac-Nair was no coward. Well, I came."

"Without telling us!" Deacon whispered.

Lucy's expression was tragic.

"What else could I do? If you had come with me nothing would have happened and we would have been no further ahead. MacNair was counting on this. And if he had the courage to challenge me, was I to be lacking in the courage to meet him? Of course I might have left my notebook where you would find it later—if things went wrong—but MacNair would have discounted its value with his story of Furie shooting me and himself shooting Furie. Anyhow, MacNair was prepared to take the risk. Furie, I concluded, was safe until I arrived."

I then recounted what had happened up to the moment when I had knocked Furie out.

"Aye, that's it!" Furie suddenly shrilled from his position on the floor. "The white-bellied coyote told me you wuz a-goin' to break me neck fer me and stake me out in six foot o' Californy dust. 'Tis a good thing ye bust me under the chin. Git on with it, will ye!"

This was encouragement, indeed, and I proceeded.

"You see, if MacNair had won, his story of the shooting would have been *true*. Furie *would* have shot me and he *would* have shot Furie a second or two later. How could you have disproved what was true, Henry? As I swept up my pistol I looked for MacNair to come pouring in. But he didn't. He was still waiting. My eye fell on the dummies and I thought of that psychological trick Andrew used thirty years ago. We meet a man wearing a striking article of attire—a hat, for example—and thereafter when we see any one wearing that hat, or a similar one, we are likely to assume at first glance that it is the same man. Our second glance corrects or confirms the assumption.

"Very well. MacNair was familiar with Furie's astonishing hat and shirt. As you see, I put both on Napoleon, at the same time pretending that Furie was on the point of shooting me. Then I fired my pistol twice. MacNair rushed in, saw Furie's hat, as I had expected he would, and fired at the dummy three times before he took his second glance. Then he whirled upon me, bringing up his pistol to kill me. *That was the overt act I had been waiting for.* . . . Give me another drink of that abominable stuff, Jerry."

When I put the flask down they were standing around me like mourners at a burying. Even that sleek old stick Hyde looked sentimental.

"John," said Henry, blowing his nose, "you are the bravest man I have ever known."

"Henry," said I, "don't be an ass."

I ran a quizzical eye from Nathan Hyde to Roy Hammond.

"It seems to me," I observed shrewdly, "that Hammond once told me he prospected these parts as a young man—ten years ago—before he took up the gentler art of law. Is it possible that he was down here recently and discovered the new entrance to the Two Brothers? Is it possible that he went to Nathan Hyde and that between them they dug up the story of that incredible poker game?"

Hyde chuckled. "We haven't found the mine transfer yet. Have you?"

"No," and I laughed. "I suppose you were going to sell it to Andrew or Lundy's heirs for a tidy sum. Well, Lundy did a good job when he hid it. . . . You can give Hyde his snuff-box, Henry."

Lucy had dried her tears and now she managed to get in a word.

"The most wonderful part of it is that my Uncle John should turn out to be Mr. Holmes instead of Dr. Watson!" she exclaimed. "You simply don't look like Sherlock, dear." She kissed me as she said it, so I didn't mind.

"That's why he's such a good one!" Henry burst forth, and I knew it was coming out at last. "Your Uncle John always played a lone hand. And he believes in keeping things to himself. When he retired ten years ago he was one of the best men Uncle Sam's Secret Service ever had. And he doesn't seem to have lost the old knack. Eh, what, John?"

30
According to Poe

Sixty-nine is getting on for much of this sort of thing and I am glad it is over. Even though I shall have to surrender myself to Mrs. Moffit's ministrations more completely than ever. She has just been in brooding over me with a hot lemonade and a dish of warm olive oil. But now she has gone, and in my old carpet slippers, Polyandria at my feet, I am drowsing over my book and absorbing the pleasant heat from the crackling eucalyptus log in the grate. (You will honor your fireplace in California, the real estaters to the contrary, let me tell you.)

I am fearfully alone to-night. Andrew gone and Lucy going—not really going, and I am gaining something unusual in nephews, she tries to assure me, as if I didn't know better!—leaves me desolate of spirit. Ah, well! life is a series of comings and goings. Eh, what, Polyandria?

My drowsing eyes fell on a calendar hung on the wall. It is an old calendar and there are many pencilings on the curled and yellow top date sheet which records the days of the month of July, 1896. The calendar advertises Brewer's Whisky and its mount pictures a voluptuous lady. Lucy says it is inartistic, Mrs. Moffit says it is sinful, and both of them say I should burn it. Well, I'll take it down after I've had my little joke on Lucy. We elderly fellows get a chuckle on the youngsters so seldom nowadays . . . so

seldom . . . make the most . . . the most of our . . . oppor-
tunities . . .

Sitting up with a start, I saw that Lucy and Jerry had
come in. They have been making love most of the day and
I have had hardly a word with them.

"Oh, you were asleep, Uncle John," Lucy cried distressfully.

"Nothing of the sort!" I snapped. "I was reading. Why
on earth should I be asleep?"

Lucy laughed and kissed me and Jerry grinned and
dropped his arm over my shoulder; both of them then
perched on the arms of my chair. I love to have them
near me. Their bounding youthfulness warms my cooling
blood. Jerry picked up my book which had somehow slid
behind my back.

"Uncle John must have eyes in his backbone," he chuckled.

"Poe," Lucy sniffed, as she caught sight of the volume.
Lucy reads Wells and Shaw and Mencken. "You'll have a
nightmare, Uncle John."

"No," I said, with a little secret smile. "I was only
reading The Purloined Letter. I had been thinking of your
wedding present."

"What has The Purloined Letter got to do with our
wedding present?" Lucy demanded, greatly astonished.

"Not your real wedding present, my dear," I said ban-
teringly. "Just a—a temporary gift. A real wedding present
requires meditation—prayerful meditation."

"For an elderly bachelor you are wonderfully wise,"
Lucy informed me. "But—I insist. What has The Purloined
Letter got to do with our temporary wedding present?
Jerry is dying to know."

"Dear me!" I exclaimed. "Don't you remember the story
of The Purloined Letter? Listen, then:

"A minister of France has stolen an important letter and
hidden it in his house. Its recovery is imperative and the

highly trained services of the French police are enlisted.
At various times during the minister's absence, the police
examine his house with characteristic thoroughness. They
examine every square inch of his rooms, they scrutinize
his cabinets, his chairs, and his tables with microscopes;
they probe his beds, his bedding, his carpets, his curtains,
the covers of his books with long needles; they inspect his
cellars, the paper on his walls, the bricks of his courtyard;
they even go through the houses next door. And—they
fail. They fail because they are mathematicians without
imagination,—and because the minister is a poet as well
as a mathematician, Poe's detective is called in. He reasons
that the minister, knowing the conventional thoroughness
of the French police, is too clever to conceal the letter in
the conventional way; he reasons that the minister will
leave it where it is so apparent to the eye that it will be ignored. Poe's detective is right—book detectives are always
right —and the letter is found in an old envelope stuck
carelessly in a pasteboard card-rack hung on the wall. An
excellent story, my dears."

"But I still don't see what you mean!" Lucy cried impatiently. "Do you, Jerry?"

"I'm listening," he grinned. "Go ahead, Uncle John."
Jerry is a smart lad and I chuckled.

"Cast your minds back to that poker game. Lundy is
left alone in his room with his ill-gotten winnings. The
check and the mining transfer represent, in his estima-
tion, around half a million dollars. These papers are not
negotiable by anybody else, but their value is known and
if they get into unscrupulous hands they could be sold
back to either Lundy or Peterson for a considerable sum—
Hyde and Hammond had something of the sort in mind.
Torridity is full of desperate characters—doesn't it boast
of being the 'toughest town in the West'?—and Lundy de-
cides against carrying them around on his person until

he records the one and cashes the other. His desk is too
flimsy to protect them and his safe is broken. What, then,
does he do with them?"

"You know very well what he did with them!" Lucy exclaimed, shaking me.

"Come on, Uncle John," Jerry grinned. "Lucy can't
stand it any longer."

I beamed on the boy. "Now Lundy was a bit of a poet—
witness that 'secret' room—and he did much as Poe's
French minister did. He placed the check and the transfer
between the leaves of that calendar and made them secure
with three thumb tacks driven into the wall. And there
they stayed for thirty years. (Now will you laugh at my
calendar and talk of burning it!) And— here they are!"

With a dramatic gesture which I had been practicing
since last night I whipped the check and the transfer out
of my pocket and presented them to Jerry. He took them
reverently and the three of us looked at them together.
The pink check had faded a little, the transfer had yel-
lowed. That sprawling "Alex Peterson" . . . rising out of
the dust of thirty years ago . . . clutched at my throat . . .
it was like seeing his dear face again. A tender stillness
filled the room. My small triumph took wing and my eyes
grew dim. The bold "Joe Lundy" and the cramped "Tex
MacCoy" were flaunted irreverencies. A lump climbed into
my throat and I shut my eyes. When I opened them again a
tear had fallen on the signature on the check, running the
indelible writing into the brittle paper.

"I shall keep these," Jerry said presently in a queer,
choked voice.

"No. You must burn them."

He looked at me with understanding rising in his eyes—
Andrew's eyes.

"Yes," he nodded, "you are right. Dad intended to burn
them."

"His last gesture," Lucy whispered. "It will be complete, then."

Jerry slowly tore them into fragments and dropped them onto the crackling log. A burst of flame, a puff of smoke, and they were gone . . . gone as definitely as most of us are when our course is run. We sat in front of the fire with a soothing beatitude stealing into our souls . . . nearer than we had ever been. In a little while they left me.

I must have drowsed again for I came to with a start. Perhaps I had dreamed a little for my mind was occupied with the thought that to-morrow I had to swallow a bitter pill. To-morrow I shall be seventy. Ah, well, a man isn't old until he is seventy-five.

"Eh, what, Polyandria?"

But Polyandria was asleep. And so, presently, was I.

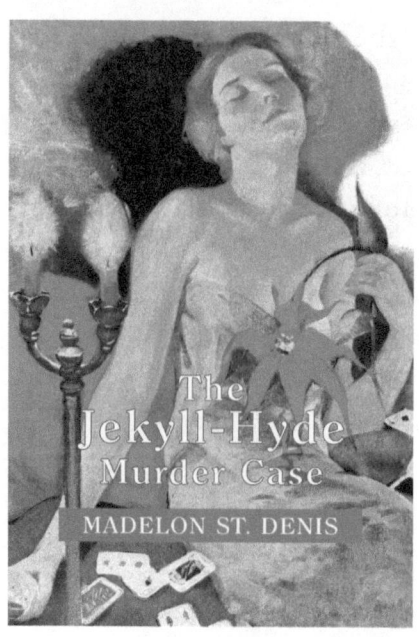

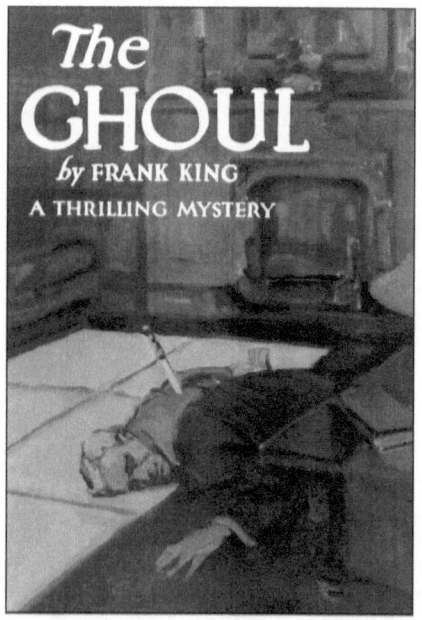

Coachwhip Publications

CoachwhipBooks.com

CLUES OF THE CARIBBEES
Being certain criminal investigations
of Henry Poggioli, Ph.D.
T. S. Stribling

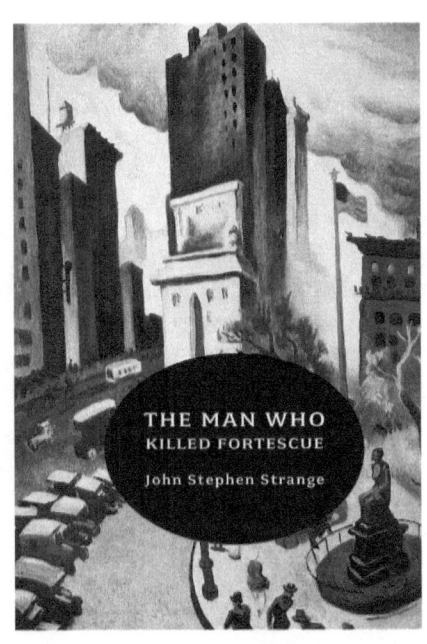

THE MAN WHO
KILLED FORTESCUE
John Stephen Strange

CRY MURDER
EDITH HOWIE

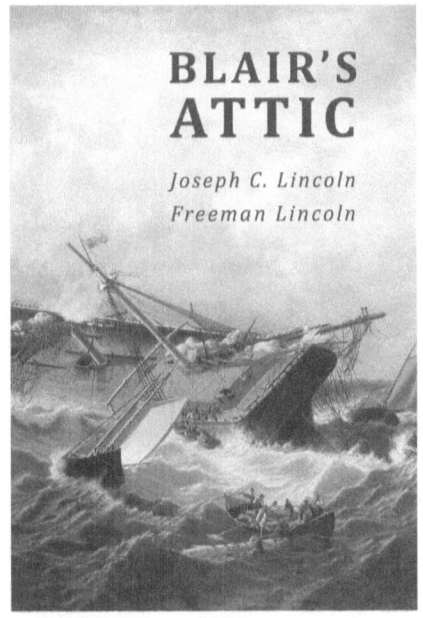

BLAIR'S
ATTIC
Joseph C. Lincoln
Freeman Lincoln

Coachwhip Publications

CoachwhipBooks.com

FULL CRASH DIVE

ALLAN R. BOSWORTH

GRIMM DEATH

DOROTHY FOSTER BROWN

LADY IN LILAC

SUSANNAH SHANE

MURDER IN THE WPA

ALEXANDER WILLIAMS

Coachwhip Publications

CoachwhipBooks.com

WHISPER
MURDER!

VERA KELSEY

DEATH
DOWN EAST

Eleanor Blake

LATE
for the
FUNERAL

Douglas and Dorothy
Stapleton

The Railroad
Murder Case
R. M. LAURENSON

Coachwhip Publications

CoachwhipBooks.com

MURDER IN THE FAMILY

NICE PEOPLE MURDER

Mary Hastings Bradley

THE 13th GUEST by ARMITAGE TRAIL

DEATH IN THE DUSK

Virgil Markham

BLOOD ON HER SHOE

MEDORA FIELD

Coachwhip Publications

CoachwhipBooks.com

MURDER
À LA RICHELIEU
THE ADELAIDE ADAMS MYSTERIES
ANITA BLACKMON

MARIAN
GALLAGHER
SCOTT

TALL MAN WALKING
THE ATTIC ROOM

THE CRIME,
THE PLACE,
AND THE GIRL

DOUGLAS AND
DOROTHY STAPLETON

CRIME IN
CORN-WEATHER

MARY MEIGS ATWATER

Coachwhip Publications

CoachwhipBooks.com

Jack Dolph

MURDER
MAKES
THE MARE GO

THE SEVEN BLACK
CHESSMEN
John Huntingdon

THE
THING
IN THE
BROOK

PETER STORME

HIDE AND GO SEEK
with, GOING TO ST. IVES

COLVER HARRIS

Coachwhip Publications
CoachwhipBooks.com

The
Hollow Tree Mystery
MADELON ST. DENIS

THE MAY DAY MYSTERY

OCTAVUS ROY COHEN

VULTURES IN THE SKY
A HUGH RENNERT MYSTERY

TODD DOWNING

SAMUEL ROGERS

YOU'LL BE SORRY!

YOU LEAVE ME COLD!

Coachwhip Publications

CoachwhipBooks.com

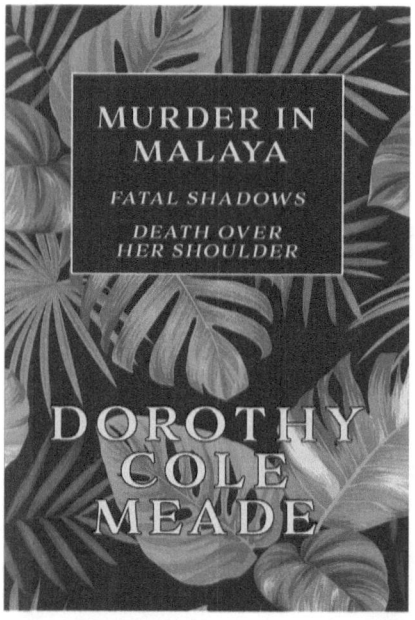

Coachwhip Publications

CoachwhipBooks.com

MARIAN GALLAGHER SCOTT

DEAD HANDS REACHING

DEATH'S LONG SHADOW

THE CASE OF THE UNCONQUERED SISTERS
A HUGH RENNERT MYSTERY
TODD DOWNING

MURDER ON THE FACE OF IT

Emma Lou Fetta

FRANCIS WALLACE
Little HERCULES
A Detective Novel CLASSIC
A FULL LENGTH NOVEL

Coachwhip Publications

CoachwhipBooks.com